With a muffled groan, he removed her gown, baring her body to his gaze, to his touch.

His tongue stroked hers, and she writhed beneath him, her body molding to his. He felt her hand caress his back and he jerked upright. "Don't."

"I'm sorry. I forgot." She gazed up at him, her dark green eyes filled with confusion and hurt. "Why can't I touch you?"

"I have my reasons." He took a deep breath. "Do you want me to go?"

"No, my lord." Her eyelids fluttered down, but not before he saw the single tear that welled in the corner of her eye.

Cursing himself, Trevayne gathered her into his arms, his hands lightly stroking her smooth flesh, slowly arousing her. When, in the throes of passion, she reached out to touch him, he captured both her hands in one of his. He kissed her and caressed her until he was on fire, until her body was ready for his; and then, with a cry of mingled pleasure and pain, he sheathed himself deep within her. And for those few moments, he forgot what he was, forgot the fate that would ultimately be his. For those few moments, he was only a man. . . .

Other titles available by Amanda Ashley

A WHISPER OF ETERNITY

AFTER SUNDOWN

DEAD PERFECT

DEAD SEXY

DESIRE AFTER DARK

NIGHT'S KISS

NIGHT'S MASTER

NIGHT'S PLEASURE

NIGHT'S TOUCH

NIGHT'S MISTRESS

NIGHT'S PROMISE

IMMORTAL SINS

EVERLASTING KISS

EVERLASTING DESIRE

BOUND BY NIGHT

BOUND BY BLOOD

HIS DARK EMBRACE

DESIRE THE NIGHT

BENEATH A MIDNIGHT MOON

AS TWILIGHT FALLS

Published by Kensington Publishing Corporation

Beauty's Beast

AMANDA ASHLEY

ZEBRA BOOKS
KENSINGTON PUBLISHING CORP.
http://www.kensingtonbooks.com

ZEBRA BOOKS are published by

Kensington Publishing Corp.
119 West 40th Street
New York, NY 10018

All Kensington titles, imprints and distributed lines are available at special quantity discounts for bulk purchases for sales promotion, premiums, fund-raising, educational or institutional use.

Special book excerpts or customized printings can also be created to fit specific needs. For details, write or phone the office of the Kensington Special Sales Manager. Attn.: Special Sales Department. Kensington Publishing Corp., 119 West 40th Street, New York, NY 10018. Phone: 1-800-221-2647.

Zebra and the Z logo Reg. U.S. Pat. & TM Off.

First Printing: September 2014
ISBN-13: 978-1-4201-3562-6
ISBN-10: 1-4201-3562-7

First Electronic Edition: September 2014
eISBN-13: 978-1-4201-3563-3
eISBN-10: 1-4201-3563-5

10 9 8 7 6 5 4 3 2 1

Printed in the United States of America

Prologue

Erik Trevayne, seventh lord of Hawksbridge Castle, stood at his wife's bedside. He watched in quiet horror as she strained to bring their firstborn child into the world.

His wife's mother, Charmion du Lac, the witch of Cimmerian Crag, stood across from him, her gaze fixed on the midwife.

"Erik." Dominique reached for his hand, her body convulsing with pain as the life slowly ebbed from her body. "Erik . . ."

The sound of her anguished cries rose to a crescendo, slashing through the dimly lit bedchamber like lightning through storm-ravaged clouds, leaving a great gaping hole of silence when, with her last feeble breath, she expelled the tiny wrinkled infant from her womb.

A low moan, rife with a sorrow so deep it would never heal, issued from Charmion's lips. Stunned, he watched the tall, dark-haired woman grasp her daughter's limp hand as if, by the sheer force of her indomitable will, she could restore Dominique's life.

Erik's gaze moved to the midwife as she quickly cut the cord.

"The child?" he asked hoarsely. "Does it live?"

Slowly, the midwife shook her head. "I am truly sorry, my lord." After wrapping the infant's body in a piece of sheeting, she placed it on the foot of the bed. "There's naught I can do."

Bowing to the lord of the manor, the midwife backed out of the chamber, afraid, as were so many others, to turn her back on the witch.

Charmion lifted her head to regard the man standing across from her. "I warned you, Trevayne," she said with quiet menace. "You should have listened."

"You cannot blame me for this, Charmion."

"I can, and I do."

"It was not my fault!" He shook his head in denial even as he accepted it for the lie it was.

"I begged you not to marry my daughter. I warned you she was not strong enough to give you an heir." Charmion lifted the stillborn child from the bed and cradled the shrouded infant in her arms. "But you would not listen . . . you would not listen! And now my daughter is dead, and her son with her." She stroked the infant's head. "You should not have planted your seed within my daughter's womb."

"It was what she wanted."

"It was what *you* wanted!"

"No." He had never wanted to marry, never wanted to be the lord of Hawksbridge Castle. For as long as he could remember, he had dreamed of dedicating his life to the priesthood, of losing himself in the silence and serenity of cloistered walls. But then his brother, Robert, the rightful heir to the estates, had been killed in a hunting accident and the title had fallen to Erik. It had been his father's dying wish that Erik marry Dominique du Lac and sire an heir to continue the family name. Stricken with grief, hoping at last to win his sire's favor, Erik had knelt at his father's bedside and sworn to do as he wished.

Charmion had vigorously opposed the marriage, but for the first time in her life, Dominique had defied her mother to marry the man she adored. At Dominique's sweet urging, they had been married in secret. She had conceived within the first month.

"Look at me, Trevayne."

Unable to resist the power in Charmion's voice, he looked up, felt himself impaled by the hatred blazing in her witch-black eyes. Her heated gaze trapped his, holding him immobile so he could neither move nor look away.

"A rutting beast you were, a beast you will become. Not all at once, my selfish one. Day by day, the change will come upon you, until you have suffered for every tear my daughter wept, for every drop of blood she shed this day."

"No!"

She nodded once. "As I have said it, so it shall be."

"Is there to be no end? Your daughter's pain is over, yet you would condemn me to a lifetime of suffering."

Charmion placed the babe on its mother's belly; then, sitting on the edge of the bed, she drew mother and child into the cradle of her arms. Bending, she kissed her daughter's waxen cheek. "When Dominique forgives you, so shall I."

"Charmion, listen to me—"

But it was too late. With a wave of her hand, the witch was gone, Dominique and the babe with her, leaving him alone with his grief, while the ominous portent of the witch's last words rang like bells of mourning in his ears.

Chapter One

Shivering uncontrollably, Kristine Arrington stood in the center of the dreary cell, her only light that of a single candle. The stones were cold beneath her bare feet; the gray walls damp and covered with mold. The single window was small and square and barred. And set too high for her to see out. Not that she would have looked, for there was nothing to see but the gallows where, on the morrow, she would draw her last breath.

She whirled around at the sound of a key in the lock, backed away from the door as it swung open.

"I've come to cut yer hair," the burly guard said, moving into the room. He shoved a three-legged stool toward her. "Sit down."

Hands clasped, she did as bidden, her nostrils wrinkling with distaste as he leaned toward her. He smelled of old sweat and ale. The stink of the prison clung to his clothing.

She recoiled at the touch of his dirty hands moving through the heavy fall of her hair, dug her fingers into her arm to keep from crying out as he made the first cut.

"Damn, girl, ye've got enough hair for a dozen women," he muttered.

The sound of the heavy shears sounded like thunder in her ears, and with each cut, another lock of hair fell at her feet. She squeezed her eyes tightly shut as he deprived her of her one true beauty. She had always been vain about her hair. Unbound, it had fallen in thick golden waves past her hips. Was this the punishment for her vanity?

"Ought to bring a fine price from the wigmaker," the guard remarked as he gathered her hair from the floor and moved toward the door. "More than enough to pay fer yer buryin'."

Kristine waited until he was gone, and then, feeling like a sheep shorn of its wool, she ran her hands over the short, spiky ends. Tears burned her eyes and she stiffened her shoulders. She was going to die. She would not cry over the loss of her tresses.

A short time later, a tall, solemn-faced priest came to hear her last confession. A single tear escaped as he gave her absolution, then traced the sign of the cross on her forehead.

Alone again, she sank down on the floor, her head cradled in her hands.

She was going to die.

Feeling numb, she sat there. Would it hurt? Would her legs hold her as they led her up to the gallows? Or would she collapse, weeping and crying like some spineless coward?

She didn't want to die. She had nothing to live for, but she didn't want to die.

Her head jerked up when the door opened again.

Was it time already?

Only it wasn't a guard who entered her cell, but a kind-faced nun bearing a wooden tray laden with a plate of broiled chicken, fresh vegetables, and a loaf of bread still warm and soft instead of hard and stale and crawling with worms. There was a glass of warm sweet wine, as well.

"For me?" After weeks of watered gruel, moldy bread, and tepid water, it seemed a feast indeed.

The elderly nun nodded.

Kristine wept with gratitude as she savored each bite of tender chicken, each morsel of the warm, yeasty bread.

The nun didn't speak, only smiled sympathetically as she patted Kristine's arm, then carried the dirty dishes away.

Later, full for the first time in weeks, Kristine curled up on the thin pallet in the corner. Seeking oblivion in sleep, she was too steeped in despair to give heed to the skinny, long-tailed rats that scurried across the stones in search of some small scrap of food. No need to worry about being bitten now, she thought glumly. What difference did it make if she caught the plague?

The rattle of the guard's keys roused her from a troubled sleep. She bolted upright, fearing that it was morning and they had come to take her to the block. Stomach churning with fear, she stared at the guard, blinking against the light of the lamp.

"That's her," the guard said. He stepped into the cell and lifted the lamp higher. "Stand up, girl. His lordship wants to see yer face."

She had learned long ago to do as she was told, and to do it quickly. Hardly daring to breathe, she scrambled to her feet.

It was then that she saw him, a dark shape that looked like death itself shrouded in a long black woolen cloak. The garment fell in deep folds from his broad shoulders to brush the tops of his black leather boots. The hood of the cloak was pulled low, hiding his face from her view. Black kidskin gloves covered his hands. He stood there, tall, regal, and frightening.

"Her name's Kristine," the guard remarked. "Don't recall her family name."

The hooded man nodded and made a circling motion with his forefinger.

"Turn around, girl," the guard demanded brusquely.

She did as the guard asked, her cheeks flushing with shame as she felt the hooded man's gaze move over her. She was barefoot and filthy. What was left of her hair was dirty and crawling with lice. Her dress, once the color of fresh cream, was badly stained, the hem torn. And worst of all, she smelled bad.

She heard a faint noise, like the rustle of dry paper, and realized the stranger had asked the guard a question.

"Just turned seventeen," the guard replied with a leer.

She heard the rasp of the hooded man's voice again and then he turned away, melting into the shadows beyond her cell.

The guard followed him, pausing at the door to look back over his shoulder. "This be yer lucky day, girl. Seems his lordship has taken a fancy to ye."

"I don't understand."

"He just bought yer freedom."

Kristine staggered back, overcome by a wave of dizzying relief. She wasn't going to die.

"He'll be comin' by to fetch ye tomorrow night."

Coming for her. Tomorrow night. Relief turned to trepidation. "What . . . what does he want with me?"

The guard threw back his head and barked a laugh. "He says he's going ta marry ye."

"Marry me!" Kristine stared at the guard in shock.

"Aye."

"But . . . he doesn't even know me."

The guard shrugged. "What does it matter?"

Why would a stranger want to marry her? And why did she care, if it would get her out of this terrible place with her head still on her shoulders? "Can you tell me his name?"

"Why, don't you know? That's his lordship, Erik Trevayne."

Stunned, Kristine stared at the guard. She would rather lose her head that very night than become the wife of the infamous Lord Trevayne. A beheading, at least, would be swiftly and mercifully over. "And he wants to marry me? Are you sure?"

"Aye, girl. It seems a fittin' match. A murderin' wench bein' wed to the Demon Lord of Hawksbridge Castle."

Chapter Two

I am to be the bride of Erik Trevayne, Demon Lord of Hawksbridge Castle.

It was the first thought that crossed Kristine's mind upon waking in the morning. And hard upon that thought came every rumor she had ever heard of the man, every bit of idle country gossip, every lurid tale.

He was a monster who hadn't been seen in public since his wife died.

He had killed his first wife and child with his bare hands.

He had been cursed by the devil himself.

He was half man, half beast.

He was old, ugly, deformed, cruel, the seventh son of Satan.

He had been beset by some rare plague that left him horribly disfigured.

Kristine huddled under her thin blanket, shivering uncontrollably. Why did he want to marry her? What manner of man took a condemned murderess for a wife? She fought back a wave of hysterical laughter. She had murdered a man. The lord of Hawksbridge Castle had murdered his wife. As the guard had said, it did, indeed, seem to be a fitting match.

Never had the hours passed so quickly. Why, she wondered, did time seem to limp along when one waited for a happy occasion, and run on eager feet for an event one dreaded?

She tried to pray for strength, for courage, but words failed her and all she could do was murmur, "Please, please, please," over and over again.

At dusk, two plump women clad in identical gray woolen gowns entered the cell. One carried a small box, the other carried a large bag.

A short time later, one of the guards dragged a small wooden tub into the cell. Two other guards followed and filled the tub with buckets of hot water, shuffling out when the task was complete. One of the women added several drops of fragrant oil to the water.

Kristine stood against the far wall, watching, wondering. Who were these women? What were they doing there? Were they also nuns? It seemed doubtful, considering the way they were dressed. Both had dark brown hair and eyes.

She looked longingly at the tub. She had not been allowed to bathe in the five and a half weeks she had been imprisoned. One needed money to procure a bath, a decent meal, a change of clothing. She had no funds of her own, nor anyone she might appeal to for aid.

She hesitated when the taller of the two women

gestured for her to step into the tub. Surely they didn't expect her to undress and bathe in their presence?

The women smiled reassuringly as they approached her. Why didn't they speak? When they began to undress her, Kristine shook her head. Stripping off her soiled clothing, she hurriedly stepped into the tub and sank beneath the water, her cheeks flaming with embarrassment.

She tried to protest when the women began to wash her, but they ignored her, their hands gentle, quick, and competent, their eyes sympathetic when they saw how thin she was. One of them vigorously scrubbed her cropped hair and scalp, the other washed her from head to toe. When they were satisfied that she was clean, they helped her out of the tub and toweled her dry, then smoothed a soothing balm over her face and neck, her breasts, her arms and legs.

Kristine was shivering with nervousness when one of the women opened the bag and withdrew a chemise, drawers, and a petticoat, all trimmed with pink ribbons and dainty pink rosettes. Next came a gown of shimmering ice blue silk.

Kristine gaped at the dress. Never in all her life had she beheld anything so lovely. The cool silk felt like heaven against her skin, so much richer and softer than the rough homespun she was accustomed to. There were matching blue slippers for her feet.

She knew a moment of embarrassment as the two women studied her hair, or lack of it. Then, with a sigh, the shorter of the two pulled out a delicate veil of cream-colored lace from the satchel. With a small shake of her head, the woman set the veil in place.

The two women walked around Kristine, smoothing her skirt, making a slight adjustment to the veil, and then they smiled at each other, obviously pleased with what they had accomplished.

One of the women rapped sharply on the door. A moment later, the guard standing watch outside the cell turned the key in the lock and the two women escorted Kristine out of the cell, down the long dank corridor, and out of the prison.

Kristine emerged from the darkness feeling like a newborn lamb about to be led to the slaughter. She took a deep breath, inhaling the scent of clean, fresh air for the first time in over a month.

As soon as she stepped outside, two men wearing the bold green and black livery of Hawksbridge Castle fell into step beside her and escorted her to the small red brick chapel located across the road from the prison.

Her heart was pounding wildly as she entered the church, followed by the two men and the two silent women.

As soon as she was inside, her gaze flew to the altar, to the tall hooded man who stood waiting for her there.

"Come, my daughter."

At the priest's words, Kristine dragged her gaze from the man who was to be her husband. Taking a deep breath, she walked down the short, narrow aisle, noticing, for the first time, that there was a woman seated in the front pew. A petite dark-haired woman dressed in unrelieved black.

Kristine was trembling from head to heel by the

time she reached the altar. A wave of panic washed over her when the hooded man took his place at her side.

The priest smiled at them. "You will please join hands."

Kristine's gaze darted toward the man at her right. He was tall, so tall the top of her head barely reached his shoulder. A cloak of finely woven dark blue wool shot with fine silver threads shrouded him from head to foot. Soft black leather boots covered his feet. He hesitated a moment, then extended his hand, revealing a long arm clad in fine white linen.

For a moment, Kristine stared at the gloved hand he extended toward her and then, wishing she could still her trembling, she placed her hand in his. His hand was large, the fine leather of his glove velvet-soft against her palm. She could feel the latent power in that hand as his fingers closed firmly around hers.

She looked up at the priest, her heart racing. If she begged the good father for help, would he offer her sanctuary? If she refused to marry, would her savior send her back to prison to face the executioner's axe?

In a daze, she listened to the words that bound her to a man whose countenance she had never seen.

Too soon, it was over.

"Lord Trevayne, you may bestow a kiss upon your bride, if you wish," the good father said cheerfully.

Kristine stared up at the man who was now her husband, every instinct she possessed urging her to flee as she waited for him to claim his first kiss. Tall and regal, he stood there, not moving, his face hidden in the deep folds of the cowl, and then, slowly, he shook his head.

She felt his fingers tighten on hers—an apology

for humiliating her, perhaps?—surprised to find that his rejection should hurt so badly.

"The Lord bless you both." The priest made the sign of the cross, then turned toward the elegant woman clad in black. "Madam Trevayne, come forward and make your new daughter welcome."

The woman in the front pew stood and walked toward Kristine, her face an indistinct blur beneath a short black veil. She was a small woman, with fine bones and small, delicate hands. Her dark brown hair was liberally streaked with gray. Kristine found it hard to believe that this petite gentlewoman had given birth to the tall, broad-shouldered man who stood so silently beside her.

"Welcome, daughter," the woman said, her voice cold, distant. She pressed a cool kiss to Kristine's cheek, but her gaze was focused on her son.

With both their faces covered, it was impossible for Kristine to see their expressions, but there was no mistaking the tension between mother and son. It crackled between them, leaving Kristine to wonder at its cause.

"Is this wise, Erik?" Lady Trevayne murmured softly. "Are you not tempting fate?"

Kristine winced as her husband's grip tightened on her hand; then, without a word, he released his hold and stalked out of the church.

Lady Trevayne looked at Kristine, then slowly shook her head. "Leyla and Lilia will see you to your new home, daughter. Fare thee well." And so saying, she moved past Kristine and knelt at the altar, where she bowed her head in prayer.

Glancing over her shoulder, Kristine saw the two

women who had assisted her at the prison waiting for her near the door.

"Do not be afraid, child." The priest offered her a reassuring smile as he firmly traced the sign of the cross on her brow with a spatulate thumb. "Go with God and fulfill your duty, as a wife should."

With a nod, Kristine followed the two silent women out of the church.

A shiny black carriage drawn by a pair of matched chestnut geldings awaited her. When she was settled inside, the two silent women joined her. She heard the crack of a whip, and the carriage lurched forward.

Trevayne paced the deep shadows of his chamber, waiting. In the adjoining room, Leyla and Lilia were preparing his bride for bed.

His bride. He had chosen her because she was marked for execution, because she had been the most pathetic of the lot, because he had looked at her scrawny arms, flea-bitten legs, and shorn head and felt nothing. Nothing at all. He had not expected her to clean up so well. Washed and scrubbed and clad in ice blue silk, her dark green eyes luminous beneath the gossamer veil, she had looked incredibly young and vulnerable, like a little girl playing dress-up in her mother's clothes.

He wished she had remained ugly and unattractive.

He raked a hand through his hair. It was time to fulfill his father's last wish, now, while he was still able. As promised, he had taken a bride. In the nights to come, he would plant his seed within the girl's womb and pray it took root quickly. Once the child was born and pronounced healthy, he would seek the peace of mind and soul that only the grave could bring.

He whirled around as the door opened. Leyla stood there. She nodded, indicating that his bride was ready.

With a sigh, he waved the buxom woman away. Then, taking a deep breath, he left his chamber to do his duty.

Kristine paced the floor, her nervousness increasing with the passing of each minute.

The women who had attended her in the prison had readied her for her bridal night. She had surmised, from their strong resemblance to each other, that they were sisters. Had they been born mute, she wondered, or had their tongues been taken as punishment, or perhaps to silence them?

They had bathed her, powdered her, and dressed her in a diaphanous white gown that revealed far more than it hid, though she had little to hide, small-breasted and skinny as she was.

Unable to help herself, she reached up again and again to finger the ends of her shorn locks, which barely brushed her ears. Her one true beauty taken from her.

In an effort to avoid thinking of what was to come, she studied her surroundings. The chamber was large, larger than any room she had ever seen. Intricately woven tapestries hung from the walls. A thick carpet covered the floor. The bed was bigger than her room at home. The soft mattress was covered with fine linens and furs and numerous pillows in all shapes and sizes.

A small writing desk and chair occupied one corner. She would have no need of that, she mused. Even if she were so inclined, she had no one to write to, no friends, no family.

A round table held a ewer and matching basin, both painted with tiny blue flowers.

Standing in the middle of the room, she turned around slowly, realizing as she did so that there were no mirrors—not on the wall, not on the dressing table. That seemed passing strange for a lady's chamber, but then, much of what had transpired in the past few days had been strange in the extreme.

With hands that shook, she poured herself a glass of water. In spite of the circumstances that had brought about her marriage, she was determined to make the best of it. She knew nothing of her husband save for the rumors she had heard. She reminded herself that rumors were seldom accurate and rarely contained more than a grain of truth. Gossip had a tendency to grow and take on a life of its own the more oft it was repeated. People had talked about her, too. Little they had said was true. Holding that thought in mind, she endeavored to put her fears away. She would not judge her husband by what she had heard or by what others thought, but by how he treated her.

Going to the window, she stared out into the darkness beyond, one hand absently massaging her neck. Her husband had paid a high price for her, had saved her from a horrible fate. She could not fathom his reasons for taking a condemned woman for his bride, but he had and she would ever be grateful.

She knew of several women in the village who had not met their husbands until the day they wed, and yet these women had grown to love their husbands, had borne them children, had grieved when their men were laid to rest.

Squaring her shoulders, Kristine took a deep breath, determined to be a good wife, to make her husband happy in any way she could and hope that, in time, she would learn to love him and that he would love her in return.

She turned when she heard movement in the hallway, all her good intentions fleeing in the face of reality. He was here! She placed the glass on the table, her heart galloping in her chest as she turned and saw him standing in the doorway. He wore the same long blue cloak he had worn at their wedding. It covered him from head to heel, his face again hidden in the shadow of the cowl's dark folds. Like a phantom from a childhood nightmare, he stood there, silent and still. His gaze moved over her in a long, assessing glance. Was he pleased? Disappointed?

Oh, Lord, she prayed, *I'm so afraid. Please let him like me . . . please let him be kind. . . . I'm afraid . . . so afraid . . .*

Wordlessly, he stepped into the room. She had forgotten how tall and broad he was. The sound of the door closing behind him sounded unusually loud in the stillness.

He crossed the floor on silent feet and extinguished the candles, plunging the room into utter darkness. "Get into bed."

His voice was low and rough, almost a growl. Just hearing it made her throat ache, causing her to wonder if it was painful for him to speak.

"Now!"

The tone of his voice propelled her into bed. She scrambled under the covers, clutching them to her breast, watching, wide-eyed, as he moved toward her, a tall black shadow gliding soundlessly through the darkness. She willed her stiff muscles to relax, told herself this man was her husband. It was her duty to submit to him.

There was a whisper of cloth as he removed his cloak and tossed it aside. He tossed the blankets to the floor. The bed sagged as, fully clothed, he straddled her hips.

She fought the urge to scream as his weight pinned her to the mattress. Fear rose within her, making her heart pound frantically as his hands slid under her gown. Apprehension skittered down her spine as she realized he still wore the glove on his left hand. Effortlessly, he positioned her beneath him.

She shifted her weight, and her hand brushed against his chest.

"Don't!"

"My lord?"

"Don't touch me."

"My lord?" she repeated, certain she had not heard him correctly.

"Don't touch me." His voice was deep, yet she thought she detected a note of pain in the harshly spoken words, a pain of the spirit rather than the flesh.

She blinked against the quick rush of tears that welled in her eyes. She had not wanted this marriage, but she had vowed to make the best of it, had promised herself she would do everything possible to please the husband whose face she still had not seen.

"Are you a virgin?" His voice, gravel-rough, broke on the last word.

She nodded, too stunned to speak, ashamed that he had felt the need to ask.

"Answer me."

"Y . . . yes, my lord."

She felt his body grow taut, heard him swear under his breath.

"It . . . it displeases you?"

"No. It's just . . . inconvenient."

"I'm sorry, my lord," she whispered.

"You needn't be sorry," he said gruffly.

The tears came then, running quietly down her cheeks. She had been a fool to think he would cherish her, a fool to hope she might come to love him, that he would learn to love her in return. She had thought her husband would be pleased with her innocence, happy to instruct her in the intimacy of the marriage bed.

His hand brushed her shoulder, and she recoiled from his touch.

"You needn't be afraid of me," he muttered. "I want nothing from you, nothing but a child."

His hands moved over her body, one rough and calloused, the other sheathed in fine leather. His naked hand slid between her thighs, readying her to receive him. And then he took hold of both her wrists in his gloved hand. To make sure she did not touch him, she mused. What kind of man was he, to be so afraid of her touch?

She heard him swear again as he unfastened his trousers, then positioned his big body between her thighs. She gasped at his weight, cried out as he breached her maidenhead with one quick thrust. He waited for the space of a heartbeat, then moved even more deeply within her, his thrusts becoming faster, harder. His urgency frightened her, and then she heard him swear again, felt him shudder violently.

For a moment, he collapsed on top of her. She felt the silk of his hair against her cheek, the warm whisper of his breath across her bare breast.

And then, as if he had never been there, he was gone, and she was alone in the bed.

Chapter Three

Back in his own room, Trevayne paced the floor, his body aching with the need to sheathe himself within his bride's warmth once more, to feel her velvet heat surround him, to inhale the warm, womanly fragrance of her skin. He cursed himself for using her so roughly, for taking her without the loving words and gentleness a bride deserved when her maidenhead was taken. But he had no gentleness left within him, no kindness for himself or anyone else. He had loved once, and it had ended tragically. He would never love again. Nor would he allow anyone to care for him.

It had been more than four years since a woman had willingly shared his bed. Four long years since he had given pleasure and received it in return.

But he could not help imagining what it would have been like to feel his bride's small, soft hands sliding over his skin, to taste her lips, to dip into her mouth and savor the honeyed sweetness within. He regretted not taking the time to explore the enticingly slim body hidden beneath the silken gown. It was his right, after all. She was his now, to do with as he pleased.

But as much as he yearned to explore the lush hills and valleys of her body, he could never allow her to learn the contours of his own. The risk of discovery, of rejection, was far too great, but even greater was the risk of letting himself care, as he had come to care for Dominique. . . .

Remorse seared his heart and soul as her image rose in his mind: Dominique, writhing in agony as her body sought to expel his child; Dominique lying still and white on bloodstained linen; Dominique, her wide blue eyes glazed with pain and empty of life.

Ruthlessly, he thrust the memories from him. He would not think of her now, nor hopefully, ever again, though he doubted that was possible. Instead, he focused on the bed he had left and the young woman who had awaited him there.

He would go to her again tomorrow night, and every night, until she was breeding, and then he would not touch her again.

He would return to the hunting lodge located high in the hills to the south and stay there until one of the women brought word that his wife had been delivered of a healthy child.

And then, his duty done, he would put an end to his life, and with it an end to his guilt, and his pain, and the hideous curse that, in its infancy, had made grown men turn away in revulsion and caused women to flee in horror.

Kristine sat with her back against the carved headboard, the thick woolen blankets pulled up to her chin. Staring into the inky blackness that engulfed the room, she fought the urge to weep. This had been her bridal night. She had not expected love nor sweet words nor tenderness from the enigmatic stranger she had wed, but neither had she expected him to take her with such blatant disregard for her feelings.

She sighed into the darkness. In truth, she hadn't known what to expect. She had never bedded a man—had, in fact, killed the man who had tried to take her by force. Ironic, that she should marry a man who had, in his own way, been more brutal than Lord Valentine.

He was a strange one, was Erik Trevayne. He had said he wanted nothing from her but a child. The bowels of a filthy prison seemed a strange place to look for a bride. But then, perhaps he didn't like women, didn't want a wife to share his life, but only a fertile belly in which to plant his seed. Strange, how that thought hurt.

She wondered what lay beneath the glove he had worn, why he hid himself from her in the dark, why he would not allow her to see him or touch him. She knew little of the marriage act, but surely it was not usually accomplished with the man fully clothed. What was he hiding?

Perhaps the rumors regarding the Demon Lord of Hawksbridge Castle were true after all. He had certainly taken her like a beast. She felt her anger rise, fueled by hurt and disappointment as her girlish dreams of love and happily-ever-after evaporated like morning dew.

Despair settled over her. She was his wife now, his property, the same as his lands and his horse.

As such, she was subject to his every whim. He could do with her whatsoever he wished. He could abuse her, beat her, even kill her, and no one would say a word against him. Why had she let herself think she might find a measure of joy in this union, that he might come to love her? Surely no normal man went hunting for a bride inside prison walls. What a ninny she had been to think she might find happiness in this huge old castle with a stranger. Her determination to make the best of her marriage suddenly seemed ludicrous.

Overcome by a wave of self-pity and remorse, she pulled the covers over her head and cried herself to sleep.

The two silent women attended her in the morning. One brought warm water so she might bathe while the other stripped the soiled linen from the bed. Kristine felt her cheeks flush when she saw the dark brownish-red stain on the rumpled white sheets, visible evidence that the marriage had been consummated, that she had come to her husband pure and undefiled.

After she bathed, the women powdered her, then dressed her in a luxurious gown of deep green velvet. Nodding their approval, they curtsied and left the room.

Kristine stood there for a moment, fingering the ragged edges of her hair and wondering what was expected of her now. At length, she put on a white ruffled cap trimmed with green ribbon and left the room, slowly making her way down the narrow stairway to the first floor. The aroma of freshly baked bread drew her toward the back of the building.

A tall, painfully thin woman wearing a blue dress and a crisp white apron hurried to meet Kristine as she stepped into the kitchen.

"My lady, what are you doing in here?"

"I'm hungry. Is it all right if I fix something to eat?"

"Gracious, no! It's not seemly for the lady of the house to be in the kitchen." The woman made a shooing motion with her hands. "Go on with you, now, have a seat in the dining hall. I did not expect you down so early this morning. I shall bring your breakfast immediately."

"Thank you . . . I'm sorry, I'm afraid I don't know your name."

"But of course you don't, love. I am Mrs. Grainger. Run along now." She turned to scowl at the scullery maids who were standing behind her, staring wide-eyed at Kristine. "Yvette, set the table quickly. Nan, take the muffins from the oven. I can almost smell them burning."

Kristine slipped out of the kitchen and peered down the long hallway, wondering behind which door she might find the dining hall.

The china clock on the carved sideboard chimed merrily as Kristine stared down at more food than she had ever seen at one time. Muffins and biscuits and tarts, bowls of fresh fruit and thick cream, a cup of hot cocoa, fat sausages, and eggs swimming in butter. She looked at the food and could not help wondering how Mrs. Grainger stayed so thin in the midst of such abundance.

She sampled everything and found it all delicious.

"Is it to your liking, Lady Trevayne?"

She looked up to find Mrs. Grainger standing beside her chair. "Oh, yes, it's wonderful. I've never tasted anything like it."

The cook beamed with pleasure. "Can I be bringing you anything else?"

"Oh, no, thank you."

The woman smiled, her eyes crinkling at the corners. "Just you wait until you see what I have planned for your supper."

"Has my . . . my husband already eaten?"

A shadow flickered in Mrs. Grainger's pale blue eyes. "Lord Trevayne takes his meals in his room."

"Oh. I . . . I didn't know."

Mrs. Grainger glanced around the opulent dining room, then sighed with regret. "No one ever eats in here."

"No one?" Kristine frowned. "I thought . . . doesn't his lordship's mother live here?"

"Not for the last year or so, my lady. Her departure was quite abrupt. Nan said she heard Lord Trevayne and his mother quarreling one night, though what they were arguing about remains a mystery." Mrs. Grainger clapped her hand over her mouth, her eyes widening. "I'm sorry, my lady. I should not be telling you this. 'Tis only kitchen gossip, after all."

"And you have no idea why she left?"

Mrs. Grainger tucked her hands into the pockets of her apron. "I think Lord Trevayne ordered her out of the house."

"He ordered his own mother out of the house!" Kristine exclaimed, shocked at the very idea. "Why would he do such a thing?"

Mrs. Grainger shook her head. "I'm afraid I couldn't say." The words *I've said too much already* hung unspoken in the air between them.

"Where does his mother live now?"

"At the convent at St. Clair."

"A convent! Whatever for?"

"It was her choice. She could have gone to live at one of Lord Trevayne's other holdings, but she said she preferred to live with the good sisters. I think she just wanted to stay close by." Mrs. Grainger cleared her throat. "Are you sure I can't be getting you anything else, my lady? More tea, perhaps?"

"No, thank you." Rising, Kristine folded her napkin in half and placed it on the table.

"It will be all right, my lady," the cook said kindly.

Kristine nodded, disconcerted by the look of sympathy in the older woman's eyes.

Leaving the dining room, she wandered through the castle. It was large, immaculately clean, furnished in the height of fashion. Imported carpets covered the floors, expensive paintings and tapestries hung on the walls. One door was locked. She thought it curious, when all the others were open.

Going into the kitchen, she queried Mrs. Grainger.

"It's the ballroom," Mrs. Grainger said.

"Why is it locked?"

"That's something you'll have to ask his lordship," the housekeeper replied.

With a nod, Kristine left the kitchen and continued her exploration of the castle. Ask his lordship, indeed.

So many rooms, she thought as she toured the upstairs. All empty of life.

Finally, she settled on an overstuffed chair in the

library, her feet curled beneath her as she tried to read. But she couldn't concentrate on the words, couldn't think of anything but the man who had come to her in the dark hours of the night. Her husband. Would he come to her again tonight?

She sat there for hours, watching the sun sink lower in the sky, watching the horizon blaze with color as the setting sun splashed the heavens with streaks of crimson and gold, her nerves growing taut as night cast her cloak over the land.

She had no appetite for supper. Mrs. Grainger hovered over her, encouraging her to eat, but the food tasted like ashes in Kristine's mouth. She couldn't enjoy the meal, couldn't do anything but wonder if he would come to her bed again.

The maids, Leyla and Lilia, were waiting in Kristine's bedchamber when she entered. Though their facial features were almost identical, Leyla was a few inches taller than her sister. Both were clad in long gray dresses and white aprons; both wore their dark brown hair in tight coils atop their heads.

As they had the night before, they brushed out her hair, dusted her with fragrant powder, and then helped her into a gown. It was a different gown from the one she had worn the night before. Made of fine black silk, it slid sensuously over her body, making her feel a trifle wicked somehow.

Leyla smiled at her reassuringly. Lilia touched her shoulder, and then, bowing, they left the room.

And there was nothing for Kristine to do but wait.

* * *

He came to her that night and every night during the following week, rarely speaking, never letting her touch him, hardly touching her. And yet, when he did touch her, she burned as bright as the sun, always wanting more, always reaching for some intangible gift that remained just out of reach, leaving her aching and yearning for something she did not understand. She wondered if he took any pleasure in her bed. He never stayed longer than was necessary; indeed, he always seemed anxious to be gone.

And the more he came to her, the more often he touched her, the more curious she became about the strange man who was her husband.

Now she stared at the door, her body still damp with perspiration, her heart pounding. He had come to her again, like a thief in the night, taking that which he desired, then disappearing into the darkness. What would he do if she refused him? Would he beat her or accept her rejection with cold indifference? Yet even as she considered it, she knew she would never turn him away. She owed him her very life, a debt she could never repay, but more than that, she sensed, deep in her heart, that he needed her in ways he would never admit.

Rising, she filled a basin with water and washed away the visible proof that he had been there, then climbed back into bed and huddled beneath the covers, wondering what it would be like to spend the night in his arms.

Too keyed up to sleep, Erik prowled the floor in front of the door that connected his chamber to his bride's. Perhaps he truly was no better than a rutting beast, as Charmion had declared. He had possessed Kristine only minutes ago, and already his body was hard with wanting her again. What spell had she cast over him, this tiny woman-child with her short, fuzzy hair and luminous green eyes? Had he come under the spell of yet another witch?

He came to an abrupt halt in front of her door, wondering if she was still awake, when he heard her scream.

Alarmed, he flung open the door, his gaze darting around the room, but there was nothing amiss, no danger that he could see. And then he heard it again, a high-pitched scream of terror.

She was having a nightmare. In the dim light cast by the bedside candle, he could see her thrashing about. She had thrown off the covers; her nightgown was twisted around her slim hips, exposing a long length of pale, slender thigh.

"No! No, please, please . . . don't make me . . ."

Moving swiftly across the room, he extinguished the candle; then, sitting on the edge of the bed, he gathered the woman, his wife, into his arms.

"Kristine. Kristine!"

She came awake with a start, her body suddenly rigid in his arms.

Kristine took a deep breath as she recognized the harsh, raspy voice of her husband. She stared up at him, wondering, as always, why he hid in the darkness. Were the rumors true? Had he killed his first wife? Had be been marked by the devil?

"Be still, Kristine," he said, his voice gruff yet kind. "It was only a bad dream."

"It . . . it was . . ." She shuddered. "It was awful."

"Tell me about it."

"No."

"Tell me." It was not a request this time.

"I was drowning," she said, her voice little more than a whisper. "Drowning in a pool of blood. And I couldn't get out. No matter how hard I tried, I couldn't get out."

"Awful, indeed," Erik murmured. "Whose blood?"

"Lord Valentine's. The man who . . . who attacked me."

Erik grunted softly. "Did you kill him?"

Kristine stared up at him, wishing she could see his face. A strange time for him to ask whether she was innocent or guilty, she mused. She had always thought it most peculiar that he had not inquired as to her guilt or innocence before they wed. Perhaps he had thought it foolish to ask. A woman charged with murder would likely have no qualms about lying as to her guilt.

"Did you kill him, Kristine?"

"Yes! I killed him! I . . . I stabbed him." Her voice rose hysterically. "He tried to . . . to . . . and I killed him!" She stared up at him through tormented eyes. "I didn't mean to. I only wanted to make him stop, to leave me alone."

"What were you doing in his house?"

"I tended his children."

"You? You're little more than a child yourself."

"I'm ten and seven."

"Ah, a vast age, to be sure. How long were you employed in his house?"

"Only a few months. My father was struck and killed by a runaway carriage early last winter. He was a teacher, and even though I was a girl, he made sure

I learned to read and write and do my sums. Lord Valentine was my father's friend. He hired me to care for and tutor his children."

Erik grunted softly. Valentine had ever been a notorious rake. "Go on, tell me what happened the night Valentine died."

Sobs wracked Kristine's body and tightened her throat as she told him what had transpired that night. She saw it all again in her mind, Lord Valentine's florid face leering down at her as he bent her back over the kitchen table, his whiskey-sour breath making her sick to her stomach, his hot, pudgy hands fondling her body, touching her in places she herself had never touched. She had struggled helplessly against him until her hand closed on the butcher knife lying on the table beside her. He had been trying to pry her thighs apart when she plunged the knife into his back.

"I didn't mean to kill him, truly I didn't," she said, sniffling. "But I was so afraid. . . ."

"It's all right, Kristine." His voice, usually a harsh rasp, was softer now, almost soothing. "There's no crime in defending your honor."

He believed her! She felt an immense surge of relief. He believed her when no one else ever had.

Minutes passed. She grew increasingly aware of the strong arms that encircled her; of his breath, warm against her cheek; of the rock-hard thighs that cradled her. Her cheeks began to burn as she remembered the times he had slipped into bed beside her, a dark phantom in the night.

She shifted in his lap and her hand brushed his. He jerked away from her touch as though she had scalded him, then quickly shoved his hand into the pocket of his trousers.

Kristine frowned. His hand had felt . . . odd somehow. Misshapen, and covered with coarse hair.

"Are you all right now?" he asked gruffly.

"Yes. Thank you, my lord."

He heaved a sigh. He did not want her thanks. He wanted nothing from her but a son to carry on the family name, to fulfill a vow made in a moment of weakness to ease an old man's passing. He held fast to that thought as he laid her back on the bed, drew her gown up over her hips, and positioned himself between her thighs.

She lay still and silent beneath him, like a sacrificial lamb awaiting the slaughter. An image of that drunken sot, Valentine, forcing himself upon her flitted through Erik's mind and he swore under his breath. He was no better than Valentine.

With an effort, he stood up and backed away from the bed. "Rest well, Kristine."

His voice seemed rougher than usual, as though he were in pain.

"My lord . . ."

But he was already gone.

Kristine rose before dawn. Sleep had eluded her the night before. Every time she closed her eyes, she had seen images of Lord Valentine lying in an ever-widening pool of blood. Now, head aching, she went to the window, drew back the heavy drapes, and gazed into the yard below.

A man rode out of the morning mist. Mounted on a high-stepping black stallion, he put the horse through its paces: a slow trot, a canter, a graceful walk that looked like the horse was dancing. But it was the man who held her attention. He wore a long gray cloak over a loose-fitting shirt made of fine white wool. Black breeches hugged his muscular thighs. He rode as if he were one with the horse, his body in perfect rhythm with that of his mount. She never saw his commands, never saw his hands or legs move, but the horse responded instantly, stopping, starting, changing direction, rearing up on its hind legs, forelegs pawing the air.

She smiled as the horse bowed. The man dismounted in an easy flowing motion. The long gray cloak he wore swirled around his ankles like fog. The cowl fell back, revealing his face. She stared at him, trying to discern his features, and then, with a shock, she realized he was wearing a mask.

As though feeling her gaze, he looked up. The mask appeared to be made of black cloth and was cut so that it covered the entire left side of his face, as well as a portion of the right. Her heart seemed to stop as his gaze met hers. Waves of anger seemed to roll toward her, like heat radiating from a fire.

With a gasp, she drew back, her hand pressed over her heart, which pounded wildly in her breast.

Erik muttered a vile oath when he saw his bride staring down at him from the window of her bedchamber. Merciful heavens, what was she doing up at this hour? Even the household staff was still abed.

He tossed the stallion's reins to Brandt, gave the horse an affectionate pat on the shoulder, and stalked toward the back of the castle. Kristine had been here for only a few days, yet she had turned his home, and his life, upside down.

She was waiting for him at the scullery door.

Erik came to an abrupt halt, his gaze moving over her in one swift glance. She wore a flimsy blue sleeping gown and matching robe. Bare feet peeked from beneath the ruffled hem of her gown. A white cap trimmed with lace covered her head. To hide her shorn locks, he surmised. The lace framed her face in a most becoming manner.

"What are you doing here?" he asked brusquely.

Kristine swallowed past the lump in her throat. She had forgotten how tall and broad he was. His size intimidated her even more than the black silk mask that covered two-thirds of his face, leaving only his mouth and strong square chin exposed.

She stared at him, mute, wondering what horror lay hidden beneath the mask. She reminded herself that this was the same man who had comforted her the night before.

He swore, the rough timbre of his voice making the oath sound even more vile, and then he swept past her, every line of his body radiating anger. And buried beneath the anger, she sensed a dark and bitter despair.

Kristine stared after him, wondering what manner of man she had wed.

She thought of him all that day. Indeed, there was little else for her to do. She had no tasks to keep her hands busy, nothing else to occupy her mind.

She wandered through the castle, then went outside and walked through the gardens. Vast gardens, well tended. A section of fruit trees, another of vegetables, all carefully weeded. She found a rose garden and followed the white stone path that wandered up one row and down the other. A bed of red blooms, one of white, another of pink, and still another of yellow. Beautiful roses, hundreds and hundreds of them.

In the center of the rose garden, she discovered a pool, and in the center of the pool, a statue of a great hawk, namesake of Hawksbridge Castle, carved of black and white stone.

Kristine walked around the pool, studying the hawk from all sides. It was truly awe-inspiring, almost lifelike as it perched there, wings spread. She would not have been surprised to see it soar heavenward.

Enchanted with the beauty of the grounds, she continued her exploration, a cry of delight erupting from her throat when she happened upon a topiary garden. Trees cleverly trimmed into animal shapes rose all around her. Elephants and horses, a giraffe and a unicorn, a bear and a tiger. Animals she had only seen in pictures. She walked slowly, pausing to study each remarkable sculpture, wondering how it was possible to make the bushes look so alive.

After a time, she returned to the rose garden and sat down on the grass, her skirts spread around her. She ran her fingertips over the smooth silk of her gown. Never before had she worn such fine clothes.

With a sigh, she removed her bonnet and ran a hand over her hair. How long would it take for it to grow out? It had never been cut short before. She felt naked without its warmth and weight, as if a vital part of herself had been shorn away.

It seemed the day would never end, but at last the moon took command of the sky. She ate a lonely supper, took a lengthy bath, then retired to her bedchamber, wondering if he would come to her that night.

Afraid he would, afraid he would not.

Surely no one else had a marriage quite as strange as hers. Curled up in a chair, she closed her eyes and fell asleep.

In his room, Erik paced the floor like a caged beast. Earlier in the day, he had watched Kristine walking through the gardens, more beautiful than any of the flowers. He had watched her and hated her, hated the soft glow in her eyes and the smoothness of her skin, the smile that curved her lips as she paused to admire his roses. He hated her vulnerability, the sweet lilting sound of her voice, the way her name echoed in his mind and lingered on his lips. He hated her for being young, for making him want things that would never again be his.

He ripped the mask away, yanked off his glove, ran his good hand over the hideous contours of his face. Charmion's curse screamed in the back of his mind: *A rutting beast you were, a beast you shall become. Not all at once, my selfish one. Day by day, the change will come upon you. . . .*

Day by day, the transformation had happened. So slowly, so subtly, that in the beginning he had been convinced it was only his imagination, his own guilt rising up to torment him. But the day had come when his acquaintances could no longer hide their curiosity about the changes in his appearance. Rumors had flown that he had been stricken with a rare disease that caused the disfiguration, and he had not denied it. Better that rumor than the truth.

Not long after that, he had risen from a troubled

sleep. After splashing water on his face, he had stared into the mirror and been horrified by the hideous half-human, half-beastly reflection that stared back at him. On that day, in a fit of horror and helplessness, he had broken every mirror in the castle, save a small one, and the floor-to ceiling mirrors that lined the ballroom, now out of sight behind locked doors.

Since then, the curse had crept over him like some insidious poison, creeping down the left side of his neck, his left shoulder, his arm, his hand. . . .

He lifted his left hand and studied it, horrified as always by the thick yellow nails, the coarse black hairs that covered his arm and the back of his hand, the pelt growing thicker with each passing day. The skin of his palm was thick and growing dark, like the pad of a wolf's paw. Soon there would be nothing human at all about the left side of his body. And in another few months, a year at most, there would be nothing human at all.

Removing the only remaining mirror in the castle from a drawer in his bedside table, he stared at his reflection, struck by the horrible realization that he would look less frightening, less grotesque, when the transformation was at last complete and he was finally, fully, a beast.

Unable to bear the sight of his reflection any longer, he dropped the mirror in the drawer and slammed it shut.

A beast . . . He felt the madness rise up within him, felt it seep into his mind, felt the darkness pulling at him, enticing him. . . . His dreams of late had been filled with images of predator and prey, of blood and death.

"No." He shook his head. "No!" He repeated the word again and again until the cry of denial became a shout, and the shout became a roar that shook the very walls. "No!"

Kristine came awake with a start, wondering if she had dreamed that awful heart-wrenching cry. But there it was again, louder this time. She covered her ears in an attempt to blot out the horrible sound. What was it? Surely no one, man or woman, could produce a cry of such complete and utter agony. It penetrated every nerve, every pore, until she thought the anguish of it would cause her heart to break.

She cried out in alarm as the door to her room crashed open and he stood there, every muscle in his long, lean body taut, his eyes burning through the slits in the mask.

"Get into bed."

Frightened, she scrambled out of the chair to obey.

He extinguished the lamps, plunging the room into darkness. After unfastening his breeches, he ripped the flimsy sleeping gown from her body, then settled himself between her thighs, his gloved hand imprisoning both of hers above her head.

He closed his eyes, hating himself for taking her as if she were no more than a harlot, hating her for letting him do it without complaint.

She moved beneath him, the slight shifting of her hips settling him more deeply within her. With a groan, he buried his head against her shoulder, his body convulsing violently. A low moan trembled in her throat when he withdrew. Had he not known better, he might have thought it a protest at his leaving.

Praying that she would soon conceive, he left her lying there, unloved, unsatisfied.

As soon as Trevayne left her chamber, Kristine slipped from the bed and drew on a robe of soft pale blue velvet lined with dark blue silk. Sitting at the little writing desk, she opened the small leather-bound book that Mrs. Grainger had procured for her. Kristine had protested that it was much too fine, that all she wanted were a few sheets of paper, but Mrs. Grainger had insisted she keep the journal, saying there were many more where that one had come from.

With a sigh, Kristine opened the book, picked up her quill, and began to write.

> *What a strange place I have come to live in. My mother-in-law makes her home with the nuns in the convent at St. Clair. My maids are both mute. By birth, I wonder, or design?*
>
> *Hawksbridge Castle is an enormous house, one that seems to shelter many secrets. I doubt I have seen it all, yet there are only a few servants. Mrs. Grainger, Leyla and Lilia, Nan and Yvette. Just the five of them, yet the affairs of the castle run smoothly enough. Mrs. Grainger's husband, Chilton, is in charge of the stable and grounds. Their two sons, neither of whom I've met, care for the gardens and help their father with the horses. Only eight servants to run this vast estate. I cannot help but wonder why there are not more. . . .*

*If the castle is strange, Lord Trevayne is stranger
still. I know all the stories, I have heard all the
rumors. I can only wonder which tales are true and
which are fables told to frighten children. Sometimes
I feel like a child. I know so little of the world, only
what my father taught me, only what I have read
in books.*

Leaning forward, she dipped the quill in the ink
again, then paused a moment to reflect on her words
before continuing on.

*My wedding night was not as I had always
dreamed. The act, which I had feared, was not so
awful as I had been warned or imagined, though
my husband holds no love for me, nor I for him. I
cannot help but wonder what peculiar circumstance
prompted him to choose a bride who brings nothing
of value to the marriage, and was also under
sentence of death.*

*Last night I had a terrible nightmare. I was
surprised when Lord Trevayne came to comfort me.
He held me so gently, so tenderly, he hardly seemed
the same man who comes to me in the dark of night.
I feel my cheeks grow hot as I write this, as I admit,
here on this page, that I look forward to his nightly
visits, strange as they might be, to those few brief
moments he spends in my bed. I wonder, does
that make me dreadfully wicked?*

*I wish I knew what he is hiding behind the
mask, why I never see him during the day, why he
dines alone in his room, why he refuses to let me
touch him. . . .*

This morning I saw him riding in the yard. He

*was surprised to see me, almost as surprised as I was
to see him. How magnificent he looked, with his
long gray cloak billowing behind him as he put his
mount through its paces. A hell-black stallion
ridden by a demon from hell, if town gossip is to be
believed. But I do not believe my husband is a
demon. Though he does seem strangely tormented,
I do not give credence to the stories that he is a
monster.*

*I have so many questions, and no one I dare ask
for answers. I suppose that means I shall have to
uncover the truth for myself. . . .*

Chapter Four

Kristine woke early the next morning, determined to discover what her husband was hiding beneath the mask. She was tired of wondering, tired of being afraid. She had married the lord of Hawksbridge Castle for better or worse, and she would not rest until she discerned all there was to know about him.

She had no idea where this sudden surge of courage had come from. She had always been a rather cowardly creature, afraid of the dark, frightened of the unknown.

Perhaps it was merely feminine curiosity, the same insatiable curiosity that had compelled Pandora to open that accursed box. Kristine only hoped that whatever she discovered would not prove to have such disastrous results!

Erik had never come to her during the day. So, if he would not come to her, she would go to him. Remembering that she had seen him riding early yesterday morning, she dressed in the clothing she had worn the day before, plucked her bonnet from the chair, tied the ribbons beneath her chin, and then looked around for her shoes.

Thinking that one of the servants might have put them in the armoire, she opened the doors. And blinked in astonishment at the sight that met her eyes. Dresses. More dresses than she had ever seen. Where had they all come from?

Frowning, she stepped forward for a closer look, her hands moving lightly over the bounty before her. Yesterday there had been only three dresses and a pair of half-boots. Today there were at least twenty gowns in a wide variety of fabrics—fine muslins, delicate silks, lush velvets and satins. And the colors! Rich blues, deep greens, warm reds. Stripes and plaids. There were matching slippers and boots. Petticoats. A dozen exquisite bonnets perched on the top shelf.

Turning away from the armoire, she opened the drawers in the highboy, a soft exclamation of delight rising in her throat at the bounty she found there—fans and gloves and lace-edged handkerchiefs, delicate camisoles and silk stockings.

As she dropped a pair of gloves in her pocket, she wondered again where it had all come from, though there was but one logical answer—Erik. She was the wife of a wealthy man. It was only fitting that she look the part.

After pulling on a pair of boots from the armoire, she ran down the stairs and across the yard toward the barn.

Hearing voices, she ducked into an empty stall, her heart pounding with fear at being discovered. Huddled in a corner, she heard footsteps as the stable boys led Erik's horse out of its stall.

A few minutes later she heard the harsh rasp of

her husband's voice, the clatter of hooves as he led the stallion from the stable.

Popping up from her hiding place, she saw Erik walking his big black stallion across the yard toward the flatlands beyond.

If she hurried, she might catch him.

"You there!" she called to the stable boys, hoping her voice had the proper ring of authority. "Saddle me a horse immediately."

The two boys whirled around. "My lady," they exclaimed, almost in unison.

"My horse, quickly!"

The boys exchanged glances. "We had best do as she says, Brandt," the taller of the two suggested.

"Yes, indeed," Kristine said with asperity.

"She should have a sidesaddle," Brandt said. "It isn't fitting for a lady to ride astride."

"Then fetch me a sidesaddle," she said impatiently. If they didn't hurry, she would never find Lord Trevayne.

"Begging your pardon, my lady," Brandt said. "But we don't have one. The master's first wife didn't ride."

"Just saddle my horse," Kristine said. "And be quick about it!"

In a matter of minutes, she was standing beside a long-legged, cream-colored mare. "Has she a name?"

"Aye, White Mist," Brandt replied, "but we call her Misty."

"Is she gentle?"

"Yes, my lady, you've nothing to fear. She has a soft mouth and a fine disposition."

Brandt helped her mount. Until then, she had not realized how tall the mare was. The ground suddenly seemed quite far away and Kristine felt her newfound courage rapidly deserting her. She had never been on a horse before; now, seated precariously on the leather saddle, with nothing to cling to, she began to think she had made a terrible mistake.

But there was no turning back, not if she hoped to follow Lord Trevayne. Casting a tremulous smile at the two stable boys, she clucked to the mare, breathed a sigh of relief when the animal walked out of the barn.

Kristine was wondering how to make the mare go in the direction she wished when Misty turned of her own accord, following the path Erik's stallion had taken.

Kristine focused all her concentration on remaining in the saddle. The thin reins clasped in her gloved hands didn't seem sturdy enough to control such a huge beast. Experimenting, she tugged on the left rein, then the right, laughing with delight as the mare turned left, then right. Reaching up to resettle her hat, Kristine accidentally tugged on the reins and the mare came to an abrupt halt, almost unseating her.

"This isn't so hard," Kristine mused aloud. It was, in fact, rather exhilarating to be out riding so early in the morning. Diamond drops of dew still clung to the grass, the birds were singing cheerfully high in the treetops, the sky was a bright clear blue.

Kristine had left the castle far behind when she heard the neighing of a horse. Erik's horse? Her heart began to pound in anticipation at seeing him. Misty whinnied a reply and then, without warning, broke into a gallop.

With a startled shriek, Kristine toppled from the saddle. She saw the ground rushing up to meet her.

And then she saw nothing at all.

* * *

Trevayne reined his stallion to a halt as a woman's cry shattered the early-morning stillness. For one swift moment, he was transported back in time as the sound of Dominique's last anguished cry rang down the corridors of his mind.

Shaking the memory away, he wheeled the stallion around and rode back the way he had come. Rounding a stand of timber, he saw Misty trotting toward him, head lifted high to avoid stepping on the dangling reins.

Catching up the mare, Trevayne urged his horse into a gallop, a sudden sense of unease knifing through him.

He reined the stallion to a halt, his heart pounding with trepidation when he saw Kristine sprawled facedown on the dew-damp grass. Vaulting from the saddle, Trevayne knelt beside her, his gloved hands skimming over her arms and legs, along her back and neck. Satisfied that there were no broken bones, he removed her bonnet and examined the back of her head. Anger flared within him as he ran his fingertips over the short frizziness of her hair. Then, as carefully as he could, he turned her over, cradling her in his lap.

"Kristine?"

Her eyelids fluttered open at the sound of his voice.

"Kristine?"

She blinked at him. "My lord."

"Are you hurt?"

"I don't think so. What happened?"

"It seems you took a fall. What are you doing out here? Who gave you permission to ride?"

"No one gave me permission," she admitted, not quite meeting his eyes.

"What are you doing out here?" he asked again.

Should she tell him the truth? Would he be angry? What was he thinking? The mask hid most of his features. Leather riding gloves covered his hands. He wore a shirt of finely woven gray wool beneath a black broadcloth coat; black riding breeches were tucked into expensive black boots.

"Answer me."

Something warned her not to lie to him. "I was following you."

"Following me?" Surprise flickered in his eyes. "Why?"

"Because I . . . that is . . ." Her gaze slid away from his. "I was curious, my lord."

"Curious?"

"About where you go. I never see you except . . ." She took a deep breath, disconcerted by his unwavering gaze. "I never see you during the day." *Or in the night.* The unspoken accusation hovered between them.

He muttered something under his breath, then eased her from his lap. Rising, he stared down at her for a long moment; then, reaching for her hand, he helped her to her feet. He released her as soon as she was steady.

"Come," he said gruffly. "I'll take you back."

Kristine bit down on her lower lip; then, summoning her courage, she asked, "Do we have to? Go back, I mean." She spread her hands in a gesture that encompassed the surrounding countryside. "It's so pretty out here. And I do like riding. It's quite . . . exciting."

"You want to ride with me?" he exclaimed, disbelief evident in his voice, in the taut lines of his body.

"Yes, my lord, very much."

"Have you ever ridden before today?"

She shook her head, wondering if such an admission was wise. Would he make her go back, now that he knew she was a novice?

"I shall have Brandt give you lessons."

Taking up Misty's reins, he led the mare to Kristine. "Are you certain you wish to ride with me?"

She nodded, feeling a rush of excitement as Erik's hands closed around her waist. He lifted her effortlessly into the saddle, handed her the reins, then swung onto the stallion's back and clucked to the horse.

Kristine urged Misty up beside him. They rode side by side, not speaking.

In spite of her earlier remark about the beauty of her surroundings, Kristine paid little heed to the passing countryside. The trees might have been blue, the sky green, for all the notice she took. All her senses were riveted on the man riding beside her. The tall, dark mysterious man who was her husband. Erik . . .

She watched him furtively. He rode easily in the saddle, the reins loosely held in his right hand. His left hand, curled into a tight fist, rested on his thigh. Her gaze moved over his broad back and shoulders. He was as well muscled as the big horse he rode. Her gaze lingered on the blue-black highlights in his hair, was drawn again and again to the mask that covered his face. What was he hiding beneath that bit of black silk?

Trevayne was acutely aware of her veiled glances in his direction. He understood her curiosity. What he didn't understand was why she wanted to ride with him. He had given her no reason to desire his company.

The silence stretched between them, thrumming like a tuning fork. Kristine glanced at his gloved hands, remembering how they felt moving over her body, wondering again if his left hand was deformed in some way. He shifted in the saddle and she watched the play of muscles beneath his coat, felt her mouth go dry as he turned to face her.

Desperate to break the taut silence between them, she cast about for some safe topic of conversation. "All this land," she said, making a sweeping gesture with one hand. "Is it yours?"

He nodded curtly. "And yours, too, madam."

She felt a rush of heat climb up her neck and into her cheeks as he reminded her, in his rough, gravel-like voice, that she was also his. She wondered if he had been injured somehow, if that was what caused his voice to be so harsh.

"Where does your . . . our . . . land end?"

"At the stream, just beyond that rise. The property across the water belongs to Lord Farthingale."

Kristine nodded, though she had no idea who Lord Farthingale might be.

She looked at Erik, her gaze again drawn to the mask. She saw his eyes narrow, his muscles tense, as he endured her scrutiny.

Muttering an oath, he reined the stallion to a halt.

Unwilling to pass the stallion, Misty planted her feet. With a startled cry, Kristine grabbed at the saddle to keep from flying over the mare's neck.

"Why did you come after me?" Erik rasped.

"My lord?"

"Answer me, damn you. Why were you following me?"

She flinched at the bitterness in his voice, the
quiet rage in his eyes.

"Answer me!"

"Because I . . . I thought that we should spend
some time together."

"Did you?"

His voice, that low, gruff voice, struck her like
shards of glass. She nodded, her hands clenching
and unclenching on the reins.

"Did it not occur to you that I might wish to be
alone?"

"Do you?"

Two words. Small words. Simple words. They drew
the anger from him as effectively as a poultice drew
poison from a wound. Of course he didn't want to be
alone. He wanted his old life back. He wanted to be
able to go riding along the public roads again, to
while away the hours gambling with his former
cronies, to dine with old friends, to dance with a
pretty woman who would smile at him instead of
turning away in horror. Alone? He was utterly weary
of being alone, of life.

She was watching him, silent, curious, perhaps even
afraid. Well, she should be afraid. Soon he would be
more monster than man. He stared into her eyes,
those luminous emerald-green eyes that haunted his
sleep, and wished he could sweep her into his arms
and bury himself in her warmth, here, now, with the
sun shining upon them like a benediction. Wished he

could strip away his mask and clothing and feel the honeyed warmth of her silken skin against his. . . .

Bitterness rose up within him anew as he considered all that was forever denied him, and with it an overpowering sense of despair.

"Go back to the house, Kristine," he said wearily.

"My lord?"

"Do as I say."

She lacked the courage to argue with him. He watched her tug on Misty's reins. The mare did not want to leave the company of the stallion, but Kristine finally managed to turn the horse around. His wife sent one last glance in his direction, her eyes filled with hurt and disappointment, and then, with a toss of her head, she left him there, staring after her, foolishly wishing for things that could never be.

That night, Kristine bent over her diary, fighting the urge to cry as she wrote.

> *He doesn't want me, and he never will. I know that now. He doesn't want warmth or affection. He doesn't want someone to share his life or his dreams. Why, then, did he marry me? What did he hope to gain?*

"A son," she muttered bitterly. "That's all he wants from you."

Fighting the childish urge to throw herself on the bed and pound the pillow with her fists, she took a deep breath, then dipped her quill in the inkwell.

I asked Mrs. Grainger why he wears a mask, but she shook her head and refused to answer me. One way or another, I shall uncover the secrets of this house, and those of the man who is its master.

I have nothing else to do with my time. . . .

Chapter Five

Kristine rose early the next morning. Dressing quickly, she went to the window and peered out into the gray dawn. As soon as she saw Erik striding toward the barn, she went to the door that separated her room from his. It was locked. Frowning, she stood there a moment, then left her room. She tiptoed the short distance to his chamber, then paused, her hand on the latch.

What was she doing? What if one of the maids found her in there? With a shake of her head, she opened the door. She was, after all, the lady of the house, and Erik was her husband. She had every right to be there.

She closed the door quietly behind her, then stood there a moment, her heart thundering in her ears. This room was even larger than her bedchamber. A huge bed with wine-colored hangings and a matching counterpane stood directly across from the entrance. Several large pillows were propped against the massive oak headboard. There were tables on each side of the bed. There was an armoire of carved oak to her left, a stone fireplace similar to the one in her room to her right. A small round table and a single chair stood to the right of the hearth. High, narrow, leaded windows were located on either side of the bed. Draperies the same color and material as the canopy hung at the windows. Tapestry rugs in muted shades of wine and blue covered the floor.

Moving farther into the room, she ran her hand over the counterpane, slid her fingertips over one of the pillows. He slept here. Did he ever think of her, dream of her?

Feeling like a thief in the night, yet unable to resist, she went to the armoire and looked inside, noting that her husband seemed to have a preference for coats and breeches in somber hues. The top drawer held a number of shirts in a variety of colors, all made of finely woven wool. Did he always wear wool, she wondered, even in summer? The second drawer held handkerchiefs of fine linen, a wide assortment of cravats and gloves. The third held at least a dozen masks, all fashioned of black silk.

Her breath caught in her throat when she picked one up. It was featherlight in her hand, made so that a portion of it fit over the top of his head. Narrow ribbons served to hold it in place. Why did he wear a mask, she wondered again. What was he hiding? A horrible scar? The disfiguring marks of the pox? A deformity of some kind?

She shook her head. He was such a large, vibrant man, she could not imagine that someone who exuded such power could be anything but perfect.

She held the mask by the edges and lifted it in front of her face, peering through the slits cut for his eyes as she tried to imagine what it would be like to wear such a thing day and night.

"What are you doing in here?"

She would recognize that gruff voice anywhere. It split the stillness with the force of a thunderclap. Kristine felt her cheeks flame with embarrassment as she whirled around to face him, the mask dangling from her hand, forgotten.

Dressed all in black, her husband loomed over her like a dark, angry cloud.

"I . . ."

"You have no business in here."

She stared up at him. Tall and broad, he blocked the doorway, effectively shutting off her only means of escape.

"I asked you a question." He spoke each word softly. Slowly. Distinctly.

She tried to swallow past the lump in her throat, tried to form a coherent sentence, and failed.

He held out one gloved hand. "Give it to me."

Kristine looked at him blankly. "What? Oh!" She dropped the mask into his outstretched hand.

"Get out." His fist closed over the silk.

"I'm sorry." She stared up at him, willing him to move. She wanted nothing more than to flee his presence, but he stood in front of the door, blocking her retreat.

"Get. Out."

"I will. I would. But . . ." She glanced longingly at the door. "I can't."

He stared down at her and then, realizing her predicament, he took a step to the left.

With a wordless cry, she picked up her skirts and ran out of the room.

* * *

Trevayne stared after her, engulfed by rage and an overpowering sense of hopelessness. He had never meant to care for her, had not thought it possible. But she was so young, so innocent. She stirred feelings within him that he had thought long dead, crushed beneath the bitterness, the hatred, that had been his constant companions since Dominique's death. He had married Kristine because she was a stranger, because she had no ties to his past. He had thought he could wed her and bed her and forget her. Now her very presence threatened to bring down the walls he had so carefully erected between himself and the rest of the world.

He paced the floor, the mask he had taken from her crumpled in his hand. He would go to her tonight and plant his seed within her. If there was any mercy in the world, his seed would take root and he could leave here, leave her. He could not bear the pain of his reawakened emotions, could not let himself care for a woman who would recoil in horror if she but knew what lay behind his mask, what kind of monster came to her bed in the dark of night.

The day passed slowly. With Kristine in the house, he felt like a prisoner in his own chambers. He wished, futilely, that he might go downstairs and engage her in conversation, but the mask he was forced to hide behind was like a wall between them. He could not abide the curiosity in her gaze, could not answer the unspoken questions in her eyes, could not pretend that their marriage was anything but what it was—the means to an end. He dared not let her become important to him for fear it would weaken his resolve and that, when the time came, he would be unable to end his life, that he would be unwilling to leave her once the child was born. It would be far better for her, and for him, if there were no tender feelings between them. If he were wise, he would cultivate her hatred. He wanted no one to grieve for him when he was gone. At his death, she would become a wealthy woman. She could remain a widow or marry again at her leisure.

The thought of another man savoring her sweetness filled him with rage. It was part of the curse, he thought, that horrible fury that rose up within him more and more often of late, urging him to strike out, to destroy those who elicited his wrath.

Filled with black despair, he paced the floor, waiting for darkness to cover the land so that he might go to his wife's bed.

He stared out the window, willing the sun to set, willing the night to come quickly and cloak the land in shadow. He, who had once loved the light, now sought the sheltering cover of darkness.

Was it a lifetime ago that he had hunted the woods with his companions, spent his days at his club, his nights drinking and carousing or pursuing the pleasures of female flesh? Hard to believe he had once been rather vain of his looks, harder still to recall that beautiful women had once sought his favor, that he had been the envy of his peers. Once, secure in his youth and virility, he had attended numerous balls and cotillions where women old and young, married and single, had vied for his attention . . . and then he had married Dominique and that life had come to an end.

A bitter laugh that resembled a growl more than

human amusement rumbled deep in his throat. His days of youth and innocence were gone now, forever gone. He was no longer the man he had been, but a freak, half beast, half man. A heavy sigh rose within him. Soon, too soon, there would be nothing left but the beast. . . .

A knock at his door roused him from his morbid thoughts. A curt word sent Mrs. Grainger away. He had no appetite for food this night.

He thought of Kristine, imagined the two silent women readying his bride for bed, bathing her in perfumed water, anointing her body with sweet-smelling oils.

He summoned Yvette and ordered water for a bath, then sent the maid away.

He bathed quickly, hating the sight of his own body . . . the right half forever reminding him of what he had been, the left side evidence of what he would soon become. He pulled on a clean pair of breeches, a wool shirt that hid his misshapen left side, the soft leather boots that were specially made, the left one larger than the right to accommodate his changing shape. He donned a clean mask, drew a glove over his deformed hand.

He swore silently as he unlocked the door between his room and hers, damning the vindictive witch who had cursed him. He could feel the curse spreading, knew that in the morning, he would have lost a little more of himself to the beast that was slowly stealing his humanity, devouring him a little more with each passing day. Soon, too soon, there would be nothing left of the man he had been.

Like a wounded animal, he felt the need to be alone, to go off by himself and hide from prying eyes. God willing, his seed would soon find fertile ground and he could seek the solitude he craved.

With his hand on the latch to his bride's bed-chamber, he sent a swift, silent plea to heaven, praying that Kristine would be with child before the night was over.

Kristine woke with a start to find Erik standing beside her bed. He had been so angry earlier, she hadn't expected him to come to her that night. Recalling the rage that had burned in his dark eyes when he'd found her in his room still had the power to make her tremble.

He had extinguished the light she kept on the table at her bedside. In the darkness, he loomed over her like the shadow of certain death.

After unfastening his breeches, he threw the covers aside, flung her gown up over her hips. Unreasoning panic rose inside her as his body covered hers. She didn't want him to take her like this, as if she were no more than a receptacle for his lust, some tawdry harlot whose favor he had purchased for the night. She knew he didn't care for her, but she was his wife. Surely she deserved some small measure of respect.

She felt his hand on her breast, and suddenly, in the darkness, it was Lord Valentine lying atop her, his hot sweaty hands groping her. She closed her eyes, and Valentine's image rose up before her, his thick lips pulled back, his pale blue eyes filled with lust as they raked her body.

"No," she whimpered softly. "Leave me alone, please just leave me alone!"

Trevayne froze as she began to thrash beneath him.

"My Lord Valentine," she sobbed, her eyes tightly shut. "Don't! Oh, please, please, let me go!"

"Kristine."

Lost in the nightmare of the past, she writhed beneath him, tears coursing down her pale cheeks.

"Kristine, it's me, Erik," he said, and then wondered why that knowledge should soothe her. He had given her no reason to trust him.

"No, don't . . . don't . . ." She sobbed the words.

Swearing softly, he sat up and drew her into his arms. "Kristine, you are safe here. Listen to me! I will not hurt you. No one will ever hurt you again, I swear it."

Opening her eyes, she stared at him blankly a moment. "My lord?"

"You're safe now, Kristine," he murmured. "I'll not bother you again."

Carefully, he lowered her back onto the mattress, drew her gown down over her hips, and pulled the covers up to her chin.

Turning away from the bed, he fastened his breeches, then walked toward the door. He was reaching for the latch when she called his name.

"Erik?"

"What?"

"Will you not stay with me?"

He went still, hardly daring to breathe. "Why?"

"I don't want to be alone. I . . . I don't want you to be alone."

"We can't always have what we want."

"Please, my lord, won't you stay with me until I fall asleep?"

Every instinct he possessed urged him to leave the

room. Instead, he retraced his steps to the side of the bed and sat down on the edge of the mattress. "Go to sleep, Kristine."

He could not see her face in the darkness, but he heard her soft sigh as she snuggled under the covers.

"Thank you, my lord."

He made a soft, wordless sound deep in his throat. He wondered how long she had spent in prison, if that was the reason she feared the darkness, the reason she kept a lamp burning at her bedside throughout the night.

He took a deep breath, his nostrils filling with the warm, sweet scent of her—the soap she had bathed with, the peppermint she used to sweeten her breath, the scent of lilacs that clung to her skin. It was part of the curse, his heightened sense of smell, of taste. His hearing was more acute than before, too. He could hear each soft breath she took.

He clenched his left hand, shoved his right hand into his pocket to keep from touching the curve of her cheek, the short, silky cap of her hair.

Desire rose within him, a desire to bury himself within her. He yearned to shed his clothes and his accursed mask and enfold her in his arms, feel the heat of her skin against his. . . .

His body hardened painfully. Why was he sitting here, torturing himself with her nearness? He was not her nursemaid, nor her governess. If she was afraid of the dark, she had a lamp at her bedside.

But he didn't leave the room, only continued to sit there, his hands tightly clenched, until the soft, steady sound of her breathing told him she was asleep.

Hating her, hating himself, he lit the lamp at her bedside and then left the room, left the house.

Outside, he removed his mask, ripped off his glove and his shirt, and then he began to run. He threw back his head, and the deep-throated sound of his despair pierced the darkness in a long, mournful howl.

Chapter Six

Kristine sat in the library a week later, trying to make sense of the history book she was reading, when one of the maids entered the room.

"Lady Charmion is here," Yvette announced.

"Who?"

"Lady Charmion."

"I'm sorry, I don't know who that is."

"She is the mother of Dominique, Lord Hawksbridge's first wife."

"Oh. I . . ." Kristine closed the book and set it on the table beside her. "Does she wish to see me?"

Yvette nodded, her blond curls bobbing. "She's waiting in the front parlor."

"I see." Kristine stood up, uncertain what she should do.

"Perhaps you would like some tea and honey cakes?" the maid suggested.

"Yes, thank you."

With a nod and a curtsy, Yvette left the room.

Kristine took a deep breath, hoping to calm her

nerves. Lady Charmion. She had heard it said the woman practiced the black arts. Why was she here?

Kristine smoothed her skirt, hoping her day dress of dark blue velvet would be acceptable for greeting her guest. A white lace cap covered her short hair.

Gathering her courage, Kristine made her way to the parlor, hoping that Erik would be there.

Opening the door, Kristine stepped into the room. A woman stood in front of the hearth, staring into the fire. She turned when she heard the door open.

Kristine stared at the woman. Lady Charmion was tall and slender. Dressed in a severe black gabardine gown and cloak, she had the look of a crow, with her sleek black hair and piercing black eyes.

Kristine bobbed a curtsy. "Good day to you, Lady Charmion."

The woman looked at her sharply. "So, he has taken another wife. I could scarcely credit it when I heard the news."

Kristine gestured at the floral damask sofa. "Won't you please sit down?"

"I'll stand."

"I've ordered tea and cakes," Kristine said.

"There is no need. I want nothing from this house."

"Then why have you come here?"

"I wanted to see you with my own eyes, to warn you to flee his presence before he destroys you, too."

"Destroys me?"

"He killed my daughter."

"He . . . he has treated me kindly thus far."

"Has he? Has he taken you to his bed? Has he satisfied his animalistic lust upon you?" The woman took a step forward, her black eyes burning like ebony fire as she placed her hand over Kristine's belly. "Has he planted his demon seed within your womb?"

Kristine took a step backward, frightened by the intensity of the woman's stare, by the cold hatred in her voice.

"You are not yet with child," Charmion said. "I urge you to come away with me now, before it is too late."

"She is going nowhere with you."

Kristine looked over her shoulder at the sound of Erik's voice, relief washing through her when she saw him standing in the doorway. He wore a loose-fitting cream-colored woolen shirt, forest green breeches, and black boots. Fathomless gray eyes regarded Lady Charmion from behind the black silk mask.

Kristine glanced at Charmion, baffled by the gleam of satisfaction she saw in the woman's eyes.

"Get out of my house," Erik said, his voice as hard and cold as winter ice.

"I should watch my tongue, if I were you," Charmion replied, her voice equally cold and hard, "lest a worse fate befall you."

"Worse!" he exclaimed softly. "What could possibly be worse than the hell to which you have already condemned me?"

Charmion smiled smugly as her gaze ran ever so slowly over Erik from head to heel, lingering on the mask, the glove on his left hand.

"For every tear my daughter shed, Trevayne," she said, her voice bitter. "For every drop of blood." With a last fulminating glance, she swept out of the room, her ebony cloak billowing behind her like a witch's malediction.

Kristine stared at Erik. He stood as though frozen in time, his hands clenched into tight fists, his whole body rigid. Behind the mask, his eyes were dark pools of anguish.

She stood rooted to the spot, wishing she could think of something to say to banish the silence, to erase the tension that lingered in the woman's wake, like acrid smoke from a pyre.

A shudder rippled through Erik. When he looked at her, it was as if he was seeing her for the first time. "Why are you still here?"

"My lord?"

"Why don't you run screaming from my presence?" he asked bitterly. "I heard what she told you. Are you not in fear for your life?"

"No, my lord."

He lifted his gloved hand and studied it a moment. "You should be afraid," he murmured, flexing his fingers. "The day may come when I'll tear you to shreds."

"My lord?" She stared at him, perplexed by his cryptic words.

"Leave me, Kristine."

"As you wish, my lord," she said.

Trevayne clenched his hand as he watched her leave the room. "Nothing will ever be as I wish it again," he murmured bleakly. "The witch has seen to that."

Her presence in the house was driving him to distraction. Two months had passed since he had taken

Kristine as his bride. The hours he had once spent immersed in running the affairs of the estate he now spent thinking about the young woman who was his wife. He spent hours watching her—spying on her, he amended with a rueful shake of his head. The castle was honeycombed with secret passageways and peepholes.

He watched her when she sat in the solar, a piece of embroidery in her lap, her brow furrowed in concentration as she took tiny, delicate stitches in the fine linen.

He watched her in the library, her head bent over a book. Sometimes she read aloud, the soft sound of her voice caressing his ears as he longed to caress her flesh. But he had vowed not to touch her again—a promise that put him at odds with the deathbed oath he had sworn to his father, for how could he ensure an heir for Hawksbridge when he had vowed not to bed his bride again?

"Kristine." Her name conjured sunlight and music, a longing to be touched, an ache so deep it caused him to groan in pain.

Kristine. If only he could seek her out, sit across from her while she dined, join her in front of the fire in the evening and tell her of the day's events. He yearned for the normal things most men took for granted—the company of his peers, an evening at the theater, the crush of people at a ball, the simple pleasure of making love to his wife in the light of day, with nothing between them but desire.

Kristine. He felt her presence as he walked through the house late that night. The lingering scent of her perfume filled the very air he breathed. The book she was reading lay on the desk in the library, tempting his hand because she had touched it. Her embroidery made a splash of color on the chair where she had left it. Her bonnet hung from a hook near the door. Because she liked flowers, the rooms were filled with them—fragrant roses from the gardens, wildflowers and lacy ferns from the woods. The rose petals reminded him of her—soft and fragile and sweet-smelling.

Unable to help himself, he went to her room and stepped inside. She had left the drapes at her window open. Moonlight filtered into the room, its pale light blending with the glow of the lamp beside her bed, bathing her face in its soft radiance.

Drawn by an irresistible force, he crossed the floor to her side and gazed down at her. How lovely she was! Her cheeks were the color of ripe peaches, her lips as pink as the petals of the roses she loved, her hair the color of sun-ripened wheat. Her womanly scent rose up to tantalize him, stirring his blood, his desire.

His breath caught in his throat when he realized that she had awakened.

She sat up, sleepy-eyed and innocent. "My lord, is something amiss?"

"No." He ground the word from a throat gone dry.

"You sound most peculiar. Are you ill?"

He was ill, all right, he mused. Ill with wanting her. Feeling like a fool, he shook his head. "Go back to sleep, Kristine. I'm sorry I disturbed you."

He was turning away from the bed when she caught his hand. "Stay, if you wish."

He stiffened, his face turned away from hers. "What did you say?"

"You need not go, if you would rather stay."

He stared down at the slender fingers curled around his gloved hand. He could feel the heat of her through the soft leather. "It would be better if I left."

"As you wish." Her hand dropped away from his.

"It's not what I wish," he replied gruffly.

"Then stay."

"I cannot." He shook his head. "I cannot stay and not touch you."

He heard the sharp intake of her breath as the implication of his words struck her.

"Good night, Kristine." He started toward the door, her unspoken rejection no less painful for being expected.

And then he heard her voice, soft and shaky. "I'm lonely, too, my lord husband."

He froze, one hand on the latch. "Lonely?"

"Yes, my lord. The days are very long with no one to talk to. And my nights are longer still."

"I'm sorry, Kristine. I did not think . . ." He shook his head. It had not occurred to him that she might be lonely, too. But, of course, she would be. She was imprisoned in this place, as was he.

Kristine took a deep breath, steeling herself for his rejection. "Will you not stay the night with me?"

"I cannot, Kristine. I cannot lie beside you and not touch you."

"You are my husband. It is your right to share my bed."

"I vowed I would not touch you again!"

"I release you from that vow."

He stood there, unmoving, hardly daring to believe that she had spoken, certain he had misunderstood.

"Kristine, do you know what you are saying?"

"Yes, my lord."

Slowly, he turned toward her, his gaze searching her face. "Are you certain?"

She nodded, her green eyes luminous in the light of the lamp.

On legs that trembled, he moved toward the bed, his gaze fixed on her outstretched hand as he blew out the lamp.

And once again, her delicate fingers closed over his gloved hand. Heart pounding, he sat on the edge of the mattress. "I'll try not to hurt you."

She nodded, her eyes widening as he lowered his head to capture her lips with his.

She was sweet, even sweeter than he remembered. He drank from her lips, heat and desire spearing through him as he pressed her back on the bed, his ungloved hand sliding up and down the length of her thigh, delving under her gown to stroke the warm, soft skin beneath.

With a muffled groan, he removed her gown, baring her body to his gaze, to his touch.

His tongue stroked hers, and she writhed beneath him, her body molding to his. He felt her hand caress his back and he jerked upright. "Don't."

"I'm sorry. I forgot." She gazed up at him, her dark green eyes filled with confusion and hurt. "Why can't I touch you?"

"I have my reasons." He took a deep breath. "Do you want me to go?"

"No, my lord." Her eyelids fluttered down, but not

before he saw the single tear that welled in the corner of her eye.

Cursing himself, Trevayne gathered her into his arms, his hands lightly stroking her smooth flesh, slowly arousing her. When, in the throes of passion, she reached out to touch him, he captured both her hands in one of his. He kissed her and caressed her until he was on fire, until her body was ready for his; and then, with a cry of mingled pleasure and pain, he sheathed himself deep within her. And for those few moments, he forgot what he was, forgot the fate that would ultimately be his. For those few moments, he was only a man. . . .

She fell asleep in his arms, and he held her for a long while, stroking the soft, silky cap of her hair, wishing he could lie naked beside her, feel the warmth of her body pressed against the length of his own.

But it was not to be, and wishing would not make it so.

Just before dawn, he kissed her cheek, then slipped out of her bed and returned to the cold comfort of his lonely room.

"Why won't you tell me what he's hiding beneath that mask?"

"I cannot tell you."

"Cannot, or will not?" Kristine asked.

"Cannot, my lady."

"But you know, don't you? You know what he's hiding."

Mrs. Grainger shook her head. "I don't know,

dear. No one has seen his lordship's face in almost four years."

"But why?"

The cook shrugged. "Rumors abound. I'm sure you've heard them all. Can I get you anything else, my lady? More tea, perhaps?"

"No, thank you." Kristine rose from the table and left the dining room.

She questioned Nan and Yvette, but both claimed they knew nothing.

Later that afternoon, she went out to the stable and questioned Mrs. Grainger's two sons, but Brandt and Gilbert only looked at her and shook their heads.

Defeated, she went back into the house. Erik had loved her so gently last night. Never had she imagined she would hunger for the touch of a man's hand, yearn to be held and kissed and caressed. There was tenderness in him, a need for love that he refused to acknowledge. But she had seen it in his eyes, felt it in his eager hands. Intuition told her that he would never let himself love her, that she would never be able to tear down the walls he kept between them, until she knew what he was hiding behind the mask.

Later that night, sitting at her desk, she took pen in hand and opened her journal.

It has been weeks since last I wrote. I have asked questions, I have wandered through the house, but I can find no answers to the riddle that is my husband. I believe the household staff knows something, but I do not believe they know what Erik is hiding beneath that mask. He is a strange man,

*silent and aloof, yet ever so gentle when he comes to
me in the night. I think I could care for him if he
would let me. I feel that he is as lonely as I, that he
needs me, yet he will not let me close to him, nor
trust me with whatever it is he is hiding.*

*I am so lonely. . . . I pray that my womb may
soon shelter a child. At least then I will have
someone to love, someone to love me.*

Chapter Seven

He stalked the night, as much a part of the darkness as the light of the moon and the glittering stars. The ground was damp beneath his feet as he tracked her across the moor. His nostrils flared, filling with the scent of her warm flesh. The smell of her fear trailed behind her, arousing his ever-growing lust for blood. He could hear the rapid beating of her heart as she realized she was being followed and began to run.

But she couldn't outrun him, could never outrun the beast. He threw back his head and howled, the long, ululating cry filled with the certainty of victory.

Dropping to all fours, he loped after her. Saliva dripped from his jaws. And then he saw her, just ahead. Excitement flowed through him. The thrill of the hunt, the anticipation of the kill, made the blood roar in his ears.

She glanced over her shoulder, her face ghostly white in the moonlight, her eyes wide with fright. She tripped over a vine, a shrill scream of terror rising in her throat as she tumbled to the ground.

And then he was on her, his teeth ripping through the thick velvet cloak, sinking into the soft skin beneath. The air filled with the sharp sting of her fear even as his mouth filled with the warm coppery taste of her blood. . . .

"No!" He howled the word, screamed it over and over again. Howled it in anguished denial as his razor-sharp teeth tore into her soft tender flesh. . . .

"Erik! My lord, wake up! Erik!"

Trevayne came awake with a start. Drenched in icy sweat, his heart pounding frantically, he glanced around the room. Had it only been a dream, then? But it had seemed so real.

"Erik!" He heard her fists pounding on the door, demanding entrance to his room. "Erik, let me in!"

He closed his eyes and took several deep breaths, then plucked the mask from the table beside his bed and slipped it over his head.

"Erik?"

"I'm coming." He took a deep, calming breath before he unlocked the door.

"Are you all right?" She lifted the lamp higher, her gaze sweeping over him.

"I'm fine," he said, his voice rough.

"Are you?"

"Merely a nightmare." He tried to smile and failed. "You've had them yourself."

"Yes. Well, then . . ." Her eyelids fluttered down, but not before he saw the sting of his rejection reflected in her eyes.

"I'm sorry, Kristine, I didn't mean to be so curt. I . . . I appreciate your concern."

"Would you like me to stay with you for a while?"

He glanced at his deformed hand, hidden behind

the door, at his foot, hidden in the shadows. He should send her away, but he could not. The thought of being alone was beyond bearing. "Give me a moment."

He closed the door, quickly removed the long shirt he slept in and pulled on a shirt and a pair of breeches. He slid his hand into his glove, stepped into a pair of soft leather boots. Taking a deep, calming breath, he opened the door and beckoned her inside.

"Can I get you anything, my lord?" She placed the lamp on the table beside his bed. "A glass of wine? Some warm milk, perhaps?"

Trevayne shook his head.

"Is there nothing I can do for you, my lord husband?"

"Why would you want to?" He sat on the edge of the bed and regarded her through narrowed eyes.

Kristine stared at him. All her life she had wanted someone to love, someone to care for. Her father had loved her, in his own way, and she had loved him, but he had ever been busy, too busy to shower a shy daughter with the affection she craved. As frightened as she had been when she learned that the lord of Hawksbridge Castle was to be her husband, she had hoped that he would come to love her, to need her, as no one else ever had. "I'm your wife."

"Why do you stay here, Kristine? Why don't you hate me? Why haven't you run away?"

Her gaze slid away from his. "I have nowhere else to go, my lord, but if you wish me to leave, I shall do so."

"You didn't answer my other question."

"I cannot find it in my heart to hate you, my lord."

Slowly, she lifted her gaze to meet his. "You saved me from a cruel death, and for that I shall ever be grateful."

"And that's why you stay, why you let me into your bed? Because you are grateful?"

He saw the blood rush to her cheeks and wished he could call back the words. "I'm sorry," he muttered. "Forgive me."

She refused to meet his eyes. "It's obvious you have no need of me, my lord," she said stiffly. "I'm sorry if I've . . ." Her voice broke and he knew she was on the verge of tears. "I'm sorry for intruding."

With a sob, she turned blindly toward the door, wanting only to get away from him. How could she have been so wrong? He didn't need her the way a man needed his wife. And he never would.

"Kristine, wait."

She hesitated, her hand on the latch, her whole body quivering with the effort to hold back her tears.

"Kristine, what do you want of me?"

"I want to be your wife."

Trevayne stared at her back, noting the tremors that shook her, the slender shape barely visible beneath her gown. "I don't understand."

"I want to share your life. I cannot abide living the way I do. I feel like a prisoner. Oh, the castle is lovely, and the servants are kind, but I have no one to talk to, nothing to occupy my time. I'm so lonely."

She had mentioned that before, he mused, but he had not really listened. "Go on."

"I want you to take your meals with me. I want to go riding with you when you tour the estate. I want to . . ." She paused, and he saw the telltale flush climb up the back of her neck. "I want to sleep beside you."

She wanted the impossible, he thought bleakly.

She wanted a normal life, but he could not give her that. He closed his eyes, remembering his vow to get her with child, then leave the castle, to end his life when she had borne him an heir. Selfish lout that he was, he had never taken her feelings into account. What would it hurt, to spend a little time with her, to keep her company if that was what she wanted? He refused to acknowledge he wanted it, too, refused to admit that his solitary existence was slowly choking him to death. . . . Ah, death, it loomed before him, shining, beckoning, the only hope he had to end the curse that was slowly robbing him of his humanity.

He took a deep breath, let it out in a slow, pain-filled sigh. "Very well, Kristine, it shall be as you wish."

"You mean it?" She turned around, her green eyes sparkling with hope. "Truly?"

"Truly."

"Thank you, my lord husband." Smiling shyly, she took a step toward him. "Will you not tell me why you wear a mask?"

"No. You have told me what you want. Now I shall tell you my terms. You will never again ask about the mask, and you will promise to respect my privacy in this matter."

"As you wish, my lord."

"I shall do my best to be your husband in every way, but I cannot stay the night in your bed." He lifted a hand to still her protest. "I do not wish to sleep with the mask on," he explained. The hours of darkness were the only time he was free of it; he could not sacrifice those hours of freedom, not even for her. "If you wish, I shall stay with you, in your bed, until you fall asleep."

She nodded, hoping her disappointment didn't show. She had thought she might be able to sneak a look beneath the mask while he slept, but he had neatly forestalled the possibility.

"Very well, I agree to your terms." Kristine held out her hand. "Will you join me in my bed, my lord husband?"

It was too soon. He needed time to adjust to her demands. "We will start our new life together on the morrow, Kristine."

"As you wish, Lord Trevayne," she replied. "Sleep well."

Their new life started the following morning. Mrs. Grainger stared at Erik, obviously stunned by his presence as he entered the dining room.

"Good morning, my lord," she said when she had gathered her wits. "Will you be dining with Lady Kristine?"

He nodded curtly as he sat down at the head of the table. He had avoided his servants as much as possible since he had started wearing the mask; had not eaten a meal downstairs in four years. He was aware of Yvette's furtive gaze as she hurried to set a place for him, of Nan's wide-eyed stare as she poured him a cup of tea.

"Good morning, my lord husband," Kristine said as she swept into the room. "Did you sleep well?"

"No," he replied candidly. "Did you?"

Twin flags of color rose in her cheeks as she lowered her gaze, her reply a barely perceptible shake of her head. She wondered if he had spent the night tossing and turning, as she had.

"Will you take me riding this morning?" she asked, determined to draw him out, to make him talk to her.

"I had planned to spend the day going over the household accounts," Erik replied, his voice cool.

Kristine glanced away, but not before he saw the disappointment in her eyes. He did not understand her, he thought. Why did she want to be with him? For all that they were man and wife, she knew nothing about him, would be horrified to know what kind of monster sat at the table with her.

He picked at his food, unable to enjoy the meal while she was watching him. It had been years since he had taken his meals anywhere but in the privacy of his room. He was acutely conscious of his mask. With its silk so lightweight, he managed to forget its presence from time to time. But not now, with Kristine sitting across from him, with the housemaids sending furtive glances in his direction each time they entered the room.

With an exasperated sigh, he pushed away from the table. "Be ready in an hour," he said gruffly.

They rode in silence for a time. Erik studied her, noting her stiff posture, her iron grip on the reins.

"Relax your hold," he said quietly. "The mare has a soft mouth."

"I don't understand."

"Her mouth is tender, sensitive to the pull of the bit. You needn't hold the reins so tightly. Nor sit so stiffly. Let yourself move with the mare."

Kristine tried to do as he said. It was hard at first.

She wasn't at ease on the horse and it was hard to relax. But, gradually, she did as he said. Erik told her how to hold the reins, how to guide the mare not only with the reins, but with the pressure of her knees, how to bring the mare to a smooth stop. It amazed her that two strips of thin leather could control so large an animal, but Misty responded instantly.

As Kristine grew more at ease, she found that riding was quite pleasant. The countryside was beautiful, the rocking motion of the mare was restful.

Erik drew his horse to a halt near a narrow stream shaded by silver birches. He dismounted in a fluid motion, then turned and helped her from the saddle.

Kristine stared at his hands at her waist as he set her on the ground. His gloved left hand felt different from his right, though she couldn't quite explain why.

Abruptly, he drew his hands away and took a step backward. "I thought you might like to rest awhile."

"Yes, I would, thank you." She sat down on the grass, spreading her skirts around her.

Trevayne felt a sudden tightness in his throat as he looked at her. She wore a forest green riding habit that emphasized her sweet womanly curves and made her eyes glow like emeralds. A wide-brimmed hat with a matching green feather shaded her face and helped hide her shorn locks. She looked beautiful, he mused, beautiful and desirable. If he were a normal man, he would take her in his arms. He would kiss her and caress her, perhaps make love to her there, on the grass, with none but the sun to know.

But he was not a normal man, and she would turn away from him in horror, repulsed by his face and body, by the thought of giving herself to a monster.

"My lord?"

The sound of her voice brought him back to the present. "What is it?"

"Is something wrong?"

Wrong? He almost laughed out loud. She had no idea just how wrong things were. The good Lord willing, she would never know.

Kristine stared up at him, at his eyes, which looked dark and haunted behind the mask. "Why will you not confide in me?"

His eyes narrowed. "Confide in you? About what, pray tell?"

"Why you feel the need to wear a mask." As soon as she spoke the words, she remembered her promise not to mention it again, but she forged on. "Why that witch woman called you a demon and urged me to leave with her before it was too late."

He stared at her, his hands clenched at his sides, his breathing suddenly harsh and uneven.

"What did she mean about every tear and every drop of blood her daughter shed?"

He opened his mouth as if to speak, but no words came out. For a moment, Kristine thought he might strike her; then he turned away, his shoulders shaking.

Kristine stared at him in amazement. Was he crying?

Rising, she went to stand behind him. "Erik? Erik, I'm sorry."

"Go back to the house."

She had ruined it, she thought, ruined what could

have been the nicest day they had spent together since their marriage. She was about to turn away when she heard a muffled sob. He *was* crying, and it was all her fault.

Without stopping to consider the consequences, she put her arms around him, her front pressed to his back, and hugged him. "My lord? Erik? I'm truly sorry. Please forgive me."

He stiffened in her embrace, his body as rigid as stone, and then, as if a dam had broken inside him, he began to cry, deep gulping sobs that shook his frame from head to foot. His tears dripped onto her hands.

"It will be all right." She murmured the words as she stroked his back. Shudders wracked his body. "Erik, please don't cry." Guilt rose within her. What had she said to cause him such pain?

Not knowing what else to do, she continued to speak to him in low, soothing tones, one arm wrapped loosely around his waist, the other stroking his back . . . his back. . . . She ran her hand over him, her fingertips detecting a difference between one side and the other. She lifted her hand a little and massaged his shoulders. Was his left shoulder larger than the right?

Her curiosity rising, she ran her hands up and down his arms. His left arm felt different beneath the fine cloth of his coat, larger.

She was pondering what it could mean when he suddenly whirled around to face her. He wasn't crying now. Anger blazed in his dark eyes as he captured both her hands in his right one.

"What are you doing?" he asked in a voice that could only be called a growl.

"Nothing . . . I . . . nothing . . ."

She stared up at him, transfixed.

"I told you not to touch me."

"I . . . I didn't mean any harm."

She trembled in his grasp, her eyes wide with fright. He had a horrible urge to fling her to the ground, to strip off his mask and clothing and let her see the monstrous horror that was slowly engulfing his face and body. He wanted to frighten her, to hurt her. To make love to her until they were both breathless.

With an oath, he released her hands. "Go back to the house."

She didn't argue this time. With a wordless cry, she whirled around and ran for her horse. He had a quick flash of one long stocking-covered leg as she pulled herself into the saddle and rode away without a backward glance.

Kristine sat at her desk, scribbling furiously, her head aching from the tears she had shed earlier.

I have ruined it all, shattered the fine thread of friendship that had bloomed between us. If only he would confide in me, if only I knew what it is that torments him so!

The memory of Charmion's visit haunts my every waking moment. Strange, I gave it hardly a thought when it occurred, but now I cannot forget the hatred in her eyes when she looked at Erik. I think she truly believes he killed her daughter. I have not wanted to believe the rumors true, but I have seen his anger firsthand. What if, in a fit of rage, he killed his first wife? After today, I no longer think him incapable of such a foul deed. . . .

Kristine froze, her pen poised over the page, as she heard the door to her room swing open. Even before she turned around, she knew he was there.

He loomed tall and broad in the doorway. His coat was gone, his cravat was askew.

"My lord?"

"Yes, wife?"

"Is something amiss?"

He shook his head, one hand braced against the wall. "I forgot about my vow."

"Your vow?"

He nodded, his words slurring together as he said, "I have come to fulfill it."

She stared at him, horrified by the realization that he was drunk.

"I promised my father an heir." He closed the door and shot the bolt home. "Get into bed."

"Now?" Her voice emerged as little more than a frightened squeak.

"Now."

She stood up, knocking the chair over in the sudden panic that engulfed her. Her gaze darted around the room, her heart beating frantically. She had never refused him, never truly been afraid of him, until this moment. Behind the mask, his eyes burned like glowing coals.

He took a step toward her, and she retreated.

A low growl rose in his throat as he reached for her.

With a shriek, she tried to slip past him, but his hand closed over her arm, holding her fast.

"Don't," she whispered. "Please don't. Not like this."

"I must, my sweet Kristine. It is the only way to end this torment."

She turned away as his whiskey-soured breath filled her nostrils.

A low groan rumbled in his throat as he drew her up hard against him, one arm holding her close. His right hand clasped her chin, holding her head still while he bent down to cover her mouth with his.

"Sweet," he murmured. "Sweet."

She tried to turn her face away, to free herself from his grasp, but it was impossible. He held her firmly, easily. She could feel every taut line of his body pressed against hers from shoulder to thigh. His tongue plundered her mouth and she tasted the whiskey he had been drinking.

She gasped when he swung her into his arms and carried her to bed. Depositing her none too gently on the mattress, he began to undress her. Clumsy in his haste, he ripped her gown and then, with a cry of frustration, he tore off her undergarments, flinging them across the room, until she lay on the bed, fully exposed to his rapacious gaze.

"Don't." She whispered the word, knowing, in her heart, that it would do no good. "Please, don't."

He stared at her for a long moment, his gaze sweeping over her body like a flame, bringing a hot flush of embarrassment to her cheeks.

He moved away from the bed to extinguish the lamp and close the drapes, plunging the room into utter darkness. She felt the bed sag under his weight as his body covered hers, pressing her down into the mattress. His gloved hand imprisoned both of hers while his other hand caressed her.

She had expected him to be rough, to take her

quickly and be gone, but his hand was infinitely gentle as it glided over her body, arousing her against her will. She heard him curse under his breath, and then he was kissing her again. There was no violence in him now, nothing but tenderness as he rained kisses over her face and neck.

She tried to remain impassive, but her body betrayed her. Had he been cruel, she might have resisted, but he made love to her with infinite care, whispering to her all the while, praising her beauty, the softness of her skin, the sweetness of her lips, and she found herself responding, found herself wishing her hands were free so that she might stroke his back and shoulders, that she might run her fingers through her hair. She tried to draw her hands from his, but he tightened his hold.

"No," he whispered. His voice was deep and husky, but there was no anger in it.

He kissed her shoulders, the curve of her neck— long, lingering kisses that excited her, until she writhed beneath him.

"Now," she begged, and lifted her hips in silent invitation.

"Now," he agreed. Reaching down, he unfastened his trousers.

A moment later, his body merged with hers. She thought she heard him whisper, "Please don't hate me, Kristine," but she couldn't be sure, and then there was no time to wonder, there was only the exquisite pleasure of his body melding with hers as he moved deep within her.

She moaned softly as heat rippled through her, warm, sweet heat that touched every nerve, filled every hollow. She cried his name as pleasure burst within her, felt him shudder as he found his own release. Needing to touch him, she tried again to free her hands.

"No, Kristine."

"Why?" she asked petulantly. "Why can't I touch you?"

She tried to see his face in the darkness, but he was only a dark shadow rising above her, a phantom lover who came to her in the night and disappeared with the dawn.

He rested his forehead against hers, his hair brushing her cheeks. "Don't ask."

She felt his body relax, felt his hand move aimlessly over her body, stroking her arm, the curve of her breast, the curly cap of her hair. She wondered if he would fall asleep, wondered if he did, whether she dared light the candle and discover what he was hiding from her.

Minutes passed. She could hear the tick of the clock on her dressing table, the faint whisper of the wind against the windows. His breath fanned her cheek.

Then, with a sigh, he rolled away from her and stood up. She could feel him watching her as he fastened his trousers.

"Good night, Kristine."

"My lord, I . . ."

"What?"

"Can we not start again?"

He blew out a deep sigh. What did she want from him? Surely she realized theirs would never be a normal relationship.

"Will you not stay with me until I fall asleep?"

He closed his eyes, his hands clenching. "If you wish."

"I do. Very much."

He heard the rustle of cloth as she drew back the blankets in silent invitation.

Wordlessly, he returned to the bed and slid in beside her. A moment later, she rested her head on his right shoulder. Why, he wondered, why didn't she hate him? He had given her no cause to feel otherwise. Was she so desperate for attention, she was willing to settle for whatever he was willing to give?

With a sigh of resignation, he slipped his arm around her shoulders and drew her against his side.

"Will you take breakfast with me on the morrow?" she asked.

Erik nodded. It would have been easier to live with her hatred, her scorn. He feared her affection would destroy him. He did not want her to care for him, did not want to care for her in return.

"Good night, my lord," she murmured.

"Good night, Kristine."

He stroked her hair, listening as her breathing became slow and even. When he was certain she was asleep, he brushed a kiss across her lips, rekindled the lamp beside her bed and then, reluctantly, left her chamber for his own.

Chapter Eight

The next few weeks passed quietly. Trevayne took his meals with Kristine. He spent his mornings looking after the affairs of the estate, took Kristine riding each afternoon. She quickly became an accomplished horsewoman. Even though the grooms were there to do her bidding and care for her horse, he taught her to saddle and bridle her own mount, insisted she learn the proper way to curry the mare, how to check Misty's feet and clean her hooves. Kristine proved to be a good student. She listened carefully to everything he told her, asked intelligent questions.

In the evenings, they usually retired to the library, which was Trevayne's favorite haunt. It was a large room, dominated by an enormous fireplace made of stone. Bookshelves bursting with all manner of books lined the walls. Heavy dark green draperies covered the windows, shutting out the shadows of the night. A large oak desk and leather chair stood in one corner of the room; a pair of overstuffed chairs covered in a dark green-and-gold stripe were placed invitingly in front of the hearth.

Some nights, he read the newspaper while she worked on a piece of embroidery. Some evenings he asked her to read to him. He taught her to play chess. Sometimes, as now, they sat in front of the fireplace, reading.

Each evening he followed her up the stairs and made love to her in the concealing darkness of her bedchamber. Ah, the hours he spent there, learning the contours of her body, exploring the softly rounded curves, the subtle hills and warm, deep valleys. Learning what brought her pleasure, what made her laugh, what made her burn like a living flame in his arms. He yearned to feel her hands on him, to feel her lips move across his flesh as she explored him in turn, but such a thing was beyond the realm of possibility.

When he had taken her to wife, he had hoped she would conceive immediately so that his vow to his father would be fulfilled and he could seek the solitude of his hunting lodge. But as the weeks passed into months, he found himself hoping his seed would not take root within her womb. It was foolish to let himself care for her when there could be no future for the two of them, no lasting happiness, yet he could not help wishing for more days in her company, more nights in her bed.

Being with her was torture of the most exquisite kind, sheer agony to know that their time together must soon end. The malignant affliction brought on by Charmion's curse was spreading to the toes of his right foot. He could feel the wretched change being wrought upon his body, an excruciating pain in bone and tissue as his flesh fought against its new shape.

Soon, it would not be a human foot at all, but a paw like the other, complete with fur and claws.

Soon, he would not be human at all, but an animal. Morbidly, he wondered if, when the hideous transformation was complete, he would lose the power of speech. Already his voice was altered, so that it often sounded more animalistic than human. Even more frightening than the possibility of losing the ability to speak was the possibility that he would lose all memory of being human . . . and he wondered which would be worse, to forget his humanity entirely, or to remain aware that he had once been a man, damned to spend the rest of his life trapped in the guise of a beast.

"Erik?"

He looked up to find her staring at him.

"Is something wrong?"

"No." He laid his book aside. "Why do you ask?"

"You seem so far away."

"I'm sorry."

"I was going to ring for a cup of tea. Would you care for some?"

"I would rather have a brandy."

She nodded, a flicker of concern giving her pause as she recalled the night he had come to her, intoxicated. That had not happened again, though she knew there were nights when he sought solace in a glass of whiskey.

A few minutes later, Nan entered the library.

Kristine relayed their wishes, then closed the book she had been pretending to read. For perhaps the hundredth time, she wondered what was troubling Erik. What secret was he keeping from her? It was more than just whatever disfigurement he hid behind the mask. She had hoped he would come to trust her enough to confide in her, prayed that, in time, he would come to care for her, as she was learning to care for him.

She knew there were times when he was in terrible pain, but he would not reveal the cause. She knew something weighed heavily upon his mind, but he would not divulge the reason. And yet she could not help but be heartened by the gradual change in their relationship. He seemed to genuinely enjoy her company. They ate their meals together, spent time together each day. Made love each night. It was a victory, of a sort, and she reminded herself again to be patient.

Nan returned a few minutes later. She handed Kristine a delicate china cup of peppermint tea sweetened with wild honey, and handed Erik a snifter of brandy.

"Will there be anything else, my lord?"

"No. Thank you, Nan."

The maid bobbed a curtsy and left the room.

Kristine regarded her husband over the rim of her cup. He drained the glass in a few quick swallows. Placing the empty snifter on the table beside him, he rested his head against the back of the chair and closed his eyes. She saw the tension drain out of him as the brandy's warmth seeped through him.

Slowly, she sipped her tea, watching him all the while. His gloved hand relaxed in his lap, the tension went out of his shoulders. Was he asleep? She watched a few more minutes, but he didn't stir.

Almost before the thought crossed her mind, she was on her feet, tiptoeing toward him, the temptation to peek beneath the silk covering on his face overpowering in its intensity.

She stood beside his chair, her heart pounding so loudly, she wondered that it did not awaken him. Now was her chance to see what lay beneath the mask. She took a deep breath, held it for the space of a heartbeat. Now. It had to be now. She might never get another chance.

She was reaching for the bottom edge of the mask when she suddenly drew back, hands clenching at her sides. She had promised to respect his privacy; if she peeked beneath the mask without his consent, she would be breaking her promise, violating his trust. And trust, once shattered, could never be fully regained.

Fighting the urge to stamp her foot in frustration, she returned to her chair and finished her tea.

Kristine stared at the invitation in her hand. It was addressed to Lord and Lady Trevayne. It seemed odd to see her married name in writing. Lady Trevayne. She rarely thought of herself as such. In spite of her luxurious surroundings and elegant gowns, she was just Kristine.

She turned the envelope in her hands. Dare she open it? She ran her finger over the heavy vellum. Why shouldn't she? It was addressed to her, after all. She broke the seal and withdrew a sheet of monogrammed stationery. It was a handwritten invitation to a masquerade ball to be given by Lord and Lady Courtney Gladstone in three weeks' time.

"What have you got there?"

Feeling suddenly guilty, Kristine whirled around,

startled by the sound of Erik's deep-throated voice. "An invitation." She thrust it toward him, wondering if he would be angry that she had opened it.

Trevayne perused it quickly, then crumpled the page in his hand. There had been a time when Gladstone had been his best friend.

"I guess you don't want to go," Kristine remarked with a wry grin.

"I don't go out. You know that."

She nodded, her gaze intent upon his face.

Trevayne regarded her thoughtfully a moment. "Is it your wish to attend?"

"No!" She shook her head vigorously. The thought of mingling with all those highborn people was intimidating in the extreme. She had no social graces to speak of. She didn't know how to dance. She considered herself lucky that her father had taught her to read and write.

Trevayne grunted softly. Perhaps they should attend. When he was gone, Kristine would be mistress of Hawksbridge Castle. She should know who her neighbors were. In spite of her former station in life, she was Lady Trevayne now. He needed to make sure that she would be treated with the respect due her title.

"I was just going for a walk in the gardens," Kristine said. "Would you care to join me?"

Trevayne smoothed the paper in his hand. "I want you to send a reply to Lady Gladstone and tell her we shall be pleased to attend."

"What?" Kristine stared at him, certain her ears were playing tricks on her.

Trevayne nodded. "It's time you met your neighbors."

"But I don't want to go. I can't go."

"I thought it would please you."

She shook her head again. "I don't like meeting strangers. And I can't dance. And . . . and what if someone should recognize me? I was in prison, condemned."

"I doubt you need worry about meeting anyone you would know," he remarked dryly, "or anyone who would know you."

"I would rather not take the chance."

"Enough. We're going. I shall teach you to dance. Leyla and Lilia can teach you anything else you need to know."

His gaze ran over her. She was young and artlessly beautiful, her heart-shaped face devoid of the garish paint and powder so many women hid behind. She wore a day dress in muted shades of green that made her eyes glow. Her hair had grown out a little, framing her face in a cap of short, dark blond curls.

"But we never go out," she said. "Why do we have to start now?"

"Ah, but Kristine," he replied, his voice tinged with bitterness, "a masked ball is the perfect place to start." He took her hand in his. "Come along," he said, "you can write our reply, and then we can take that walk."

With a sigh of resignation, Kristine let him lead her into the library. She sat at his desk, her brow furrowed, as she endeavored to pen a proper reply.

Trevayne sat in the chair near the fireplace, watching her. She had torn up her first two responses and was now laboring over a third. He could have done it for her, but something kept him from offering.

At last, she put her pen aside. "How does this sound? *Dear Lady Gladstone, thank you for your kind invitation. Lord Trevayne and I will be most happy to attend your masquerade ball on June first.*" She looked up at him. "Is it too short? Too curt?"

"No, it's fine."

"Are you sure?"

"Amelia doesn't require a lengthy reply. She merely needs to know how many people to expect."

"I wish you would write it," Kristine said petulantly. "Your handwriting is so much neater than mine."

Rising, Trevayne went to stand behind her chair. He peered over her shoulder, his gaze skimming over the short message she had written.

"It looks fine, Kristine," he assured her, and then, tempted by the slender curve of her throat and the flowery scent that clung to her hair and skin, he bent down and kissed her cheek.

At the sound of his voice, the touch of his lips, she went still all over. There had been no intimacy between them in the light of day. He came to her bed each night and left after she fell asleep. Except at breakfast, and the hour or two they spent horseback riding in the afternoon, she saw little of him until suppertime. A tiny flicker of hope peeked through the layers of self-doubt. Was he starting to care for her at last?

Startled by what he had done, Trevayne drew back. It had seemed the most natural thing in the world to brush his lips across her cheek. Almost, he had gathered her into his arms. Would she have objected? With a mental shake of his head, he went to stand near the hearth, his back toward her. It would be best for them both if he remembered that theirs was a marriage of convenience. He did not want to care for her, did not want her to care for him.

Once he had her with child, he would no longer be a part of her life. He would be wise to remember that.

"Have Chilton deliver your reply," he said tersely. "And tell Judith you will need a costume for the ball."

"Judith?"

"Mrs. Grainger. I shall see you at dinner." Hands shoved deep into his pockets, he headed for the door.

"My lord . . ."

He paused, not looking at her. "Yes, Kristine?"

"You were going to walk in the gardens with me."

"Not now." He gentled his voice. "I shall teach you to dance after supper." Without looking at her, he left the room.

Erik twirled her around the floor, faster and faster, until she was breathless. It was glorious to be in his arms. He was incredibly light on his feet for such a large man, infinitely patient as he taught her to waltz. It was dizzying, to be so close to him, to see the heat in his eyes when he looked at her. She had felt clumsy at first, tripping over her own feet, stepping on his, but he had counted the steps for her, urged her to relax, to forget about her feet and listen to the music provided by Mrs. Grainger's sons, who were out of sight in an adjoining room.

As Erik twirled her around the floor, Kristine watched their reflection in the mirrors that lined the walls of the ballroom. There were no mirrors in any of the other rooms in the castle. She had been surprised to find them here, behind locked doors.

He moved effortlessly, gracefully, leading her through the steps. No longer needing to concentrate on her feet, she smiled up at him.

"You are a most wonderful teacher, my lord husband."

"And you are a most apt pupil, my lady wife, and as light as a feather in my arms."

Pleasure engulfed her at his words. Her heart began to pound as his steps slowed, and then he was bending his head toward her, his lips claiming hers.

With a sigh, she melted against him, her hands clutching at the lapels of his coat, her eyelids fluttering down as he deepened the kiss. Wordlessly, he lifted her into his arms and carried her to one of the plush couches that lined three of the walls. After setting her on the cushions, he moved through the room, extinguishing all the lights save one at the far end near the door.

She watched him through heavy-lidded eyes, admiring the height and the breadth of him, his long-legged stride. She opened her arms in welcome when he returned to the couch and he sank into her embrace, his lips seeking hers, his hands loosening the ties of her gown, fondling her breasts as he removed her dress and chemise.

She yearned to caress him in return, but knew he would not welcome her touch. In all the months of their marriage, she had never seen him naked, never felt the touch of his naked flesh against her own. Always, his clothing stood like a barrier between them.

She ran her hands over his shoulders, her fingertips stroking the rich velvet of his coat, wondering if his skin would be as soft, as smooth. It never failed to astonish her that she could want him so quickly. How was it that one man's touch could arouse her to heights of ecstasy she had never dreamed existed, while another's evoked only loathing?

She moaned with delight as their bodies merged. She loved the weight of him pressing her down upon the cushions, the touch of his hand stroking her flesh, the urgency that caused him to groan with need as he drove deeper inside her, burning away every thought, until they melted together, one into the other, and she was complete at last. . . .

He held her close in his arms afterward, held her tight, as if he cared for her, as if he could not bear to let her go.

"Why?" he asked after a long while had passed. "Why did you not look under the mask the other night in the library?"

Startled by his question, she blinked up at him, though she could not see his expression in the dimly lit room. "Why, my lord? Why, because I promised I would not." She sat up, her eyes narrowing with suspicion as she put her dress to rights. "You were not asleep, then?"

"No." He sat up, his arm curling around her waist.

"You were only pretending to be asleep, then, trying to trick me?"

He lifted one shoulder in an elaborate shrug. "I needed to know if I could trust you."

With a little *humph* of annoyance, she tried to thrust him away from her. It was like trying to move a mountain.

"Don't be angry, Kristine."

"Let me go!"

He laughed softly, amused by her show of temper.

"Not yet." He dropped tender kisses along the curve of her cheek, down the length of her neck, across her shoulder. "Not quite yet."

She tried to hold on to her anger, but it evaporated beneath the heat of his kisses, banished by the husky tremor in his voice as he whispered endearments in her ear, his tongue a wicked flame as it moved across her skin.

She ignited like dry tinder in his arms, everything else forgotten as she clung to him. Once, turning her face to the side, she found herself staring at numerous shimmering images of the two of them reflected back at her from the mirrored walls. They were a study in ivory and ebony, she mused, her skin seeming extraordinarily white against the darkness of his clothing, his black mask and hair a striking contrast to her pale flesh.

How well we look together, she mused, and then he was kissing her again and there was no more time for thought. . . .

"No! No!" She screamed the words as she clawed at his face, her nails raking deep furrows down his florid cheeks. "No!"

Her hand closed around the knife and she drove it into his back, her stomach roiling as she felt the blade pierce skin and flesh, gagging as his hot blood spurted over her hand. "No!"

"Hush, Kristine, it's all right. Hush now, hush, it's over."

The deep timbre of a familiar voice, the solid strength of familiar arms, chased the nightmare away.

"Erik? Oh, Erik." With a sob, she buried her face against his chest.

"You're safe, Kristine," he whispered. "Nothing can hurt you here."

She nestled against him, her arms twining around his waist. "It's so awful. I wish I could forget."

He stroked her back, pressed a kiss to the top of her head, his lips moving softly in the fine silken curls of her hair. "It's over now," he said. "Try to get some rest. It will be morning soon."

"Stay with me. Please stay with me."

With a nod, Trevayne eased her under the covers, then stretched out beside her, one arm holding her close. She felt so small, so fragile, he could only imagine how terrified she had been when she fought off Valentine's unwelcome advances. Damn the man. If she hadn't already killed him, he would gladly do it for her.

A soft sigh escaped her lips as she rested her head on his shoulder. He felt the tension drain out of her, felt her body relax as sleep claimed her once more.

Trevayne trailed his fingertips over her cheek. They were a fine pair, he mused, both haunted by nightmares—hers brought on by memories of the past, his filled with fears of the future.

He lifted his left hand. What lay beneath the glove could no longer be called human. It was deformed, covered with coarse black fur, the nails thick and long. His entire left side was covered with a heavy pelt of black fur, his left foot was misshapen, transformed by the same coarse black fur and thick yellow nails as his left hand. His right foot now looked the same as his left.

He fought back a rising tide of panic, praying that

Kristine would soon conceive, knowing that, all too soon, he would not dare go near her bed for fear she would discover his secret. But more than that, he was terrified that he would lose control of the beast rapidly devouring his humanity; that, in a moment of mindless need, he would do her harm.

He turned onto his side and watched her sleeping. Her nightmares had been eased; he feared the worst of his were just beginning.

Chapter Nine

Kristine gazed in wonder at the colorful lanterns that lined the long, curved drive that led to Gladstone Manor. It looked like a fairy place. The windows on every floor were also ablaze with light.

Erik assisted her from the coach and took her by the hand. Portraying the Angel of Death, he was attired all in black. A black broadcloth cloak lined in ebony silk fell in graceful folds from his shoulders, the hem brushing the tops of his knee-high black boots. A hideous death's-head mask that was genuinely frightening to behold completed his costume.

Representing the Norse goddess Freya, Kristine wore a long white gown trimmed in gold satin, her short hair covered by a long blond wig. They made a striking pair, she mused, like midnight and moonlight.

The sound of conversation and laughter filled the air, vying with the music. She had never seen such a crush of people. She couldn't stop staring. Zeus waltzed by with Cleopatra, a lion stood in the corner, conversing with a shapely ghost in a diaphanous gown.

There were all manner of costumes. Some were comical, some were grotesque, some quite bizarre. Kristine would have melted into a corner if given a choice, but it was not to be.

"Come," Erik said, leading her onto the dance floor, "let us see how well you remember your lessons."

She moved woodenly at first, conscious of people staring at them. She didn't belong here with these elegant people. They would be appalled if they knew they were entertaining a convicted felon. She tripped on her skirt, stepped on Erik's toes.

"Relax, Kristine," he said, giving her hand a squeeze. "You have nothing to fear."

She gazed up into his eyes and everything else faded away. She forgot to watch her feet, forgot to count the steps. Effortlessly, he waltzed her around the room. She was aware of his hand, large and firm, at her waist, of his gaze burning into hers. They dipped and swayed as if they had been waltzing together for years.

When the music ended, there were a dozen men waiting to claim her for the next dance.

Trevayne surrendered her with good grace, though inside he was seething with resentment. Making his way to a shadowed corner, he watched her waltz by in the arms of another man. This was what he wanted, he reminded himself. He wanted her to get to know other men. She was young, far too young to spend the rest of her life alone. She would undoubtedly wish to marry again. She would want companionship, a man's protection. His child would need a father. . . .

Jealousy rose within him like bitter bile as he watched the young fops fawn over her, vying for a smile, a dance, bringing her a cup of hot spiced punch, seeking to make her laugh.

Shy at first, she was soon at ease in their midst. He knew she had never been taught to flirt, yet she came by it naturally. The men swarmed around her like bears to a honey pot.

Trevayne watched as long as he could and then, unable to endure it a moment longer, he made his way through the crowd. Ignoring the protests of those paying her court, he led her away from her admirers.

"Are you having a good time, madam?"

"Yes, very." She looked up at him, her eyes alight with merriment, her lips parted in a smile, until she saw the expression in his eyes. "Have I done something to displease you, my lord?"

He choked back the harsh reply that sprang to his lips. How could he chastise her? He had left her alone, like a fawn among a pack of wolves, and now he was angry because she had held her own, because she had not come running to him for protection.

"My lord?"

"No, Kristine, you have done nothing to displease me." He offered her his hand. "Come, my lady wife, and dance with me."

He was aware of the stares that followed them as they twirled around the floor, conscious of the whispered voices as his neighbors speculated on why he had not been seen in public for the last four years.

When the waltz ended, Lord Dunston claimed Kristine for the next dance. Erik kissed Kristine's hand, inclined his head in Dunston's direction, and left the floor.

It seemed odd to be in the midst of so many people after his self-imposed exile, strange to hear music and laughter. A few of his old cronies guessed who he was and urged him to join them for a game of cards. At first, he was reluctant, but the thought of being in their company again, of being able to pretend, if only for a little while, that he was still the man he had once been, was far too tempting. He sent one of the footmen to tell Kristine he would see her in an hour, and followed Gladstone into the card room.

"Erik, it's good to see you out again," Gladstone remarked as he sat down and began to shuffle a deck of cards.

"It's good to be out."

"That new bride's been keeping him busy, I'll wager," Robert Jordan said with a leer.

"Ah, without doubt, without doubt," Fitzroy said. "Our Erik always had a way with the ladies. Shall we remove our masks while we play?"

"I think I shall keep mine on," Jordan declared.

"I shouldn't wonder," Erik muttered with a wry grin. It was a well-known fact that Jordan was unable to keep from smiling when he was dealt a good hand. "I shall keep mine on, as well."

They played with the ease of men who had grown up together and were comfortable with one another. Gladstone kept the whiskey flowing, Dunston relayed the latest court gossip, Fitzroy complained loudly each time he lost a hand.

The hour passed all too quickly. With regret, Erik stood to leave.

"You're not going!" Dunston exclaimed. "Surely you intend to give us a chance to recoup our losses."

Erik grinned beneath his mask. "I am sorry, gentlemen, but I have left my bride alone far too long already."

"Yes, I'd keep an eye on that one myself," Jordan remarked.

"My plan, to be sure," Erik said. He slipped his winnings into his pocket. "Gentlemen, it has been a pleasure, as always."

"Of course," Fitzroy muttered irritably. "You won. As always."

Erik sketched an exaggerated bow, then left the room. Taking a glass of wine from one of the footmen, he made his way to the ballroom, his gaze skimming over the crowd until he found Kristine.

She stood out from the other women like a rose in a field of clover. Her face was flushed from dancing, her eyes bright as she stood in the midst of a group of admirers. Lady Trevayne was the belle of the ball, he mused. Once he was gone, she would have suitors aplenty at her door, men eager to woo and wed her. And bed her.

"But for now, she's mine," he murmured, and placing his empty glass on a table, he crossed the floor to claim his bride.

"May I have this dance, wife?" he asked.

Kristine looked up at him, eyes shining. "I'm afraid I've promised it to Lord Hoxford."

"Lord Hoxford can wait," Erik said curtly, and before the lord in question could protest, Erik swept her into his arms. "You are my wife," he said as he whirled her out among the other couples, "and I want to dance."

"As you wish, my lord."

He gazed down at her. "How much wine have you had to drink?"

"Only a few glasses."

"No more."

"My lord?"

"I don't want you tipsy."

"I'm not . . ." She hiccupped. "Tipsy."

"Indeed?"

She looked up at him, obviously offended. "I'm sober as . . . as a judge." She shuddered at her poor choice of words. A judge. All too well she remembered the dour-faced magistrate who had sentenced her to death, who had refused to believe she had killed Lord Valentine in self-defense.

"Kristine?" Erik frowned, wondering at the sudden change in her mood. "Are you sick?"

"No." She looked up at him, her eyes filled with sadness. "I didn't mean to kill him."

"I know." He drew her into his arms and held her close. "I know."

The Gladstones' butler chose that moment to announce dinner.

Because of the large number of people, and the rather cumbersome costumes of some of their guests, Lady Gladstone had decided on a buffet.

Kristine watched in amazement as the doors at the far end of the ballroom opened to reveal a dozen long tables covered with white damask cloths and laden with food: whole roast pigs, game hens stuffed with wild rice, racks of lamb, platters of seafood, huge bowls of vegetables in rich sauces, baskets of bread and rolls. Just looking at so much food made her feel suddenly queasy.

She placed her hand on Erik's arm. "Could we go outside for a moment? I feel the need for a little fresh air."

"Of course."

Tucking her hand into his, he led her out into the vast gardens that surrounded the estate. "Better?"

"Yes, thank you." She removed her mask and placed it on a wrought-iron bench. "It was quite warm in there."

Erik smiled indulgently. How young and innocent she was, and how beautiful. An angel, caressed by moonlight.

"Why are you looking at me like that?" she asked.

"Like what?"

"Like a hungry cat about to pounce on a poor little mouse."

"Perhaps because that is exactly what I am thinking."

"Really?" She blinked up at him, her eyes wide, her cheeks as pink as the roses that grew in profusion all around them.

"Really."

She swayed toward him. "Will you not kiss me then, my lord?"

It was a thought to tempt a saint, but he could not indulge her now, could not remove his mask without revealing the ugliness beneath.

"My lord?" She took a rather unsteady step toward him.

"Kristine!" He reached out to steady her. "I think you are in your cups, my dear."

"I don't feel so good," she mumbled.

"I'll take you home."

"But I don't want to go home," she protested. "I'm having such a good time. And I owe Lord Hoxford a waltz."

"There will be no more dancing for you tonight, my sweet," Erik said. "I'm taking you home. I shall send Brandt in to make our apologies."

She looked up at him in horror. "You're not going to tell him I'm . . . I'm . . ."

"Of course not. I shall say you're feeling a little under the weather."

"I'm fine, really." She took a deep breath, intending to argue further, then pressed a hand over her mouth. "Oh, Erik, I'm going to be sick!"

Scooping her into his arms, he ran toward the far end of the garden, then set her down. No sooner had her feet touched the ground than she dropped to her knees and began to retch.

Erik knelt beside her, one hand supporting her, silently offered her his handkerchief when she was through. "Are you all right?"

"I think I'm dying."

He laughed softly. "Not quite. You will most likely feel better now. Not used to spirits, are you?"

Kristine shook her head, then groaned. "No."

"One shouldn't overindulge on an empty stomach," he said sympathetically. "Come, let us go home."

She was unusually quiet in the carriage on the way home.

"Is something wrong?" Erik asked.

"I made a fool of myself," she replied, not looking at him. "I made you leave the party early."

He laughed softly as he drew her into his arms. "Did you have a good time?"

"Yes."

"That's all that matters."

"You are so good to me, Erik." She rested her head on his shoulder. "Why are you so good to me?"

He gazed down at her, at her lips, pink and slightly parted, at the long dark lashes that lay against her cheeks. Why, indeed, he mused as he gave her shoulders a squeeze. Why, indeed.

"Will you make love to me when we get home?"

"You should get some sleep."

"I am not tired." She lifted her arms and wrapped them around his neck. "Come, my lord, you must do your husbandly duty."

He told himself it was the champagne talking, but he didn't care. She wanted him, and that was all that mattered.

"Yes," he said gently, "my duty."

Chapter Ten

Kristine felt slightly nauseous the morning after the ball. She attributed it to a very late night and all the champagne she had consumed. By noon, she felt better. By evening, she had forgotten all about it, so she was surprised to find herself ill again the following morning, as well, and every morning for the next two weeks.

"I don't know what's wrong with me," she groaned as she rinsed her mouth with warm water.

Lilia and Leyla smiled at each other as they changed the soiled linen on her bed.

"You don't suppose I'm coming down with something, do you?" Kristine asked.

Leyla's smile widened as she placed her hand over Kristine's belly, then pretended she was cradling a baby in her arms.

Kristine stared at the woman a moment, and then her mouth dropped open. "A baby? You think I'm with child?"

Leyla and Lilia looked at each other and nodded. Cocking her head to one side, Leyla pressed lightly on Kristine's breast.

Kristine frowned. Her breasts had been tender for the last few days.

Lilia and Leyla looked at each other and smiled.

"A baby," Kristine murmured. "Oh, my." A slow smile spread across her face as she contemplated telling Erik he was going to be a father. It was what he wanted, the reason he had married her in the first place. He had told her so himself. *I want nothing from you*, he had said, the words cold and blunt and implacable. *Nothing but a child.*

She felt the smile die on her lips. Would he stop coming nightly to her bed now that the deed had been accomplished and she was carrying his child? Though she was certain it was unseemly, she treasured their lovemaking, had grown accustomed to falling asleep in his arms. And though he was gone in the morning when she awoke, his scent permeated her bedclothes, her pillow, her skin.

She wasn't ready to give all that up, not yet. "Promise me," she said, looking from one woman to the other, "promise you won't tell anyone."

Leyla and Lilia exchanged glances.

"Promise me," Kristine insisted. "This is my news, and I wish to tell my lord husband in my own time, in my own way."

The two silent women both nodded. They helped her dress, then left the room.

"A baby," Kristine murmured.

Taking her diary from the drawer, she sat down and picked up her quill.

It has been so long since I've written, I don't know where to start. I feel, at last, as though I am truly married. Erik still refuses to spend the night in my bed, but I feel that he has come to care for me, at least a little. As for me, I think I could love him if he would let me. We spend a part of each day together, but it is the quiet evenings we share that bind us together.

Leyla and Lilia made it known to me this morning that they think I am with child. The thought had not occurred to me, but I know now that it is true, that Erik's child is growing within my womb. I am to be a mother. It is almost beyond comprehension, a miracle. I wonder, will it be a boy or a girl, though I care not, so long as it is strong and healthy and whole. . . .

With a sigh, she put her pen aside, her happiness marred by doubts. What if Erik was horribly misshapen beneath the mask? What if he had been born that way, if the same deformity should be passed on to their child? But surely, if that were true, he would not be seeking an heir.

Keeping her secret was harder than she had expected. A dozen times a day the words rose in her throat. At night, in his arms, after they had made love, the words begged to be said and yet she kept them locked inside. She could not put aside her fear that, once he knew his seed was growing within her, he would no longer have need of her.

* * *

They went riding every morning. She knew she would soon have to stop, for safety's sake. A fall could be dangerous for her child. But not on this beautiful day. It was the first of July and the sky was a clear, azure blue. As always, she lost herself in the joy of riding, in the beauty of the landscape. The grass spread before them like a carpet of lush green velvet. Flowers dotted the countryside, as bright as gems scattered by a careless hand.

They paused after an hour or so to rest the horses. It was then, as she watched Erik dismount and walk toward her, that she noticed the stiffness in his movements.

"Are you in pain, my lord?" she asked as he lifted her from Misty's back.

"It's nothing." He set her on her feet. Gathering the horses' reins, he led them to a small pool and let them drink.

Kristine frowned as she watched him walk away. He was limping. She was sure of it.

Plucking a bright yellow dandelion, she twirled it between her thumb and forefinger, her gaze focused on Erik's back. The sun glinted in the blackness of his hair. She watched the muscles ripple beneath the fine wool of his shirt, and her fingers ached to touch him.

He turned and caught her watching him. Heat suffused her cheeks, not the heat of shame at being caught staring, but the heat of desire. The attraction between them sizzled like summer lightning.

Hardly aware of what she was doing, she crushed the dandelion in her hand as he tethered the horses to a tree and crossed the distance between them.

"Kristine . . ."

She looked up at him, her green eyes bright. "Yes, my lord?"

Erik's gaze swept the surrounding countryside. They were alone, quite alone.

Taking her by the hand, he led her to a small copse of trees.

"Here, my lord?" she asked as he drew her down beside him.

"Here, now." He was running out of time, he thought desperately. The right side of his body ached, the pain reminding him that time was one thing he didn't have to waste. If he was going to sire an heir, it had to be soon, before even layers of clothing and a mask would not hide what he was becoming.

He undressed her quickly, his heart pounding with need and desire, his gaze drinking in the beauty of her face and form. Her skin was soft and smooth and he wished that, just once, he dared remove his clothing and feel the heat of her body against his. And even as his body became a part of hers, he knew she deserved so much more than the half man, half monster cradled between her thighs.

Release came quickly for both of them.

With a sigh, he drew her into his arms and held her close, one hand lightly moving over her belly, her breasts . . .

Muttering an oath, he sat up, eyes narrowed thoughtfully as he cupped her breast, spread his hand across her belly.

"Is there something you want to tell me?" he asked, his voice sharp.

A dark flush stained her cheeks as her gaze slid away from his. "I'm . . . that is, we . . ."

"Are you breeding?" he asked curtly.

"Aye, my lord."

"How long have you known?"

"Nearly a month."

"And you saw no need to tell me?"

"I . . ." She looked up at him, tears welling in her eyes.

"Why did you not tell me, Kristine?"

"I was afraid."

"Afraid? Of what?"

The flush that stained her neck and cheeks crept up into her hairline.

"Answer me!"

"I was afraid," she stammered. "Afraid you would no longer come to my bed if you knew."

He stared at her, speechless. "Why would you think that?"

She grabbed her riding habit and drew it over her, as if it would protect her. "You once told me that you wanted nothing from me but a child."

Erik nodded, still not understanding.

"I . . . I . . ."

He would have wagered half his estate that her cheeks could get no pinker than they were. He would have lost. "Go on."

"I didn't want to lose your company in my bed, my lord."

"Ah, Kristine," he murmured. "What a delight you are, and how I shall miss you."

"Miss me, my lord? Where are you going?"

"Nowhere," he said quickly. "When is the child due?"

"I'm not sure. Mrs. Grainger thinks sometime after Christmas." Kristine bit down on her lower lip. "Will you be terribly disappointed if it is a girl, my lord?"

"No." He plucked the habit from her hand and tossed it aside, then placed his hand over her belly. His child was growing there, beneath his hand. It was a powerful thought.

She glanced at his hand, then frowned up at him. "I don't even show yet. How did you know?"

He shook his head. She was right. How had he known? He shied away from the answer that quickly came to mind even as he knew that it was somehow tied to the curse that plagued him, to the heightened senses that enabled him to see things, hear things, that others could not.

Kristine's gaze slid away from his as she wondered how to phrase the question that plagued her without hurting his feelings.

"My lord, may I ask you something?"

"Anything."

"You won't be angry?"

"No."

"You promise?"

"I promise."

"I know you said I was not to ask about the mask, but I should very much like to know why you wear it." She lifted a hand to silence him. "You needn't tell me what you're hiding. I should only like to know if . . . if it's an affliction you were born with and if . . ." Her voice trailed off.

"You need not worry, Kristine," he replied stiffly, "your child will not be cursed with my affliction."

Right or wrong, his words removed a huge weight from her mind. "I'm sorry, my lord."

He shook his head. "Don't be. You have every right to be concerned for your child's welfare." He spread his fingers over her belly. His hand was large and very brown against her pale skin. "Now I would ask you a question, and beg you tell me the truth honestly. Is this child something you want?"

"Oh, yes!" She placed her hand over his. "Never doubt that, my lord husband. I am happy to be carrying our child."

With a sigh, he drew her into his arms and held her close.

"May I ask another question, my lord?"

He smiled at her. "Today you may ask anything."

"You are in pain, are you not?"

"Yes."

"Is there anything I can do to help?"

"No."

"What of your physician? Can he do nothing to ease your suffering?"

Erik rested his chin on top of her head and stared into the distance, the sound of Charmion's voice roaring like thunder in his mind. *When my daughter forgives you, so shall I.*

"No," he said heavily. "There is nothing anyone can do."

He had planned to see less of her now that she was with child, to gradually withdraw from her presence, thinking it would be less painful that way. Instead, he resolved to spend as much time as he could with her, to store up a wealth of memories against the day when he would no longer be able to hide his affliction and he would be forced to leave the castle for good.

True to her word, Kristine asked no more questions, but accepted the peculiarities of their life together. She grew accustomed to dimly lit rooms, to making love in the dark to a man who was fully clothed, to being unable to touch him.

As time went on, they took their rides after sunset, when the world was gray. He cherished the quiet times they spent riding together. He could see her clearly in the darkness, and he memorized every inch of her face and form, every expression, the happy sound of her laughter. She was radiant now, with a new life growing within her. Her eyes seemed to glow from within, her skin was soft and pink, her breasts were fuller, often tempting his touch. She never pulled away, never denied him.

Loving her was a mix of pleasure and pain. He delighted in touching her, holding her, caressing her, and ached because he could not accept her touch in return. And she wanted to touch him. He saw it in her eyes, in the way she sometimes forgot herself and reached out, only to have him stay her hand. Soon, he would not be able to share her bed. Soon, there would be no hiding what he was becoming.

Shortly after their attendance at the masked ball, Kristine began receiving invitations to other events—horse races and luncheons, card parties and afternoon teas. At first, she refused to attend, but he urged and then insisted that she accept. It was not good for her to spend all her time in the castle. She needed to make friends of the other women in the district, needed a life of her own.

Kristine argued at first, afraid to venture out of the house without him, afraid her manners would be found wanting. And so he had Mrs. Grainger and the mute women instruct her in every art of polite society he could imagine, and then he sat back and watched her blossom. Her hair, longer at last, framed her face with honey-gold curls. Her green eyes sparkled like the emeralds he had given her. The sound of her merry laughter filled the rooms of the once-gloomy castle.

He knew a sense of pride as he watched her accept invitations, watched her confidence grow. He gave her leave to have company whenever she wished, though he made himself scarce on days she was entertaining. In the city, it was unheard of for a pregnant woman to entertain or to accept invitations, but here, in the country, it was common for women to go out in society until their condition was quite pronounced.

Now, sitting upstairs in his room while she entertained a handful of new friends, he listened to the sounds of merriment rising from below, and knew that when the time came that he must leave her for good, she would not be alone.

Chapter Eleven

"I should like to have a party, my lord husband," Kristine decided at dinner one night.

"Indeed?"

She nodded, her eyes twinkling. "A masked ball, such as the one we attended at Lord and Lady Gladstone's." She smiled at him, pleased with the idea.

"And when is this auspicious occasion to take place?"

"On All Hallows' Eve."

Erik lifted one brow in wry amusement. "Indeed? And shall I come dressed as the devil?"

"If you wish. And I shall be one of your angels."

"You are already that," he murmured.

"I have your permission, then?"

He nodded, knowing he would willingly grant her anything she desired.

Her gaze slid away from his, and he could see she was trying not to laugh.

"Will you not share the joke with me?"

"I knew you would agree," she said with a bright smile. "The invitations went out this morning."

"Vixen," he muttered. "What would you have done if I had said no?"

Rising, she rounded the table and sat in his lap. "I would have convinced you to change your mind, my lord."

It would have been an easy task, he mused, for he could deny her nothing.

He gave her free rein to plan for the ball, letting her order whatever she wished in the way of food and decorations for the house. He hired extra servants to help Mrs. Grainger in the kitchen, gardeners to work in the yard, maids to clean the place from top to bottom. It had been years since he had opened his doors to his neighbors; if he was going to do it now, then Hawksbridge Castle must shine as bright as its mistress.

The night of the ball, he walked through the house, thinking that all the fuss and preparation had been well worth it. The castle shone like a rare jewel, the perfect setting for his lovely lady wife.

Clad all in red, with a horned mask firmly in place, he went into Kristine's room. She was sitting at her dressing table while Leyla and Lilia fussed with her hair. Glancing over her shoulder, she smiled at him.

She was a vision, he thought, a true angel in every sense of the word. She wore a long red gown that clung to every curve, displaying her creamy shoulders and a good bit of cleavage. No one looking at her would suspect she was six months with child. Her body was still slim, though her breasts were fuller. He frowned at the thought of other men staring at her beauty, then forced his jealousy aside. She was young and beautiful. She would marry again.

"My lord, is something amiss?"

He wiped the frown from his face and smiled at her. "If that is how the angels in hell look, I can hardly wait to go there."

"My lord!" she exclaimed in horror, "what a dreadful thing to say. Say a prayer, quickly!"

"You say it for me."

"I will," she replied soberly.

He had prayed, in the beginning, promised to do anything, anything, if only the curse would be lifted, but to no avail, making him wonder if Charmion had been right and he had truly caused Dominique's death. But it no longer mattered. His soul was indeed bound for hell. As soon as he knew his child had been born, he would take his own life and thus put an end to the hideous curse that plagued him.

"Here now." He put a finger beneath her chin and lifted her face to his. "Smile. We're having a party, remember?"

"You look quite frightening," she said.

"Do I?" He caressed her cheek, thinking she would be far more frightened if she knew what lay beneath his costume.

Leyla and Lilia applied the finishing touches to Kristine's hair. Smiling and bowing, they left the room.

Kristine stood up and kissed Erik on the cheek. "Ready, my lord husband?"

With a nod, he placed her hand on his right arm and they went downstairs to greet their guests.

* * *

Erik stood in the shadows, watching Kristine play Lady of the Manor. She charmed their guests, from young Edward Randolph to the old dowager, Lady Rowena Silverstone. He heard several young ladies whispering about Kristine's short hair, wondering if perhaps it was the result of a high fever. The young men swarmed around her, their eyes hot as they devoured her.

It seemed strange, to see the house and grounds lit up, to hear the sound of laughter ringing from the walls. Not since Dominique died had there been so many people within Hawksbridge Castle.

He watched as his guests went in to dinner. Mrs. Grainger had planned a buffet, and she had done herself proud. Several long tables nearly groaned beneath the weight of food being offered—succulent hams, pheasants, chickens swimming in wine sauce. Vegetables and fruit, bread and rolls. The air was redolent with the varied aromas.

He frowned as he watched young Lord Hoxford escort Kristine into the dining room. Hoxford had been hovering near Kristine all evening, smiling at her, paying her outrageous compliments, claiming her for every waltz, holding her far too close.

Erik felt his anger rise when Hoxford leaned in to whisper something in Kristine's ear. The man was far too bold, and yet he would make an excellent match for Kristine. He came from an old family. He was tall and broad-shouldered and handsome. And discreet in his liaisons.

Taking a deep breath, Erik forced himself to relax. One of the reasons he had agreed to this elaborate affair was so that Kristine could get better acquainted not only with her neighbors, but with possible suitors.

He did not join the others at dinner. One of the advantages of the buffet was that he did not have to sit at the head of the table. There was no formal seating. Some of his guests sat at the dining table, others wandered into the parlor or the library, or found seating in the gardens.

Grabbing a glass of wine, Erik sought the darkness beyond the house. Dark gray clouds were gathering overhead. He could smell the moisture in the air. There would be rain before morning. He wondered how many of his guests would look at the weather and decide to spend the night.

He drained his glass and tossed it aside. Laughter and music drifted on the breeze as he wandered through the gardens. He lifted his head, sniffing the wind, then swore as he realized what he was doing. The beast within him was growing stronger. More and more he found himself behaving in feral ways, found himself feeling hampered, confined, by his clothing, found himself asking Mrs. Grainger to serve his roast beef rare instead of well-done.

He lifted his left hand and removed his glove, staring at the animal-like paw as if, by doing so, he could make it disappear. And then he lifted his right hand and wiggled his fingers. What a wondrous thing a hand was, he mused. He could hold a glass, pick a flower for his wife, caress her warm, soft skin. . . .

He closed his eyes as pain ripped through him. It was constant now, the pain that throbbed through his body as it fought the transformation, the anguish of knowing he was running out of time. And the worst pain of all, that of knowing that he was going to lose Kristine. He had known her such a short time, yet he loved her beyond all reason. He longed to tell her so, to hold her in his arms and pour out his love. It took all his willpower to keep the words locked inside. Once said, they could not be taken back. It was better for her to go on thinking that all he wanted from her was an heir. She knew he was fond of her, but there was a vast difference between fondness and what he felt. Better for them both if the words remained unsaid.

With a sigh, he turned back toward the house. He was the host; it was his duty to mingle with his guests.

As he neared the back of the castle, he heard whispered voices. And then he saw a couple standing near one of the hedges. Young lovers. The thought filled him with a bittersweet longing, and then, catching Kristine's scent on the air, he felt a surge of anger rise up within.

On silent feet, he padded toward them.

"You are most fair, Lady Trevayne," Hoxford was murmuring. "Truly, you are the most beautiful woman here this evening."

"You mustn't flatter me so, Lord Hoxford," Kristine protested.

"I speak no flattery," Hoxford replied. "Only the truth." He lifted her hand to his lips and kissed her palm. "Your skin is like the finest satin, your hair shines like the sun."

Kristine tried to withdraw her hand from his. "Lord Hoxford, you must not say such things to me. It isn't proper."

"Not proper to compliment my hostess?" Hoxford laughed softly as he drew Kristine into his arms. "Don't be absurd."

A low growl rose in Erik's throat as Hoxford kissed Kristine. She struggled for a moment, then stood passive and unresponsive in the young man's arms.

Hoxford released her immediately, his expression curious. "Do you find me so repulsive?" he asked quietly.

"No, my lord. I am flattered by your words and your interest, but I am, after all, a married woman."

"You take your vows seriously, then?"

"Yes, very seriously. I would do nothing to shame my husband, or myself."

Hoxford nodded. "My apologies, my lady. I hope you will not think the less of me for my impetuousness."

Kristine shook her head. She knew that flirting was to be expected, knew that many women, forced to marry men they did not love, sought affairs. She was not one of them. Her marriage might be a strange one, but she had no wish to end it, no wish to cuckold Erik.

Hoxford offered her his arm. "Come, I'll walk you back to the house."

"Thank you, but I think I shall stay outside and take the air for a few minutes," Kristine said.

Hoxford bowed over her hand. "As you wish, Lady Trevayne. Again, my apologies for my behavior. I pray I have not offended you."

"Apology accepted, Lord Hoxford."

"We can remain friends, then?"

Kristine smiled. "Of course."

With a nod, Hoxford returned to the house.

Kristine watched him walk away, her emotions in turmoil. He was a very handsome young man. At another time, before Erik had entered her life, she would have found young Hoxford most attractive, would have been extraordinarily pleased by his admiration.

In truth, she had found his kiss quite pleasant, though it lacked the fire and excitement of Erik's kisses. Erik. She wished he was here with her now, wished he would take her in his arms. . . .

She whirled around, suddenly aware that she was no longer alone. As if conjured by her desire, he was there before her, a dark silhouette in the blackness of the night.

"My lord," she murmured. "You startled me."

"Indeed?" He closed the distance between them, until they were only a hand span apart. "What are you doing out here, alone?"

"Nothing. I . . ." Her gaze slid away from his. How much had he seen? How much had he heard? She felt a wave of heat sweep into her cheeks. "I wasn't alone."

"No?"

She shook her head. "Lord Hoxford was with me."

"A fine young man," Erik remarked, his voice cool.

"Yes."

"He's to your liking, then?"

"Yes. But only as a friend, my lord. You are my husband."

"And if you were free, would you accept Hoxford's suit?"

"Erik, my lord . . ." She couldn't keep the fine edge of panic from her voice. Had she displeased him in some way? Was he planning to put her aside? "What are you saying?"

"Nothing, my sweet." He drew her into his arms and crushed her close. "Nothing."

"You don't think that Lord Hoxford . . . that I . . ." She looked up at Erik, wishing she could see his face.

"No." He drew her against him once more, his

hand stroking her back. She was warm and soft in his arms, a temptation like none he had ever known. With a sigh, he rested his chin on the top of her head, wishing he could hold her thus forever, wishing that he had years to spend with her instead of only a few more months at best. Wishing . . .

The strains of a waltz filled the air. Kristine placed her hand on his shoulder. "Dance with me, my lord?"

With a nod, he led her onto a small expanse of smooth stones, then swept her into his arms. The music and the night seemed to close around them, shutting out the rest of the world.

She was light as a feather in his arms as she followed his lead, and he thought how well they danced together, how well they fit together. Had it not been for the awful curse that plagued him, they might have enjoyed a long and happy life together.

He drew her closer. Soon, her belly would swell with his babe. It amazed him that she wanted his child, amazed him still more that she didn't despise him, that she welcomed his touch, that she had feared he might cease coming to her bed once she conceived. What had he done to inspire her affection, her trust? Or was he fooling himself into thinking she cared? Perhaps she welcomed him in her bed out of a sense of duty because he had saved her from the executioner's axe and given her a comfortable home. Perhaps her smiles were merely her way of expressing her gratitude. The thought filled him with a strange sense of anger and sadness. He wanted her love, her affection. He wanted her smiles and her laughter, knew he would hoard each precious moment he spent with her from now on so that he could take them out and look at them later.

"Is something amiss, my lord?" Kristine asked. "You seem very far away."

"Do I? How could I be, when I'm holding you in my arms?"

His flattery warmed her down to her toes. "You're not angry with me, then?"

"Angry?"

"About Lord Hoxford."

"No, I'm not angry."

A slender ray of moonlight broke through the clouds, haloing her hair. She was gazing up at him, her eyes dark, her lips slightly parted.

"Kristine . . ." Murmuring her name, he lifted the lower edge of his mask, bent his head, and claimed her lips. She tasted of sweet wine and he deepened the kiss, his tongue stroking hers. She pressed against him, her breasts warm against his chest, her breath quickening.

"Sweet," he said, his voice thick, "so sweet." His hand slid down her back, over her buttocks, drawing her up against him, letting her feel the need thrumming through him.

Feeling suddenly bold, she grabbed him by the hand and led him away from the house, her destination the little cottage she had found near a small pond. It was a tiny little house, one that might have been fashioned for a child.

Erik allowed her to lead him along, saying nothing. They had almost reached the cottage when it began to rain, a light mist that quickly became a downpour.

Kristine, dressed only in a gown of thin red silk, was soaked to the skin by the time they reached the cottage. Erik, clad in shirt, breeches, and a heavy woolen cloak, fared better.

As soon as they were inside, Erik pulled her into his arms and kissed her. She surrendered willingly, wondering at the desperation that seemed to grip him.

Gradually, his hold loosened. With a sigh, he released her. "You're shivering," he said. "You need to get out of that wet gown."

She nodded.

"I'll build a fire."

While he laid the fire, she went into the bedroom and took off her ruined slippers, then peeled off her clothing, draping her gown and undergarments over a chair to dry. There were several blankets in the chest at the foot of the bed. She wrapped one securely around her, then carried two more into the parlor.

A small fire blazed in the hearth, casting heat and shadows into the room.

Erik stood with his back to her, one hand braced against the mantel. He had removed his cloak; it was spread over a chair.

She bit down on her lower lip. She knew without asking that he wouldn't undress in front of her; knew better than to light one of the lamps.

With a sigh, she walked up behind him and draped one of the blankets over his shoulders.

"Thank you."

"What is this place?" she asked, looking around.

"My brother and I played here when we were young."

"Your brother?"

Erik nodded. "My elder brother. Robert," he said heavily. "He was the rightful heir. He died in a hunting accident when he was nine and twenty."

"You've never mentioned him before."

"No." He gazed into the flames, thinking how different his life would have been if his brother had lived. Robert would be lord of Hawksbridge Castle and he, Erik, would be living with the good brothers in poverty and obedience, his life dedicated to the church. He never would have married Dominique, or been burdened with this hideous curse.

He never would have met Kristine. . . . Meeting her, loving her, was almost worth all the rest.

"My lord, you should get out of those wet things."

"They're only damp," he replied with a shrug. "They'll dry soon enough."

She stared at his broad back, wondering at the change in him. Only moments ago he had been on fire for her; now he seemed almost indifferent to her presence. What was he thinking?

"Have you other brothers?" she asked. "Sisters, perhaps?"

"No." Slowly, he turned to face her. He had removed the horned mask and replaced it with one of black silk. "Have you?"

She shook her head, thinking how rare it was for him to ask about her family, her past. "All I have is you," she said, very softly. And then she smiled. "And our babe."

Pain lanced through him at her words, a pain so deep he thought he might die of it. He would never see his child. He knew it with gut-wrenching certainty.

"My lord? Erik?" She reached out, her hand closing over his arm. "Are you ill?"

"No."

She looked up at him, her green eyes filled with worry.

"I'm fine, Kristine," he said reassuringly. "Only cold all of a sudden." He opened his arms. "Come, warm me."

She stepped into his embrace, her arms wrapping around his waist, content to be there. "Tell me of your childhood. Was it happy?"

He rested his chin on the top of her head. "Happy enough. I never wanted to be lord of Hawksbridge. I knew the title would go to Robert, and I was glad of it. I was a solitary child, happiest when I was alone with my books. It was my intention to join the good friars at Hawksbridge Abbey and devote my life to God. It seemed a fine ambition at the time. I know now I was not cut out to be a monk any more than I was cut out to be the lord of Hawksbridge Castle."

"Why do you say that? Hawksbridge flourishes under your care."

"I never wanted wealth or lands or title, or the responsibility that they entail. But now . . ." Now, when he was about to lose it all, he realized how much he had grown to love the land and its people. He would miss the rolling green acres, miss galloping through the early-morning mists. He would miss his library, and Mrs. Grainger's apple dumplings, and the sense of accomplishment he felt at the end of each year.

But most of all, he would miss Kristine. . . .

With a groan, he slanted his mouth over hers and

kissed her hungrily, desperately. His good hand moved restlessly over her body, stroking her breasts, her thighs, her buttocks, pressing her intimately against him. He kissed her cheeks, her nose, her eyes, her chin, ran his tongue down the slender column of her neck, tasted the soft, sensitive skin behind her ear.

With an impatient cry, he tossed the blanket aside so that she stood bared to his heated gaze, her body glowing in the light of the fire. Bending down, he rained kisses over her swollen belly, knowing this was as close to his child as he would ever get.

He closed his eyes as he felt Kristine's hands move in the hair at his nape.

"What is it?" she asked. "Please, Erik, what is it that troubles you so?"

"Don't ask," he said with a low growl. "Not now. Not tonight."

His lips moved up over her belly, his tongue laving her breasts, and then he was kissing her once more, kissing her as if he would never stop, could never have enough.

Sweeping her into his arms, he carried her into the bedroom, away from the light cast by the fire. The bed was small and narrow, the mattress soft. It was a child's bed, and it sagged beneath their weight.

She embraced him, taking him into her arms, into her heart, holding him close, lifting her hips to receive him into herself.

As always, she longed to touch him, to explore his body, to know his body as intimately as he knew hers.

As always, he refused to let her touch him.

As always, he saw to her pleasure first. His climax followed quickly.

Lying there, their bodies still pressed intimately together, she closed her eyes. Listening to the sound of thunder and her husband's ragged breathing, she felt a tear slip down her cheek, and knew that it was his.

Chapter Twelve

"What about our guests?" Kristine asked. She snuggled against Erik's right side. She had noticed that he was always careful to keep her to his right and she wondered if his left side pained him greatly. She wanted to question him about that but knew he would not answer, knew that it would spoil the beauty, the intimacy, of this precious moment.

"I doubt anyone will miss us," Erik replied. He ran his hand through her hair, watched the fine golden strands curl around his fingers. It was silky soft against his skin. He wished he could have seen it before it had been cut, wished he could have seen her standing in moonlight clad in nothing but her hair.

"Are we to spend the night here, then?" she asked.

"If you wish."

She nodded. Contented as a well-fed cat, she didn't want to move, didn't want to get dressed or go back to the party.

"Tell me of your childhood, Kristine. Was it happy?"

"Yes, very. For a while anyway. My father was the

schoolmaster in our town. We had a comfortable home. He was well-respected in our community."

"You loved him."

"Of course. Didn't you love your father?"

"No, but I respected him. He was a wise man."

"Why didn't you love him?"

"Because he didn't love me. Robert was his first-born, his heir. I was nothing." He ran his knuckles over her cheek. "We were speaking of you, of your life. What of your mother? You have not mentioned her."

"She was very beautiful. Everyone thought so. She was much younger than my father and after a while she became discontented with our small village, our quiet life." She sighed. "The summer I was two and ten, a troupe of players came to town."

"Go on."

"My mother took me to see the play. I don't recall what it was, but I thought it was wonderful. The actors were fascinating. I wanted to stay and see the play again. So did my mother. When the first performance was over, we went outside and walked around, looking at the people, the animals. My mother was fascinated with everything. We were sitting in the shade, waiting for the next performance to start, when a young man approached us. He was one of the actors." She took a deep breath. "When the troupe left town a week later, so did my mother. I never saw her again."

"I'm sorry, Kristine. That must have been difficult for you. And for your father."

"Yes." She placed her hand over her belly in a protective gesture. "I couldn't believe my mother had left me, left my father, for a man she scarcely knew. I still can't believe it. At first, I told myself he had taken her by force, that she would never have gone with him willingly. Several days later, my father received a letter from my mother. She said she was sorry and begged him to make me understand why she had run away. Of course, at the time, there was nothing my father could say to make me understand."

"And now?"

"I would never leave my child," Kristine said vehemently. "Never!"

"And you never heard from your mother again?"

"She wrote me at first, on my birthday and at Christmas, telling me about all the wonderful places she had seen, how happy she was, promising to come and see me the next time the troupe came to town. But she never did. When I was four and ten, the letters stopped coming."

"I'm sorry, love," Erik murmured.

Love . . . It was the first time he had used such an endearment. It drove every other thought from her mind. Turning on her side, she looked into his eyes, so dark and mysterious, behind the mask. "Erik?"

"Hmm?"

The words *do you love me* trembled on her lips, but she swallowed them, unsaid. "Nothing," she whispered, and leaning forward, her hands braced on his broad chest, she kissed him with all her heart and soul, and understood, for the first time, why her mother had run off with another man.

He rose with the dawn, knowing he would not be able to resist holding her, kissing her, when she woke, knowing he dared not risk making love to her in the light of day. He felt safe, protected, in the darkness.

Moving quietly, he went into the main room of the cottage to stand at the window. The rain had stopped and the sky was a bold dark blue. The scent of rain lingered in the air, and with it the smell of damp grass and earth. Water dripped from the eaves of the cottage, from the leaves of the trees. Birds chirped a welcome to the new day.

"Good morning."

He glanced over his shoulder to see Kristine standing in the doorway, a blanket wrapped tightly around her. "You're up early, wife."

"So are you."

He made a vague gesture with his hand. They both knew why he had left her bed; there was no need to fabricate a lie. "We should go back. Our guests will be preparing to leave soon."

She nodded in agreement, but didn't move.

Slowly, he walked toward her. "Thank you for last night," he said, and watched her cheeks bloom with color.

"Thank you," she replied with a saucy grin. "Won't you kiss me good morning?"

He smiled indulgently, then kissed her, long and hard. "Go get dressed."

"And if I refuse?"

"Go," he said. "Mrs. Grainger is fixing breakfast. I smell ham and eggs cooking."

"You do not!" Kristine exclaimed, but the mention of food made her stomach growl, and she realized she was ravenous.

He sniffed the air. "And fresh-baked scones with honey butter."

"All right, I'm going," she said. "And there had better be scones when we get there."

* * *

It was late afternoon by the time the last of the guests took their leave. As Erik had expected, their absence the night before had not been noticed.

Now he and Kristine were sitting at the dining room table, nibbling on bread and cheese. Erik picked up his glass and sipped his wine. It was an excellent vintage, he mused, and added it to the list of enjoyments he would miss.

Leaning back in his chair, Erik regarded Kristine over the rim of his wineglass. "I should say your first soiree was a huge success."

"It was fun, wasn't it?" Kristine mused with a smile. "We shall have to have another soon."

Erik nodded, knowing that he would not be present the next time. He took a deep breath as a sharp twinge ran the length of his right arm. He clenched his hand. The curse was spreading.

Placing his glass on the table, he stood abruptly.

Kristine frowned as wine splashed over the white cloth. "What's wrong?"

He shook his head. "Nothing. I'll see you this evening."

"Erik? Erik!" She turned in her chair, watching as he rushed out of the room.

Kristine sat at her dressing table, her head bowed over her diary.

Our first ball was a huge success. What fun, to be able to spend however much money I wish, to be able to order gowns and flowers, to entertain our

*neighbors in grand style. In truth, I had thought
they might refuse, for Mrs. Grainger told me it has
been several years since my lord husband has
welcomed visitors to Hawksbridge Castle.*

*Lord Hoxford was most attentive throughout the
evening. He is a handsome young man, with light
brown hair and dark brown eyes. He is tall, though
not so tall as my Erik . . . my Erik . . . He kissed
me in the gardens, and then we went to the little
cottage I found the other day. For the first time, he
told me something of his past, his childhood.
Imagine my surprise when I learned he'd had a
brother! No one has ever mentioned him. Erik told
me he had once thought to enter the priesthood. I
cannot imagine my lord Erik in a monastery,
cannot imagine my life without my strange
husband. I wonder if I will ever see what lies
behind his mask, if he will ever come to trust me
enough, or love me, as I have grown to love him. As
I love our unborn child. I pray it will be a strong,
healthy boy, with Erik's beautiful dark eyes. . . .*

She paused, rereading what she had written. "My
strange husband," she murmured. Why had he left
the parlor so abruptly this afternoon? Where had he
gone? She had not missed the look of torment, of
pain, in his eyes. He had told her before he was often
in pain. Was he hiding some dreadful illness from
her, some fatal malady?

Fear clutched at her heart at the thought of
losing him.

Slipping the book back in the drawer of her dresser,
she left her chamber in search of her husband, but he
was nowhere to be found.

At loose ends, she wandered down to the stable to visit Misty. She was currying the mare when Erik rode up.

The stallion was breathing heavily, its sides covered with foamy yellow lather, its legs smeared with mud.

Kristine smiled tentatively as Erik swung out of the saddle and patted the horse on the neck.

"Cool him out," he said as he passed the stallion's reins to Brandt. "And give him an extra ration of oats."

"Yes, my lord," Brandt said. With a polite nod in Kristine's direction, the boy led the horse away.

"Did you have a good ride, my lord husband?" Kristine asked.

Erik nodded curtly. He had ridden long and hard and, for a short while, he had forgotten everything but the sheer joy of racing across the meadow. Once the stallion had lost its footing and Erik had wondered, even as he pulled up on the reins, if it wouldn't be better for all concerned if he took a fall and broke his neck.

"I would have gone with you," Kristine remarked quietly.

"Next time," Erik replied. He brushed a kiss across her cheek. "I shall see you at dinner."

He was silent and withdrawn at the dinner table that night. She didn't know how or why, but she felt that he was withdrawing from her, erecting a wall between them. He had not said whether he planned to continue sharing her bed, and she couldn't summon the courage to ask. She felt his furtive gaze often during the meal, noticed that he ate nothing, though he drank several glasses of wine.

As was their wont, they went into the library after dinner. Erik perused the day's accounts while she sat in her favorite chair, frowning over a bit of embroidery. It was busywork, nothing more, she thought glumly, and then smiled.

"Erik?"

"Hmm?"

"I'll be needing some material, you know, to make things for the baby."

He grunted softly. "Make a list of what you want. I will send Leyla to fetch them in the morning." He looked up. "You will be needing some material for yourself, too, I should imagine."

Kristine rested a hand over her belly, imagining how it would look in a few months' time. "Yes, I suppose so."

"Purchase whatever you need. Whatever you want."

"Thank you, my lord. You are most generous."

His gaze met hers, his eyes dark with an emotion she could not name and then, before she could do more than wonder what was troubling him so, he turned away so she could not see his eyes. Something was bothering him, she knew it in the deepest part of her, but what?

At ten, Mrs. Grainger brought them a pot of tea. At eleven, Kristine rose to go to bed. She folded her embroidery into a neat pile and placed it on the chair, then walked round the desk to kiss Erik's cheek.

"Good night, my lord husband."

"Good night."

"Will you . . ." She bit down on her lip. "Will I see you later?"

He didn't look at her but he nodded, once, curtly.

She yearned to touch him, to wrap her arms around him and press his head to her breasts, to beg him to tell her what it was that caused him such anguish, but he had never welcomed her touch. With a sigh, she turned and left the room.

A muscle clenched in Erik's jaw as she closed the door. He sat there, staring at nothing, remembering the warmth of her lips on his cheek, the faint flowery scent that clung to her hair and clothing, the slightly husky sound of her voice as she asked, in her own shy way, if he would join her in bed later. It never failed to amaze him that she invited his touch, that she had not told him of her pregnancy for fear he would no longer warm her bed. If he had one wish, it would be to always share her bed, her life, to cradle her in his arms each night, to kiss her awake each morning. But it was not to be.

Despair rose within him, darker than the night outside his window, deeper than the lake near the hunting lodge.

Driven by some primal urge that frightened him even as it compelled him, he left the house and turned toward the deep woods, discarding his clothing as he went, until he ran naked through the night.

The wind whipped through his hair, stung his eyes, chilled his body, and still he ran. The ground felt strange beneath his feet . . . and yet he knew it was his feet, and not the ground, that had changed. He ran for miles, tireless, mindless, his nostrils filling with the scents of the night—the damp earth, the leaves he crushed, the stink of something long dead. He heard the screech of an owl and then he caught the strong scent of blood.

Fresh blood.

It drew him like a beacon in the darkness.

The wolves growled as he approached. Three of them, a male and two females, huddled over the carcass of a deer.

Breathless, the blood teasing his nostrils, he walked toward them. The dominant female whined softly, then turned and trotted away, followed by the other, smaller female. The male stood his ground, teeth bared, hackles raised. A low growl rumbled in his throat.

An answering growl rose in Erik's throat as he bared his teeth and took a step forward.

The wolf growled again, then turned and disappeared into the night.

With a howl of triumph, Erik dropped to his hands and knees and sniffed the carcass.

A purr of satisfaction rumbled in his throat as he lapped at the blood, and then he reared back, a cry of horror erupting from his lips as he realized what he was doing.

"No! No!" Scrambling to his feet, he scrubbed the blood from his mouth with the back of his good hand. "No." He backed away from the carcass, appalled by his feral behavior.

"Kristine," he moaned. "Help me. Someone, please, help me."

* * *

She woke from a sound sleep, the melancholy cry of a wolf ringing in her ears. "Erik?" She patted the bed beside her and knew he had not been there.

Rising, she drew on her night robe and padded barefoot to the window. The moon hung low in the sky, silvering the trees, shining on the pond in the middle of the garden. All was quiet.

She was about to go back to bed when she saw it: a dark form making its way toward the back of the house. She leaned forward, eyes narrowed as she tried to see who it was. An intruder? One of the Graingers' sons coming home from a night in town?

The figure stepped into a pool of moonlight and she caught a glimpse of long black hair, the flash of a naked thigh.

"Erik!" Grabbing the small lamp burning beside her bed, she hurried out of the room and down the stairs toward the kitchen.

She got there as the back door opened. "Erik?"

"Put out the light!"

"What?"

"The light. Put it out."

Frowning, she turned down the wick, plunging the room into darkness.

"What are you doing here?" he growled.

"I . . . I saw you from my window. What were you doing out there? Are you . . . I thought . . . are you naked?"

"Go to bed, Kristine."

"Erik, please tell me what is troubling you. Please let me help."

"Kristine, go to bed." He bit off each word.

"Yes, my lord."

Turning on her heel, she ran out of the kitchen, through the dining room and hallway, then ducked behind the long curved settee in the parlor. A narrow shaft of moonlight shone through a slit in the draperies. Heart pounding, she waited.

And suddenly he strode into her line of vision. The moonlight slid across his bare shoulders. She could not see his face, only one arm and a long length of muscled thigh. He was carrying a wadded-up bundle that she assumed were his clothes.

She squinted, trying to see better in the darkness, but it was no use. He crossed the room quickly and disappeared up the stairs, leaving her to sit there, more confused than she had ever been in her life.

Erik felt every muscle in his body tense as he walked through the parlor, his face averted. He knew she was there, hiding behind the settee. Her scent filled his nostrils, as tempting as the deer's warm blood. Revulsion rose up within him. He had hoped to spend one last night in Kristine's bed, to hold her close one more time, to make love to her slowly, tenderly. To memorize every soft curve, but he dared not go to her now, nor ever again.

Tonight, he would gather what few things he would need. When he was certain she was asleep, he would go to her room and take one last look, and then he would leave the estate. He had left written orders for Mrs. Grainger, informing her that she was to tell no one where he had gone. After the babe was born, she was to send him word. When the time came, he wondered morbidly if he would still be human enough to care that Hawksbridge had a new heir.

When he reached his chamber, he locked the door, and then locked the connecting door between his room and Kristine's.

He heard her footsteps in the corridor a few moments later, heard the sound of her chamber door open and close.

Fighting the urge to go to her, Erik shoved a few items of clothing into a bag, grabbed a mask to replace the one he had lost in the woods.

He heard the soft rap of her knuckles on the door between their rooms. "My lord husband, are you in there?"

Heart pounding, he stared at the door, everything within him urging him to go to her, to seek the warm shelter of her arms. She had such a soft heart, surely she would be able to find some small shred of pity for the beast he was becoming. And then he looked down at the left side of his body, the thick dark hair, the deformed hand and foot, and knew she would run screaming from the sight of him.

"Erik, please answer me. Are you hurt?"

"No," he replied, his voice sounding harsher than ever in his ears. "I am not injured. Go to bed."

"I thought, that is, you said you would come to me tonight."

"I cannot."

"Very well, my lord husband. I understand."

He heard the coldness in her voice, the hurt, the disappointment. She thought he no longer wished to bed her now that he had gotten her with child. Nothing was further from the truth, but he could not tell her that. There was no point in trying to explain.

Let her think him callous and cruel. In the long run, it would be a kindness.

He sat on the edge of his bed, staring at the paw that had once been his left hand, at the thick black nails, fascinated and horrified by the sight. *A rutting beast you were, a beast you will become.*

"Are you happy, Charmion?" he wondered aloud. "Does it give you pleasure to know what I've become? Does the horror that I'm living ease the pain of your loss? Do you think Dominique rests more peacefully because of what you've done to me?"

With a weary sigh, he pulled on a black shirt and a pair of trousers, donned his mask and gloves and boots. Unlocking the door that connected his room to Kristine's, he stepped into her chamber. She was lying on her side, asleep.

He padded quietly toward her, his heart breaking when he saw that she had been crying.

"I'm sorry," he whispered. "Forgive me."

"There's nothing to forgive, my lord."

"I thought you were asleep."

She shook her head, too proud to admit she had missed him beside her.

He looked at her and knew he could not leave without making love to her one last time.

Sitting on the edge of the bed, he wrapped his right arm around her and crushed her close, his mouth hungry for the taste of her, his hands desperate in their need to touch her.

She came alive in his arms, his desperation conveying itself to her. As always, when she would have caressed him, he caught both of her hands in his right one, denying her that which she sought.

He lifted her sleeping gown over her hips, unfastened his breeches, and settled himself between her thighs.

Their coupling was violent, passionate, burning as hot and bright as a comet streaking across the sky. It left her breathless and aching and satisfied as never before.

She was smiling when she fell asleep.

Chapter Thirteen

He was gone in the morning. Kristine stared at Mrs. Grainger, unable to believe her ears. "Gone? What do you mean, gone? Gone where? When is he coming back?"

"He has gone on an extended holiday, my lady."

"A holiday? But . . . where has he gone?"

"I'm sure I don't know, my lady." The house-keeper's gaze slid away from Kristine's; nervous fingers plucked at the spotless white apron.

Kristine frowned, certain the housekeeper knew more than she was telling. "Did he say when he would be back?"

Mrs. Grainger hesitated a moment, and then sighed. "No. I am sorry. Truly I am."

"Why didn't he tell me?"

"I'm sure I couldn't say, my lady. Would you be caring for some breakfast?"

Kristine shook her head. Gone on holiday? With Christmas coming? She didn't believe it, refused to believe he would go off and leave her without a word after the night they had spent together. Surely it was a joke, a cruel prank. And even as the thought crossed her mind, she knew it had to do with the anguish she had frequently seen in his eyes, not pain of the body, but of the soul.

Her appetite gone, she left the dining room. He couldn't be gone.

Never had the time passed so slowly. She walked through the castle a dozen times, hoping to find him, but to no avail. She found rooms she had not seen before—a bedroom on the third floor that she guessed had been his mother's, several rooms that held cast-off furniture, trunks filled with old-fashioned dresses and baby clothes, bonnets and blankets. At any other time, she would have been intrigued, but not now.

She went outside and wandered through the gardens, and then she ran to the stables, wondering why she hadn't thought of it sooner.

She stared at Raven's empty stall and tried to convince herself that Erik had just taken the horse out for a very long ride, but she knew, deep inside, that she was only lying to herself. He was gone, perhaps for good.

Back in the house, she went to his room and fell across his bed, certain her heart would break. Why, why, why?

He had never said he loved her, yet he had seemed to enjoy her company.

He had been pleased with the news of her pregnancy.

Hurt and confused, she wrapped her arms around his pillow. His scent surrounded her, kindling memories of days spent riding together, of nights in his arms. The tears came then, tears that burned her eyes and left her feeling weak and empty.

She was overcome with a sense of listlessness in the days that followed. She sought forgetfulness in sleep; she had no appetite, though she forced herself to eat for the sake of the child she was carrying.

She went to the stable to visit Misty each morning, tormenting herself with the memory of the hours she had spent in Erik's company, remembering the day they had made love in the meadow.

Sometimes she felt as if time had stopped and she would be pregnant forever. Mrs. Grainger and the maids tried to cheer her, talking about how good it would be to have a babe in the house again, but even that failed to cheer her.

Erik had left her and all she could do was wonder why. Had she displeased him in some way? She went over every minute of the last few days they had spent together, looking for some clue that would explain his sudden departure.

She recalled the day she had told him she was pregnant. What was it he had said? Something about her being a delight and that he would miss her. She recalled asking him about the pain he was suffering, and his reply that there was nothing anyone could do.

Was he dying? The thought made her stomach roil with nausea. Was that it? Did he have some horrible wasting disease? Was that why he wore the mask, why she had never seen him unclothed, why he refused to let her touch him?

Determined to find the answers to her questions, she arranged to have Chilton bring the carriage around the following morning.

"Where to, my lady?" Chilton asked as he handed her into the conveyance.

"The convent," Kristine said, "at St. Clair."

Lady Trevayne received her in a small, austere room. Dressed in a severe black gown, her dark hair caught in a tight coil at her nape, she managed to look both fragile and regal at the same time.

At the wedding, Kristine had guessed Erik's mother to be in her sixties. She realized now that Lady Trevayne was probably ten years younger.

"I hope I haven't come at a bad time," Kristine said.

"No. Please, sit down."

Kristine sat on one of the hard-backed chairs, her hands folded tightly in her lap. "Thank you."

"Why have you come here?" Lady Trevayne asked.

"I wanted to ask you about Erik."

A shadow passed through the older woman's eyes; her fingers went white around the rosary clutched in her hand. "What about him?"

"Is he ill?"

"Ill?"

"Yes, there's something wrong with him, I know there is."

"Have you asked Erik what it is that troubles him?"

"Yes, but he refuses to speak of it. I know he's in pain, but he won't tell me the cause."

"I'm sorry, I cannot help you."

"But you know, don't you? Please, I just want to help."

"You care for him, don't you?"

"Yes. I love him." She spoke the words without thinking, only then realizing that it was true.

"I'm sorry for you, my dear."

"Sorry for me? Why?"

Lady Trevayne shook her head. "You are with child, are you not?"

"Yes, I am. Did Erik tell you?"

"I have not seen my son since the day of your wedding."

"He left me."

A soft sigh escaped Lady Trevayne's thin lips. "It's for the best. Go home, Kristine. Forget about Erik. Think of your babe." She rose to her feet, a small, slender woman whose eyes seemed to hold all the sadness of the world. "God bless you, Kristine. Please send one of the boys to let me know when your child is born."

Kristine stared after Erik's mother, more confused than ever.

Heavy-hearted, she left the convent.

Because she didn't know what else to do, she spent the next several days trying to follow Lady Trevayne's advice. She spent hours sewing baby clothes, thinking of names, furnishing the chamber next to her own.

And yet, each morning, she woke hoping to find that Erik had returned. And each night she cried herself to sleep.

Kristine stood at the window, staring outside. The day was gloomy, overcast, and perfectly suited to her mood. It was but a few weeks until Christmas, but she had refused to let Mrs. Grainger and the serving girls decorate the house. She wanted no reminders of the season. There was no joy in her heart, only a cold, lonely emptiness.

Moving away from the window, she pulled on her riding boots, donned a thick woolen cloak and hood, and went to the barn.

Brandt met her at the door. "Ye're not thinking of riding this afternoon, miss?"

"Yes, why?"

"We'll have rain before nightfall."

"I won't be gone long."

"Very well." Grumbling under his breath about the danger of riding in her condition, Brandt saddled the mare and helped Kristine mount. "Be careful now," he warned.

"I will."

Mindful of her unborn baby, Kristine kept Misty at a sedate walk, even though she yearned to let the mare run. Once, she had found pleasure in the beauty of the land, in the sense of freedom that riding gave her, but no more. She feared she might never be happy again, that nothing would ever make her smile, or laugh.

She shouldn't be riding at all. Mrs. Grainger and the maids had all tried to dissuade her, but she had refused to listen. Riding did not provide the pleasure it once had and yet, it made her feel closer to Erik to do something they had once enjoyed together.

Reaching into her pocket, she curled her fingers around a mask she had taken from Erik's room. The material was soft, warm from being in her pocket. It was the only thing that gave her comfort.

Lost in a world of despair, she rode farther afield than she ever had before. Only when the sky turned dark and she heard the rumble of thunder did she realize she was hopelessly lost.

Misty snorted and tossed her head as a gust of

wind shook the trees and sent a handful of dead leaves skittering across her path.

Glancing around, Kristine urged the mare in the direction she hoped led home. A sharp crack of lightning rent the clouds, unleashing a torrent of rain. Thunder shook the ground.

Another crack of lightning spooked the mare and she stretched out in a dead run, oblivious to the hand on the reins or Kristine's voice demanding that she stop. The ground flew by at an alarming rate.

Terrified, Kristine prayed that the mare wouldn't fall, that she would make her way safely back home.

Misty splashed across a narrow creek that was already beginning to swell and raced up the rocky incline on the opposite bank.

They were going the wrong way. Kristine had no doubt of it now. A forest of dark trees grew at the top of the rise. Wind and rain shook the leaves so that the trees seemed to be alive, swaying to the turbulent music of the storm.

Kristine tugged on the reins in a vain effort to halt Misty's flight, but the mare had the bit between her teeth and she ran on and on.

Kristine shivered violently, chilled by the rain and the fear spiraling through her. Why hadn't she listened to Mrs. Grainger and the maids? Even Brandt had tried to dissuade her, but she had foolishly refused to listen.

She tugged on the reins again, but Misty ran steadily onward, almost as if she had a destination in mind.

Please, please, don't let her fall.

She repeated the prayer over and over again, knowing that a fall now could be fatal not only for herself, but for the babe she carried. Erik's son.

After what seemed an eternity, Misty slowed. She

whinnied, then whinnied again as she burst through the trees into a small clearing.

Kristine blinked the rain from her eyes, certain she was seeing things. But no, it was still there. A rugged-looking house built of sturdy logs and gray stone. A small barn was set back from the house.

With a sigh of relief, Kristine slid from the saddle and ran up the stairs, drawn by the possibility of a warm fire and shelter from the storm. She felt bad for leaving Misty in the rain, but comforted herself with the knowledge that wild horses remained outside in all kinds of weather.

She hesitated a moment; then, summoning her courage, she knocked on the door. She waited several heartbeats, then knocked again. Still no answer.

A gust of wind chilled her to the bone. Biting down on her lower lip, she stared at the latch, wondering if the door was unlocked, wondering if she dared go inside, uninvited.

A sharp crack of thunder ended her indecision. She lifted the latch and the door swung open. "Hello? Is anyone home?"

When there was no answer, she stepped inside and closed the door behind her.

It was cold inside the house, too, but at least it was dry. There was a thick woolen blanket draped over the back of a settee and she drew it around her, grateful for its warmth.

It was a large, square room. The fireplace looked big enough to roast an ox; the mantel was higher than her head. The furniture was large and sturdy, built for a man's comfort. A bookshelf was set against one wall. There were several low tables. A rack of antlers hung above the fireplace.

Clutching the blanket around her shoulders, she went exploring. A quick glance showed that the kitchen was little more than a stove, a table, and two chairs. Turning away from the door, she walked down a short hall. A large bedroom took up most of the back of the house. A huge, rough-hewn bed dominated the room. A large armoire stood against one wall. An intricately carved chest with a domed lid rested at the foot of the bed. She took a step into the room, then drew back as she heard a crunching sound. Looking down, she saw the shattered pieces of a large mirror scattered on the floor. Frowning, she backed out of the room. There was a smaller bedroom next to the first, furnished with only a narrow bed, a three-drawer oak chest, and a commode.

Returning to the front of the house, she looked longingly at the hearth, wishing she had a way to start a fire.

Wrapped in the blanket, she sat down on the settee and closed her eyes. She would just sit here until the storm passed, and then she would go home. . . . Home.

It would never be home without Erik.

He smelled her the moment he stepped into the lodge. Her scent filled his nostrils, seemed to permeate every fiber of his being. For a moment, he forgot the pain that engulfed him, forgot everything but the fact that she was there, within reach.

And then he looked down at his hand that was no longer a hand, at the bloody bits of hair beneath the thick black claws, and a long, shuddering sigh rippled through him.

He could not go to her, could not let her see him. If he was lucky, he would bleed to death.

But surely he could risk a look. Just one look. He knew she was asleep, though he didn't know how he had come by that knowledge.

Padding quietly across the kitchen floor, he made his way into the lodge's main room and peered over the back of the settee. And she was there, sleeping soundly, her head pillowed on her hand.

His gaze slid over her. She was as beautiful as he remembered, her skin soft and smooth, her cheeks rosy, her lips pink and inviting. He yearned to touch her, to taste her, but he dared not.

Slowly, he backed out of the room and left the lodge. Outside, he drew in a deep breath. The cold air stung his wounds. He stared at the long claw marks that ran down his arms, at the bites across his chest and legs and shoulders. Blood continued to ooze from the deepest gashes. He had a sudden, overpowering urge to lick his wounds.

The idea should have been repulsive, and yet it wasn't. It was what animals did, after all, and wasn't that was he was now? A beast?

Even the wolves thought so. Earlier, driven once more by the same urge that had compelled him to run naked through the night, he had shed his clothing and gone running through the darkness. He had felt the cool, damp earth beneath his feet. A thousand different odors had assailed his nostrils, but it had been the scent of blood that had drawn him into the woods.

He had come upon the wolves deep in the forest. He had recognized them as the same ones he had seen near Hawksbridge Castle. They had been wary of him then. But not now. They walked toward him, stiff-legged, teeth bared. He had never known a wolf to attack a man. Too late, he realized they no longer perceived him as a man to be feared, but a rival, a threat to their kill.

They had circled him, moving in closer, closer. Fear had chilled his spine. And then there was no time for fear. The larger female had darted forward, her fangs sinking deep into his forearm. Erik had growled low in his throat, then turned to ward off the male's attack.

He looked down at the bits of bloody fur beneath his nails, remembered the taste of blood in his mouth. He had fought them as if he was one of them, growling and snapping, until one of the wolves bit deep into his right arm. Only then did sanity return, and with it the instinct to survive. Rising to his full height, he had yelled at the wolves.

Startled, they had backed away from him, then turned and ran back into the woods, disappearing into the shadows.

Overcome with weariness, Erik sank down on the ground, his wounds throbbing with every breath. He was cold, sick to his stomach. And he was thirsty, so thirsty. He licked his lips, desperate for a glass of water to ease his thirst, to wash the coppery taste of blood from his mouth.

He sat there for a long moment, trying to ignore his thirst, but it was impossible.

Gaining his feet, he returned to the house and poured himself a cup of water from the jug sitting on the table in the kitchen. The water was cold and sweet and he drank deeply, easing his thirst.

And then, hearing her footsteps, he froze.

"Erik?"

"Stay where you are!"

He heard the breath catch in her throat as she paused, then took another step. "What's wrong?"

"Nothing. Do not come any closer."

"All right."

He could sense her standing just beyond the door, waiting, wondering what was wrong. "What are you doing here?"

"I went riding and I got lost. What are *you* doing here? What is this place?"

"A place where you're not wanted." He spoke bluntly, wanting to hurt her. "Go back the way you came. When you reach the stream, follow it eastward. It will lead you back to the castle."

"You want me to leave? Now?"

"Yes."

"But it's dark outside."

"In the morning, then."

"Why, Erik? What have I done?"

"Nothing. You've done nothing." He took a deep breath. "I want you gone in the morning."

He heard the sharp intake of her breath, knew she was trying not to cry. "When are you coming home?"

He clenched his right hand. She sounded so young, so uncertain. So unhappy. Was it possible she had been missing him?

"Erik?"

"I don't know." He closed his eyes and wished for things that could never be. Wished he had two good hands to hold her close, wished he dared take her in his arms just once more. Wished he could lay his head in her lap and feel her hands moving over him. He needed the touch of her hand, needed the comfort only she could give. He was alone, so alone. And so afraid. The fear was a constant sickness in his gut; fear of what he was becoming, of what he was losing.

"It will be Christmas soon. Will you not come home for the holidays?"

His eyelids flew open and he saw her standing in the doorway. He turned sideways, hiding his left side in the dark shadows behind him.

She took a step forward, one hand outstretched. "Erik, are you bleeding?"

"Don't touch me!"

She came to an abrupt halt. "I won't. What happened to you?"

"I was attacked by wolves."

Even in the darkness, he could see her eyes widen in horror. "Wolves!"

"I'll be all right. Please, just go away."

"Not until I have looked at your wounds. They'll fester if they aren't treated."

"I'm not dressed."

A rush of heat climbed up the back of her neck. They had been married for almost a year and she had never seen him naked. "It's all right. I . . . I don't mind."

"I do. Wait for me in the other room."

"Very well."

He watched her go, then went out the back door to gather up his discarded clothing. He felt better when he was dressed, his mask once again securely in place. The worst wounds were on his right side. He had not stopped to wonder why before, but he knew the answer. His human side was fragile, easily bruised. The skin on his left side was thicker, protected by a heavy layer of coarse black hair.

Desperate for her touch, needing to be near her, he would let her tend his wounds, and then he would never see her again.

When he was as presentable as possible, he went into the main room.

She was sitting on the edge of the settee, looking like a bird poised for flight. She glanced over her shoulder as he stepped into the room.

"Sit down," she said. "Do you have any matches? I'll need to heat some water to clean your wounds. And light a lamp so I can see what I'm doing."

"There are matches in one of the drawers in the kitchen."

He sank back on the settee as she left the room. He could hear her moving about in the kitchen, filling a pan with water, opening the drawers, tearing a tea towel into strips.

Every muscle in his body ached, his wounds throbbed with a dull monotony. Overcome with weariness and a sense of hopelessness, he closed his eyes. How much longer did he have? How many more days and nights until the hideous transformation was complete?

He opened his eyes at the sound of her footsteps. She had lit a small lamp. He squinted against the light, his gaze moving over her. Her body had changed. Her breasts were fuller, her belly swollen with his babe.

She knelt at his feet. Lifting his right arm, she rolled up his shirtsleeve and began to wash away the blood. Her face paled as she stared at the deep gashes that ran the length of his arm. "You need a doctor."

"No. No doctor."

"But these wounds are deep. They need stitching."

"Just wash them and wrap them up."

"Why are you being so foolish about this?"

He closed his eyes and took a deep breath in an effort to calm his anger. It was a mistake. Her scent rushed into his nostrils, warm and womanly and uniquely hers, reminding him of the nights he had gone to her bed, the pleasure he had found in her arms.

"Erik, answer me!"

"No doctor. Just do the best you can."

"I . . ." She swallowed the bitter bile tickling the back of her throat. "Do you have a needle and thread? I can . . . that is, I can try to . . . to stitch the wounds."

"I don't know." He rested his head on the back of the sofa. He felt light-headed from the blood he had lost, and weary, so weary. All he wanted to do was sleep.

He heard the faint rustle of her skirts as she stood up. He wondered where she was going, but he was too tired to give it more than a passing thought.

Time passed. A few moments, a few hours, he didn't know or care.

"I found a sewing basket in the bedroom."

He grunted. Dominique had spent a few weeks here the summer she was pregnant. She had left her embroidery basket behind. He had promised to fetch it for her before winter set in, but he had forgotten, and then there had been no need. . . .

The settee sagged a little as Kristine sat down beside him. Gently, she took his arm and laid it across her lap. "Hold still. This is going to hurt."

"It already hurts. Just do what you can."

He watched her face as she began to sew the ragged edges of his flesh together. She bit down on one side of her lower lip, her brow furrowed in concentration. He watched the color drain from her face as she guided the shiny silver needle through his skin. Drops of blood ran down his arm, staining the cloth she had spread over her skirt. She swallowed several times and he knew she was fighting the urge to retch.

Well, so was he. He had a strong urge to laugh, to tell her there were worse things to see than a few bites and scratches. No doubt she would faint dead away if she discovered that a monster had fathered her child.

"That's the last one." She removed the blood-stained cloth from her lap, wadded it up in a ball, and dropped it in the pan of bloody water. "Can I get you anything?"

"No."

"You should go to bed."

He nodded, but made no move to rise.

"Do you want me to help you?"

"No. Go to bed, Kristine. You have a long ride ahead of you in the morning."

"You never answered my question."

He blinked at her. "What question?"

"Will you come home for Christmas?"

"I don't know."

He flinched at the hurt in her eyes. She looked at him for a long moment, then turned and walked out of the room.

He waited until he heard the bedroom door close and then, with a sigh, shrugged out of his shirt and trousers and began to wash the blood from the bites and scratches that ran along his left arm and leg and chest.

She stood in the bedroom, her back against the door, trying not to cry. What had she done? Why did he hate her so? The last night they had spent together had been wonderful, at least for her. She had thought he was starting to care for her. How could she have been so wrong? Did he find her so repulsive, now that she was pregnant?

She placed her hand over the burgeoning swell of her belly. He had seemed pleased when she'd told him about the baby. Had she been wrong about that, too?

She couldn't sleep, couldn't go back to Hawksbridge Castle without knowing what had gone wrong between them, why he had left her without a word. Couldn't wait until morning for answers to the questions that plagued her.

Gathering her courage, she opened the door and walked swiftly down the hallway.

She came to an abrupt halt, a scream rising in her throat as she stared at the figure illuminated in the lamplight. Thick black hair, like that of a wolf, covered the left side of its body. But this was no wolf . . . nor was it a man. Tales of werewolves flitted through her mind, and then, slowly, the creature turned toward her, and she saw the mask.

The room began to spin before her eyes. A hoarse whisper of denial rose in her throat and then she was falling, spinning down, down, into blessed oblivion. . . .

Chapter Fourteen

Erik reacted instinctively. Lunging forward, he caught Kristine in his arms. She felt so light, so fragile. In the pale glow of the lamp, he could see that all the color had drained from her face. He held her for several moments, then carried her swiftly down the hallway toward the larger of the two bedrooms. Gently, he placed her on the bed. After a moment's hesitation, he removed her riding boots, his hand lingering over the soft swell of her calf. Knowing she would not welcome his touch, he jerked his hand away.

Unfolding the heavy quilt at the foot of the bed, he drew it over her, his gaze lingering on her face. How beautiful she was. It hurt too much to look at her, and he turned away.

Mindful of the storm raging outside, he drew the heavy drapes over the window and lit a fire in the small hearth. A last look, and then he stalked out of the room.

He dressed quickly, his mind numb, his heart bleeding, his soul shattered. After months of hiding, she had seen him for what he was, what he was becoming. He did not fault her for her reaction. It was what he had expected.

Taking his greatcoat from the hall tree, he slipped it on, then left the lodge.

Misty stood outside, her head lowered, her back turned against the storm. She whinnied softly as he took up the reins.

Leading the mare, Erik made his way through the thick mud to the stable.

Raven snuffled a soft greeting when he opened the door.

"Easy, boy," Erik murmured. He dropped the heavy bar in place, locking the door behind him, then walked to the horse's stall, the mare at his heels. He ran his hand down the stallion's sleek neck. "I brought you some company."

Moving quickly, grateful to have something to occupy his mind, he stripped the saddle and blanket from the mare, then dried her with an old piece of sacking.

After settling the mare in the stall next to Raven's, Erik shrugged out of his greatcoat and hung it from a nail in the wall, thinking, as he did so, that he would soon have no need for clothing or a coat.

Overcome with a sense of despair, he sank down on the straw in an empty stall and closed his eyes. Man or beast, he knew he would never forget the look of horror he had seen reflected in Kristine's eyes.

Kristine woke feeling groggy and disoriented. It was the worst nightmare she had ever had, she thought as she sat up, worse than her dreams of being locked in a dark place when she had been a child, worse than the nightmares she'd had after stabbing Lord Valentine.

She shook her head, hoping to dispel the lingering images of the beast that had troubled her dreams. She frowned, surprised to find herself in bed. She didn't remember coming in here last night.

Throwing back the covers, Kristine slid her legs over the edge of the mattress and stood up, noting, as she did so, that someone had swept up the broken glass.

Padding to the window, she parted the drapes and looked outside. The rain had stopped, but dark, heavy clouds hung low in the sky. Chilled, she pulled on her boots, thinking that she didn't remember taking them off. She wrapped the quilt around her shoulders, then went to look for Erik, determined to make him tell her why he had left Hawksbridge Castle, to tell him she missed his company and beg him to please come home.

He was not in the house, but he had lit a fire in the hearth and filled the wood box. She peered out the front window. Her horse was gone. No doubt Erik had gone out to feed the horses. He would be chilled when he returned.

She hummed softy, hoping to shake off the lingering vestiges of her nightmare as she went into the kitchen. A search of the cupboards turned up a tea canister and several delicate china cups. Taking the teapot from the stove, she went to the sink. She was reaching for the pump handle when she saw the bowl. But it was the rag inside the bowl that held her gaze. The dark brown stains could only be blood. . . .

The teapot fell from fingers gone suddenly numb as she stared at the rag. It hadn't been a nightmare after all. It was then that she saw the note, written in Erik's bold hand. There were only two words: *Go home.*

Heedless of the impending storm, she left the house and slogged through the thick mud toward the stable. She took a deep breath to calm her nerves, then lifted the latch. The heavy door opened with a creak.

"Erik? Erik, are you in here?" She stepped warily into the shadowy barn. "Erik?"

She moved deeper into the barn. Misty snorted softly and shook her head.

Kristine stroked the mare's neck as she glanced around the barn. There was no sign of Erik's horse, or of Erik.

Grateful that he had taught her how to saddle the mare, Kristine quickly saddled Misty. She led the mare back to the lodge and tethered her there. Inside, Kristine put out the fire in the hearth. Grabbing the quilt from the settee where she had dropped it, she went back outside and climbed into the saddle. Draping the heavy quilt around her shoulders, she rode toward the woods. When she found the stream, she followed it eastward, as Erik had instructed.

She was going home, and then she was going to find some answers.

Kristine stood in the guest parlor of the convent, waiting for Lady Trevayne. Too nervous to sit still, she paced the floor in front of the fireplace, chilled to the marrow of her bones in spite of the cheerful fire that blazed in the hearth.

"You wanted to see me?"

Kristine whirled around at the sound of Lady Trevayne's low, well-modulated voice. "Yes."

Lady Trevayne crossed the room, her black skirts swaying gracefully. She sat down, her back straight, her hands folded neatly in her lap. "What did you wish to see me about?"

"Your son."

Lady Trevayne stiffened visibly. "Has something happened to Erik?"

"Not in the way you mean," Kristine said. "But there is something wrong with him. Something horribly wrong. And you know what it is, don't you?"

Lady Trevayne stared down at her clasped hands. "Yes, I know."

"What is it that afflicts him so grievously?" Kristine placed her hands over her womb, horrified by the thought of giving birth to a child who was deformed. "He told me it would not affect our child. Was he telling me the truth?"

"You need have no fear. Erik's . . . malady will not affect your child, Kristine. Have no fear of that, but your life might be in danger."

"My life? Why?"

Lady Trevayne took a deep breath. "My son was married before."

"Yes, I know."

Lady Trevayne nodded. "His wife, Dominique, died in childbirth. Dominique's mother is a powerful sorceress."

"A witch!" Kristine exclaimed.

"Yes. She blamed Erik for her daughter's death. It was she who put the curse on my son."

Kristine shivered. "What kind of curse?"

"She accused him of behaving like a rutting beast and declared that a beast was what he would become."

"A beast . . ." Kristine sat down heavily. She wanted to say it wasn't true, couldn't be true, but it explained so many things.

"You should leave Hawksbridge Castle immediately," Erik's mother said quietly. "Go anywhere you wish. I will see to it that you and your child want for nothing."

"Leave?"

"You can return, in time, and claim your child's birthright." Lady Trevayne paused a moment. "Should your babe be a boy, he will be the eighth lord of Hawksbridge Castle."

"In time?" Kristine looked at the other woman in horror. "You mean when Erik is . . . is . . ."

"When the transformation is complete," Lady Trevayne said.

"No . . . I can't leave him. How can you suggest such a thing? He's so alone." She stood up again and began to pace the floor. "Why did you leave him when he needed you most?"

"I did not leave him," Lady Trevayne replied sharply. "He sent me away, and when I returned, he sent me away again. He did not want me there, did not want me to see . . ."

"I'm sorry."

The anger left the older woman's eyes and she inclined her head in a gesture of acceptance. "No one can help Erik now." She lifted a hand to the rosary she wore around her neck. "I only pray that . . . that once the transformation is complete, he will have no memory of who he was before."

Kristine stared at Erik's mother. Wrapping her

arms around her waist, she rocked slowly back and
forth as the reality of the curse, the sheer horror of
it, flooded her mind.

She remembered a day some months ago when
Charmion had come to the house, remembered Erik
asking her if she was afraid. She had said she was not.
You should be afraid, he had said. *The day may come
when I'll tear you to shreds.*

She had not understood his meaning at the time;
now she feared she understood all too clearly. "Is
there no way to end this curse?"

Lady Trevayne shook her head. "None that I
know of."

"But there might be," Kristine said desperately.
"There must be! Surely the witch could remove it."

"Yes, I'm sure she could, but she will not. She is an
evil woman, one who has always taken pleasure in in-
flicting pain. There is no forgiveness in her, no
mercy, nothing but an unholy desire for vengeance."

"There has to be something we can do!" Kristine
said vehemently. "I've got to try."

"Don't be a fool! There's nothing you can do for
Erik. You must think of your child now."

"I am thinking of my child," Kristine retorted.
"I'm thinking that he will need a father's love and
guidance."

Color flooded Lady Trevayne's pale cheeks. "Erik
cannot be a father! Do you not understand? Soon he
will not be a man at all, but a wild beast. Is that what
you want for your child? A father who is a wild animal,
a beast who will likely have no memory of his humanity, who might attack both you and your child?"

"No." Tears that had been hovering close to the
surface for days filled Kristine's eyes and ran in twin

rivers down her cheeks, unleashed by the gruesome images created by her mother-in-law's words. "No."

She bent at the waist, her head cradled in her hands, certain she would die from the pain knifing through her heart. She remembered the sight of the long dark hair that had covered one side of Erik's body and imagined what it would be like when the transformation was complete, when all trace of his humanity was gone and he was truly a beast.

She moaned, "No, no," and then she felt a hand on her shoulder. Looking up, she saw Lady Trevayne standing at her side. Tears shimmered in the older woman's eyes.

"I'm sorry, daughter," she said quietly. "Would you like to pray with me?"

Kristine sniffed back her tears. "Yes."

Lady Trevayne reached for her hand and together they walked down the long, narrow corridor that led to the chapel.

The light from dozens of tall white candles filled the room with a soft amber glow. Kristine glanced at the painted faces of the saints as she made her way down the center aisle. They all looked so serene; she wished she could find that same sense of inner peace in her own life.

She knelt in one of the pews beside Lady Trevayne, bowed her head, and closed her eyes. Kneeling there, she poured out the desires of her heart, praying for a miracle that would thwart Charmion's curse, praying for a strong, healthy child, begging, pleading, for help.

She lost track of time as she knelt there. She had

forgotten what a blessing it was to pray, to lay one's burdens at the feet of a loving Heavenly Father. She seemed to hear the words *Only ask and ye shall receive*, felt a reassuring presence near her, comforting her.

Blinking back tears, she rose to her feet, then offered Lady Trevayne her hand. "Why don't you come home with me?" Kristine asked.

"Thank you, Kristine," Lady Trevayne said with a smile. "But . . ."

"Erik has gone. I should dearly love to have your company."

"And I should love to spend more time with you, daughter, but . . ." She squeezed Kristine's hand. "I should not like for him to come home and find me there." Lady Trevayne took a deep breath. "It's not because I'm afraid of him," she explained softly, "but because he does not want me there. He does not wish me to see him as he is now, and I must respect his wishes."

"I understand."

"Thank you, child. I hope you will come and see me often."

"I will. And I hope you'll come and spend Christmas Day with us."

"I should like that very much. Ask Mrs. Grainger to send the coach for me."

"I will." Bending down, Kristine kissed the older woman's cheek. "Pray for us."

"I shall. Mind my words, Kristine, stay away from Charmion."

"Does she live nearby?" Kristine asked, wondering why the thought had not occurred to her before.

"She dwells at the top of Cimmerian Crag, less than a day's ride from Hawksbridge."

Kristine nodded. Cimmerian Crag was a familiar landmark, though she had never known that anyone lived there.

Lady Trevayne laid her hand on Kristine's arm. "Stay away from her," she warned again. "There is no way to soften that virago's wicked heart."

It was dark by the time Kristine returned to Hawksbridge Castle. She bathed and dressed, then went down to supper. Mrs. Grainger hovered over her. Kristine knew the cook was about to burst with curiosity but, being a servant, it wasn't her place to ask where Kristine had been, and Kristine was not of a mind to explain.

She ate because it gave her something to do, because she would need her strength for the journey to Charmion's dwelling.

She would leave in the morning and hope her courage didn't desert her along the way. After dinner, she went into the library and sat in Erik's favorite chair. The house seemed so big, so empty without him. Even when he had been busy in another part of the house, she had felt his presence, had known that, sooner or later, he would come to her bed. She had not truly realized how much she had looked forward to being in his arms until he was gone.

She moaned softly, aching for him, for what he must be feeling, thinking. Seeing him had explained so much—why he never left the estate, why there were no mirrors in the house, other than those behind locked doors, why he preferred wool to the fine lawn and linen shirts that were favored by wealthy men, why he had refused her touch. Her fingers curled into a tight fist as she thought of the nights she had yearned to touch him, to caress him. He had been wise to prevent her. Look how she had behaved when she saw him! Fainted dead away like some spineless ninny. Did he hate her for that? Heaven knew she hated herself.

She thought of all Lady Trevayne had said, all Erik had said, and knew she couldn't run away, couldn't hide inside the house. She would go to Charmion and beg the witch to lift the curse.

She felt a sense of calm, of resignation, as she made her decision. She had failed Erik once. She would not fail him again.

She rose early the following morning. Sneaking out of the house, she went to the barn and saddled Misty, then led the horse outside to the mounting block.

She was congratulating herself on getting away, unseen, when Brandt rounded the corner. Rubbing sleep from his eyes, he blinked up at her, obviously surprised to see her out and about so early in the day.

"Good morrow, my lady," he said. He covered a yawn with his hand. "Why did you not tell me you were riding this morning? I would have had Misty ready for you."

Kristine smiled brightly. "I felt like an early ride, that's all. There was no need to bother you when I can saddle my own horse."

Brandt nodded, then yawned again. "No trouble at all, my lady. Next time you come, wake me up."

"I will."

"Enjoy your ride," he said, and walked past her into the barn.

Touching her heels to Misty's flanks, Kristine urged the mare into a canter. Charmion lived at the top of Cimmerian Crag. If she hurried, she could be there before nightfall.

Chapter Fifteen

Erik stayed away for four days before returning to the hunting lodge. He knew as soon as he entered the dwelling that she was gone. There was a hollowness inside, a feeling of emptiness.

He stood before the fireplace, his heart as cold as the ashes in the hearth. Why, of all places, had she stumbled upon this one? It had been the one place where there were no memories of Kristine to haunt him, but that was changed now. He could smell her scent all around him, had only to close his eyes to picture her sitting on the settee, lying in his bed, kneeling at his feet as she washed the blood from his wounds. But the memory that tormented him most was the look of complete and total horror on her face when she'd seen him for what he was.

A moan rumbled low in his throat, deepening to a growl. He stared at his left hand, at the thick pads, the long claws. He would never caress a woman with that hand again, he mused, nor lift a glass of wine.

He would never hold his child. . . .

Throwing back his head, he let out a long, anguished

cry that emerged from his throat in a wolflike howl, echoing off the walls and spilling into the night. A moment later, he heard an answering howl from the woods, where it was picked up by another, and then another, until the air rang with the melancholy sounds.

He went to the window and stared out into the night, and knew he had to go back to Hawksbridge Castle, had to know that Kristine had made it safely home.

He had to see her just one more time, had to know that she would be well and truly cared for. How many times, he mused ruefully, how many times had he promised himself just one more time? But this would have to be the last.

Heavy-hearted, he swung into the saddle and started for home.

"Gone? What do you mean, she's gone? Gone where?"

"I don't know, my lord." Mrs. Grainger took a step backward, alarmed by the rage blazing in Trevayne's eyes. "Brandt was the last to see her. He said she went riding day before yesterday. She never came back. I sent Gilbert to the lodge to tell you, but there was no one there." She twisted her apron in her hands. "I'm sorry, my lord. We've looked everywhere."

"She didn't say anything to anyone?"

"No one here, my lord."

Had he driven her away, then, frightened her so badly with his monstrous appearance that she had fled Hawksbridge? She had no family, no friends. Where would she go?

"My lord?"

"What is it?"

"She went to see your mother."

"What? When?"

"The day before she disappeared. She asked me how far it was to the convent at St. Clair. I never dreamed she would go there alone."

He was gone from the room before the woman finished speaking.

Outside, he swung onto the stallion's back and urged the weary horse into a gallop. His mother! Why had Kristine gone to see his mother?

The convent was locked up tight when he arrived. Refusing to be thwarted, he rang the bell, then pounded on the heavy wooden door until someone came to answer it.

A woman peered at him through a small barred window cut into the door. "Yes?"

He turned so that his left side was hidden in the darkness. "I must see Lady Trevayne."

"I'm sorry, my lord, but everyone is asleep. Come back tomorrow."

"I cannot wait until tomorrow."

"I am sorry, my lord."

"I'm her son. I'm sure she will see me."

"I am sorry, my lord," the nun repeated firmly, "but no one is allowed inside the convent after dark." And with that, she closed the portal.

It took every ounce of self-control he possessed to smother the rage that bubbled up inside him, to keep from breaking down the door.

Wrestling with the beast struggling to break free

inside him, he whirled away from the door and strode into the night.

He was at the convent door early the following morning. A different nun answered the bell.

"I need to see Lady Trevayne," he said. "It's urgent."

"She is just now breaking her fast."

He clenched his hands. "I'm her son. I'm sure she would wish to see me."

"Very well." The nun took a step backward, her eyes widening as she got a clear glimpse of his mask. "Just wait in there." She gestured to a door on her left, then hurried down the corridor.

Erik entered the room she had indicated. It was a sitting room of sorts, with a fireplace, a sofa covered in a dark fabric, a low table, and several chairs. He assumed it was here that the nuns visited with family and friends.

He paced the floor, his steps restless, impatient.

"Erik."

He came to an abrupt halt at the sound of his mother's voice. He took a deep breath and then turned to face her.

"Mother."

Lady Trevayne's gaze moved quickly over her son. He had once been tall and strong and handsome. Now, a black mask covered half of his face. She noted the subtle changes in his posture, noted that his gloved left hand seemed malformed, as did the shape of his boots. His voice, too, was changed.

"Are you well, Erik?"

"Where is Kristine?"

"What do you mean?"

"She's gone. No one knows where."

"Gone?"

Erik watched the color drain from his mother's face, felt the first tendrils of fear twine around his heart. "She came here, did she not?"

"Yes." Lady Trevayne sat down heavily, her shoulders sagging. "Charmion. She's gone to Charmion."

"What!" he roared. "Why would she go there?"

"She wanted to know what she could do to help you. She seemed to think she could persuade Charmion to lift the curse."

"You told her?" He stared at his mother in disbelief. "Why would you do such a thing?"

"She's your wife, Erik. Who has a better right to know the truth?"

He paced the floor, his right hand clenching and unclenching. "Why did you let her go?"

"I tried to talk her out of it, truly I did. I warned her that Charmion would have no pity, that it would be dangerous not only for her, but for her child." Lady Trevayne gazed at her son, her arms aching to hold him, to comfort him as she had when he was a lad. "She loves you very much."

Erik stared at his mother. "What are you talking about?"

"Kristine loves you. She told me so in this very room. Why else would she risk her life and that of her child?"

Erik closed his eyes. Could it be true? Did Kristine love him? And what if she did? It solved nothing.

"You are going after her, are you not?"

"Of course." She had been gone for four days. He

had no doubt that if she had reached Cimmerian Crag, she was being held there against her will.

"Hurry, Erik. My prayers will go with you."

He took a step forward, then stopped. "I'm sorry I sent you away. It was wrong of me."

"I should not have let you send me away when you most needed me," his mother replied quietly. "That was wrong of me." She smiled up at him, her eyes damp with tears. "Come, kiss me good-bye."

"I'll find her," he promised, and bending down, he kissed his mother's cheek. "I'll send Chilton to bring you home."

"There's no need. I am content here."

"Kristine will need you." The words *when I'm gone* hovered, unspoken, between them.

"As you wish. Go with God, my son," Lady Trevayne said. She watched him leave the room, and then she went into the chapel to pray.

She had a four-day head start on him. That was all Erik could think about as he raced back to Hawksbridge Castle. He wanted to hurry toward Charmion's dark castle, but instead he swung by Hawksbridge, hoping, praying that he would find Kristine there, but it was not to be.

He stayed just long enough to change his clothes and arm himself, though he feared his weapons would be little protection against Charmion's witchcraft.

Mrs. Grainger pressed a burlap bag into his hands as he went out the kitchen door. "She'll be fine, I know she will."

With a curt nod, he took the sack of foodstuffs and ran toward the stable.

Brandt and Gilbert had replaced Raven's sweaty saddle blanket with a dry one. The stallion had been brushed, his hooves cleaned. Erik stuffed a bag of oats into one of his saddlebags, the sack of food into the other.

"We'll be praying for her, my lord," Brandt said as he handed Erik the reins. "All of us."

Gilbert's head bobbed up and down in agreement. "Godspeed, my lord."

With a nod, Erik swung into the saddle. Kristine had won all their hearts, he mused as he rode out of the yard. Heaven knew she had his.

Leaving the manor grounds, Erik urged Raven northward, ever northward, his heart burning with a cold and bitter rage.

"Please, please, please . . ." Just that one word, repeating over and over again.

Please don't let me be too late.

Please don't let Charmion take her hatred for me out on Kristine and the babe.

If anything happened to Kristine, he would never forgive himself.

He lifted his left hand, the long black claws hidden beneath a leather glove. If anything had happened to Kristine, he would rip Charmion's heart from her body.

As the morning wore on, dark clouds gathered overhead, blanketing the sun. Lightning slashed through the lowering skies. He heard the low roar of distant thunder.

Raven snorted and tossed his head.

A blinding flash of lightning sizzled across the skies, unleashing a torrent of icy rain. Erik huddled deeper into his heavy cloak. Driven by an ever-growing sense of urgency, he bypassed the shelter of a small town he passed along the way.

An hour later, he reined the stallion to a halt, giving the big horse a much-needed rest.

Dismounting, Erik patted the weary horse on the neck, then paced back and forth for a few minutes to stretch his legs. Taking shelter under a tree, he braced one shoulder against the trunk and closed his eyes.

When he opened his eyes, he found himself surrounded by a half dozen men brandishing weapons. They wore the drab clothes of peasants.

"We're here fer yer money, yer lordship," said the man standing directly in front of Erik. He wore a ragged cloak, a dingy white shirt, trousers in need of mending, and a black top hat cocked at a rakish angle. It added a rather incongruous note to the rest of his attire.

"And yer horse," added a tall, skinny lad with a mouthful of rotten teeth. "'Tis as fine a piece of horse-flesh as ever I've seen."

Pushing away from the tree, Erik lowered the hood of his cloak. The men gaped at him when they saw the mask.

"Looks like he's one of us!" exclaimed a short, stocky man wearing a tattered jacket, and a stocking cap.

A few of the men laughed nervously.

"Why the mask?" Rotten Teeth asked.

"That's my business."

"I'm afraid not, yer lordship," Top Hat replied. "Take it off."

Erik shook his head. "No." He tensed as the man in front of him cocked his pistol. The other men did likewise.

"Take it off."

"No."

"Stubborn, ain't he?" Stocking Cap said. He drew a knife from inside his shabby jacket and ran his thumb over the blade. "I could maybe persuade him for ya."

Top Hat nodded. "Have at him, Harry."

Harry grinned, exposing a row of crooked yellow teeth. Tossing the blade from hand to hand, he swaggered forward.

Erik took a step backward. He should just take the mask off, he thought. No doubt the sight of his face would scare the devil out of them, but he could not bring himself to do it.

"The mask," Harry said, pointing at it with the tip of his knife. "Take it off and show us what yer hiding."

Erik reached into his pocket and withdrew his purse. "Take the money."

"We will," Top Hat said. "Have no fear of that."

"All in good time," Harry said. Grinning, he reached for a corner of the mask.

Rage boiled up inside Erik. It spilled out in a growl as his hands closed around Harry's throat. Lifting the man off his feet, he hurled him away as if he weighed nothing at all.

Top Hat yelled, "Kill him!" and fired his pistol.

Erik reeled backward, his hand clutching his right

shoulder. The other men fired their weapons as well. One ball struck him in the left arm, another struck him low in the left side. With a roar of pain and rage, he lunged forward, but the men scattered like chickens before a fox.

He saw one of the men spring onto Raven's back. Leaning out of the saddle, the man grabbed Harry's arm and swung him up behind him in the saddle, and then they were gone.

Soaked to the skin, his wounds bleeding profusely, Erik sank to his knees.

"Kristine." He murmured her name as darkness descended on him. "Kristine . . ."

He woke slowly, frowning into the darkness, his nostrils filling with a sharp feral odor and the scent of smoke. He started to sit up, only to fall back as pain splintered through his arm, side, and shoulder. A low whine sounded to his right and when he turned his head, he saw a huge gray wolf sitting beside him, pink tongue lolling out of the side of its mouth. Moving just his eyes, Erik glanced to his left. A black wolf sat near his feet; another slept curled up at the side of the black wolf.

"Don't be afraid."

He turned toward the voice with a start and saw a woman kneeling beside a small fire near the back of the cave. "Who are you?"

"Who are you?"

"Erik Trevayne." He struggled to sit up, only then realizing he was naked. He didn't mind the lack of his clothing, but he felt vulnerable without the mask. "Where are my clothes?"

"The robbers came back after you passed out and took them, but don't worry." A smile crept into her voice. "We took them from the robbers."

He knew without asking that the men who had accosted him were no longer a threat to anyone. "And my horse?"

"He is being well cared for, have no fear."

"What is this place? Where am I?"

"You're safe, for now." She raised a slender hand and made a sweeping motion that encompassed the cavern. "I live here."

"I've told you who I am. Now, who are you?"

"I am called Valaree."

"And you live in this cave? Why?"

She rose to her feet and walked toward him. She was a tall woman, with waist-length black hair and luminous brown eyes. She wore a loose-fitting white robe that seemed to glow in the dim light of the fire.

"How do you feel, Erik Trevayne?" She peeled back the bandages from his injuries, then bent down and sniffed the wounds. Nodding, she replaced the bandages.

He let out a long sigh. The transformation was spreading. His body was in constant pain as muscle and bone and tissue fought against the Change. But there was no need to tell her that.

"I feel fine, all things considered. Who are you? How did I get here?"

"All in good time, Erik." She went back to the fire and picked up a bowl and spoon. "You need to eat to replenish your strength."

She sat beside him and offered him a spoonful of thick, dark broth. He hesitated a moment before swallowing it.

She lifted one brow in wry amusement. "Afraid I'm going to poison you?"

"It doesn't make much sense for you to save my life only to drag me in here to poison me." He regarded her curiously for a moment. "You're not afraid of me, are you?"

"Should I be?"

He lifted a hand to the left side of his face. "Most people would be repelled by this."

"I am not most people."

He nodded. There was no doubt of that. He glanced around the cave, at the wolves sitting patiently nearby. He had the peculiar feeling they understood everything that was being said. "Are the wolves your pets?"

"Pets?" She laughed at that, a deep husky sound that reminded him of distant thunder. She stroked the gray wolf's head. "This is my father. The pretty black one is my mother, and the sleepy one is my sister, Elsbeth." Valaree cocked her head to one side, her gaze studying him intently. "What happened to you? I've never seen anyone trapped in the midst of the Change."

"I don't know what you mean."

She offered him another spoonful of broth. "You're one of us, are you not?"

"One of you?"

"Never mind." Frowning, she fed him the rest of the thick soup. "You should rest now. You will feel better after a good night's sleep."

He didn't want to sleep, he wanted answers to the

questions tumbling through his mind, needed to find Kristine, but his body, warmed by the broth and weakened from loss of blood, cried out for rest. Valaree covered him with a thick quilt, then went to sit beside the fire once more.

He stared at her through heavy-lidded eyes until sleep claimed him.

Chapter Sixteen

It was after dusk the following night when Erik awoke. He sat up, surprised to find himself alone in the cave. A small fire burned near the rear of the cavern. His first thought was for Kristine. He had to find her before it was too late, had to get her away from Charmion while he was still human enough to accomplish it.

He sat there for several minutes, gathering his strength. His right shoulder throbbed painfully, but other than that, he felt remarkably strong. He removed the bandages from his left arm and side. Both were healed, with only faint scars to show he had been hurt at all. He ran his hand down his left side, scarcely able to believe his own eyes.

Rising, he found his clothes and boots and put them on. He searched for several minutes, but couldn't find his mask. He felt naked and vulnerable without it.

He was prowling the cave for something to eat when he caught the smell of fresh blood. Turning, he saw the wolves enter the cave. The gray one was carrying a lamb in its jaws.

Erik frowned. There had been three wolves last night; this evening there were four.

The gray wolf dropped the lamb carcass near the fire, then sat down. Two of the black wolves stretched out beside the male.

The fourth wolf lifted its head and let out a long, heart-wrenching howl and then, while Erik watched in slack-jawed astonishment, the creature began to change shape. It was an awesome thing to watch, frightening yet fascinating to see the thick black pelt recede and become soft human flesh, to hear the pop and crackle of bones and muscles realigning themselves, until Valaree stood before him, her long black hair falling down her bare back and over her shoulders.

She smiled at him, apparently not bothered by her nudity. "Good evening, Erik."

He nodded, unable to speak. The word *werewolf* rose in the back of his mind. He knew now why they had saved him. They thought he was one of them, trapped between his human half and his wolf half. He had never believed the tales he had heard of werewolves, had thought them only idle tales told to frighten children. Until now. "Does it hurt?"

"The Change?" There was a pile of clothing near the wall of the cavern. She reached for a long gray robe and slipped it over her head. "There is a certain amount of pain."

She picked up the lamb and the scent of blood and raw meat filled his nostrils. "Do you want it raw," she asked, "or cooked?"

Erik's mouth watered at the thought of tearing into the lamb's still-warm flesh. Horrified, he shook his head. "Cook it!"

Valaree regarded him curiously. "You have not yet fully accepted what you are, have you?"

"What do you mean?"

"There is no shame in being what we are. Our kind have walked the earth for countless centuries." She gestured at his left side. "You see what denying it has brought you."

"I am not like you," he replied quietly. "I am not a werewolf."

"No?" She cocked her head to one side in a gesture that was becoming familiar. "What are you, then?"

"Just a man."

"Indeed?" She glanced pointedly at his left side, and he knew she was remembering the long black hair now covered by his clothing.

"I would rather be what you are than what I am becoming!" he exclaimed. "At least you can be human when you wish. My humanity will soon be lost to me and I will be nothing but a beast."

"What do you mean?"

"I am under a powerful curse, one that can never be broken."

Understanding dawned in Valaree's deep brown eyes. "Surely there is a way to break the spell."

Erik laughed bitterly. "Yes, but only a woman long dead can end it."

Valaree closed the distance between them and laid a slender hand on his shoulder. "I am sorry. Truly I am." She regarded him for a long moment, her dark eyes filled with sympathy. "You are welcome to stay here, with me and my family. We will help you in any way we can."

"You are most generous, Valaree." Erik glanced at

the wolves who were lying beside the fire, watching him through dark, intelligent eyes.

"You will stay with us, then?"

"As tempting as your offer is, I cannot. There's something I must do."

Valaree looked up at him. He could smell her desire for him. She ran her fingertips over the half of his face that was no longer human, softly stroking his transformed cheek. Her touch, so gentle, so accepting, made him ache deep inside for things that could never be.

"I hope you will come back to us, Erik."

Not knowing what to say, unwilling to make a promise he might not be able to keep, he didn't say anything, merely smiled down at her.

"I will be here, waiting," she said softly. "If you ever have need of our help, you have only to call my name, and I will answer."

It gave him a curious sense of comfort to know that when he was fully a beast, there was a place where he would be welcome, accepted.

He left the cave that night, his hood pulled low over his face. Without his mask, he dared not travel during the light of day. With luck, he would reach Charmion's fortress at the top of Cimmerian Crag before dawn.

Driven by an unrelenting sense of urgency, he pushed Raven hard, pausing only briefly to rest the stallion. And always, in the back of his mind, he said a prayer for Kristine's safety.

Dawn's fingers were lifting the cloak of night from the earth when he reached the foot of Cimmerian

Crag. He stared up the long, winding road, a shiver of apprehension sending icy tendrils down his spine. He had learned to his sorrow just how powerful Charmion was, and only his fear for Kristine's safety compelled him to confront the witch now. He glanced at his left hand, felt the familiar horror unfurl within him. No matter how often he looked at his deformed body, he never got over the shock, the revulsion. Always, he felt the sickening fear in his gut, and with it an overpowering helplessness.

He stared up at the dark fortress that sat atop the mountain like a great bird of prey. Gathering his courage, he urged Raven forward.

Trees dripping gray-green moss grew on both sides of the narrow path, their extended branches hovering over him like the bony fingers of death. He heard the croaking of frogs. The hoot of an owl sounded nearby, ominous somehow. Some thought the screech of an owl signified bad luck; others thought it was an omen of impending death.

He drew in a deep breath. There had been a time when he hadn't believed in such nonsense, but Charmion had changed all that. A shiver of unease snaked down his spine as a huge white owl flew past his shoulder.

As he climbed higher, a strange silence fell over the land. No birds sang in the trees; even the wind was still. Raven snorted as they rounded a sharp bend in the trail. The left side of the path fell away into a deep abyss.

And still the trail climbed upward, higher and higher, winding round and round the mountain until, at last, they reached the top.

Built of black stone, Charmion's fortress rose up

from the earth like an enormous beast of prey. Two huge stone gargoyles flanked the entry.

Erik reined the stallion to a halt several yards from the front door. Evil radiated from the fortress like smoke from a funeral pyre. It seemed to reach out to him, beckoning him with skeletal fingers.

The stallion shook his head and backed up.

"Easy, boy," Erik murmured. He stroked the horse's neck as he studied the fortress. No lights burned from within. The lower windows stared back at him, watching him like dark, empty eyes.

Fighting off a sense of impending doom, Erik urged Raven toward the fortress, but the horse refused to obey. Lowering his head, the stallion pawed the ground and then backed up another step.

It was then Erik saw it, a crypt made of glistening white marble. A single bronze cherub knelt beside the door, its arms folded in prayer. He didn't have to see the name etched above the tomb to know it was Dominique's final resting place.

He stared at the crypt for a long while, guilt rising up within him. A lifetime of regrets lay behind that cold stone edifice. He had never truly loved her. He should never have married her.

With a sigh, Erik slid from the stallion's back. Tethering Raven to a wind-blown birch, he walked across the rocky ground toward the entrance of the fortress.

Kristine was inside, and no one, not Charmion, not the devil himself, would keep him out.

Chapter Seventeen

Kristine stood at the window, staring out into the rain-swept night. Why hadn't she listened to Lady Trevayne? Why hadn't she stayed home where she belonged? Why hadn't she told someone where she was going when she'd left Hawksbridge?

Blinking back the tears that were ever close to the surface these days, she looked toward the west, toward home, and knew she would never see Hawksbridge, or Erik, again.

Overcome by despair and loneliness, she wrapped her arms around her stomach and rocked back and forth, a low, keening wail rising in her throat.

Lightning ripped through the dark clouds like daggers. Thunder rumbled through the night like the sound of distant drums. A lusty wind pummeled the grass and the trees, moaning like a soul in torment.

Dropping to her knees, Kristine added her own cries to those of the wind and the rain.

Chapter Eighteen

Charmion sat back in her chair, one hand idly stroking the fur of the large black cat sleeping in her lap. He was here. She needed no crystal ball to tell her who approached the castle entrance, no magic of any kind. His hatred flew ahead of him like the wings of the storm, strong and black; a loathing that would have been as virulent as her own had it not been tempered by fear—fear for his young wife and unborn child.

Excitement stirred within her as she contemplated seeing him again. The transformation should be almost complete.

He was at the door now. She lifted one hand, breaking the wards that guarded the front portal so he could enter. She didn't rise, didn't go to welcome him. He would find his way to her soon enough.

And then he was there, striding across the black stone floor, his dark eyes alight with barely suppressed fury. "Where is she?"

Charmion lifted one brow and made a small tsking sound. "I see you have forgotten your manners, Lord

Trevayne. Apparently you are even more of a beast than you appear."

A growl rumbled in his throat. "Where is Kristine? What have you done with her?"

"I have done nothing to the girl. She is quite well."

"She is here, then?"

Charmion allowed a slow smile to curve her lips. There was no warmth in the expression. "She came here several days ago, demanding that I release you from the curse I had placed upon you." She sighed dramatically. "Alas, I told her it was quite impossible. There was only one person who could release you."

Charmion's black eyes burned with fury. "I told her it was most unfortunate that the only one who possessed the ability to end the curse had died at your hand."

"I did not kill Dominique," Erik retorted.

"You planted your seed within her frail body, and it killed her."

"Every woman knows the risks of childbirth. It was a risk Dominique was willing to take."

Anger flowed from Charmion. The cat in her lap awoke with a hiss, its yellow eyes narrowed.

"I warned you!" Charmion said, her voice echoing off the walls. "I told you she was not strong enough to bear a child!"

"The choice to have a child was not mine alone!" Erik said harshly. "I did not take her to bed by force." He took a step forward, his right hand clenched. "She came to me willingly, lovingly. I told her of your fears, and she laughed them aside. She said you had always coddled her, but she was not afraid."

The big black cat leaped to the floor as Charmion surged to her feet.

Eyes blazing, body shaking with fury, the witch extended her arm. Erik's clothes disappeared at a wave of her hand.

She stared at him intently, at the long black fur that covered his left side from his shoulder to his feet. She smiled with satisfaction as she saw his transformed left hand, his feet, which were now paws. His left ear was that of a wolf.

Soon, she thought, soon the transformation would be complete.

Erik called on every ounce of courage he possessed as he stood naked and ashamed before her. But he would not cower. He would not try to hide what he was becoming. She had concocted the hideous curse. Let her look her fill.

"Are you satisfied, Charmion?" he asked quietly. "Does what I am becoming give you pleasure? Does it ease the pain of Dominique's loss?"

"Yes!" she hissed. "Yes, and yes, and yes again."

She walked toward him, one long-fingered hand reaching out to stroke his furred side. She laughed softly when he tried to draw away and realized he couldn't move.

Frozen in place, he could only stand there, repelled by her touch, as she ran her hands over him, a look of evil delight in her black eyes as she slowly examined the results of her spell.

"What are you going to do with Kristine?"

"Nothing. For now." Charmion walked around him, her hand stroking his fur as if he were a pet. "She has something I want."

Fear unlike anything he had ever known churned in Erik's gut. "What do you mean?"

"She's carrying a child. A girl child. I shall call her Dominique."

"No!"

Charmion stood in front of him. "Oh, yes. I shall have a new daughter to replace the one you stole from me."

"Charmion, please . . ."

"You wish to beg me for your child's life? It would be more effective if you were on your knees."

She waved her hand, and he dropped to his hands and knees, forced there by her power.

"Beg me, Erik. Beg me for your daughter's life as I once begged you for mine."

"Please," he said hoarsely. "Take Hawksbridge, take all my holdings, only please don't take my daughter from Kristine."

She laughed in cruel amusement. "How the mighty have fallen!" she said, her voice filled with mockery. "You should see how you look! Erik Trevayne, mighty lord of Hawksbridge Castle. A few more months at most and the transformation will be complete. Perhaps I shall keep you here for a pet. Yes, I think that is a most wondrous idea. You will be able to watch your daughter grow up." A laugh of pure evil spilled from her lips. "Yes, I shall enjoy watching that. I shall enjoy looking into your eyes when you gaze at her. Think what it will be like! You will remember everything. Everything. But you will be a beast, lacking the power of speech, totally in my power."

He fought off a sense of growing horror to ask, "And what of Kristine?"

Charmion shrugged. "I fear I shall have no need of her once the child is weaned. Perhaps I shall let her go. Or perhaps I shall turn her into a beast, as well. Would you like that?"

"No!" He struggled to break free of her power, to rise to his feet, but he couldn't move, could only kneel there, helpless, while she stroked his head, her eyes thoughtful.

"Both beasts. Perhaps the two of you will mate and have more children," she remarked. And then she laughed. "Though I suppose it will be more like a litter, really."

"No! No . . . please." A howl of anguish rose in his throat, and with it an overpowering sense of guilt. This was all his fault. He should have ended his life when Dominique died.

"Come along, my pet," Charmion said. She lifted one hand, beckoning him, and he had no choice but to obey.

On hands and knees, he followed her through the great dark castle. The black cat padded after him, hissing softly.

Erik tried to free himself from the grip of Charmion's awesome power. He willed himself to stop, to stand, but his body refused to obey.

They turned right at the end of a long corridor and went down a winding flight of cold stone stairs that led to a dark, dank dungeon. The cat sat down at the bottom of the stairs, yellow eyes glowing in the dark.

The rough stone scraped his right knee, his right hand. He began to shiver as the dungeon's cold crept into him, and with it the certain fear that he would never see Kristine again, that Charmion would keep him down here until the transformation was complete, until he was fully a beast, incapable of speech, his mind and his humanity forever trapped in the body of an animal.

He heard a whispered word and a candle sprang to life, its pale light illuminating an iron-barred cell.

"Your new home," Charmion said as she opened the door.

He summoned all his willpower, all his strength, in an effort to resist her, knowing if he entered the musty cell, he would not leave it again, at least not in his present form. "I. Will. Not."

"Ah, but you will, my lord Erik. You are not strong enough to resist me." She crooked her finger at him. "Come, my pet."

"No." The word was torn from his throat, but even as the sound of his voice echoed off the damp stone walls, he was crawling inside the cell.

The door shut behind him, closing with the finality of life's last breath.

He collapsed on the cold stone as she withdrew her power, his body feeling as weak as that of a newborn colt.

Charmion stared at him a moment, and then she turned away. The candle guttered and died as she retraced her steps toward the stairway, leaving him alone in cold and utter darkness.

Shaking with pain and rage, he grabbed hold of the bars and drew himself up. He was a man still; he would not lie on the floor like some dumb beast. But, try as he might, his legs refused to support him, and he dropped to his knees, his forehead resting against the bars.

"Kristine . . . Kristine . . ." Her name trembled on his lips. What was to become of her, of their child?

Steeped in bitter despair, his body aching as the hideous transformation continued toward its inevitable end, he closed his eyes and surrendered to the darkness.

He woke to a blaze of light. He sprang to his feet, a curse issuing from his lips as he glanced around the dungeon. Mirrors, nothing but mirrors. Large and small, gilt-edged, framed in wood, veined with gold. Mirrors everywhere he looked, and for the first time since the curse had made itself known, there was nowhere to hide from what he was becoming. His reflection stared back at him at every turn, mocking him.

When the transformation first began, he had removed every mirror from the castle save the small one he used when he shaved. Never since that day had he looked into a full-length glass, never had he seen just how truly hideous he had become. Daily, he had examined his left hand, his feet, but never before had he seen the sum total of what he now was. It was his worst nightmare magnified a hundred times, illuminated by a hundred flickering candles.

"Charmion!" He clutched one of the bars with his good hand as he bellowed her name. "Charmion!"

One minute he was alone, the next she was standing outside his cell. "Is something amiss, my lord?" she inquired with sugary sweetness.

"Take them away!"

She smiled at her reflection as she glanced around the dungeon, inordinately pleased with her cleverness. Mirrors of every conceivable size and shape hung from the walls outside his cell, from the ceiling above, out of his reach but never out of sight.

"Take them away," he repeated. "I beg of you."

Her hell-black eyes met his, filled with hatred. "For every tear my daughter wept, my lord Erik, for every drop of blood she shed."

Drawing himself up to his full height, he stepped away from the bars. He would not beg, would not humiliate himself before her. He summoned his own hatred, felt it wrap around him, strengthening his resolve. He would not be brought down by his own reflection, monstrous as it was. He would not grovel. Nor would he surrender to the despair that flowed through him. He was still alive, and while he lived, he would resist her. Somehow, he would find a way to escape and free Kristine. Somehow . . .

"Has your lady wife seen you as you are now?" Charmion wondered aloud.

Muttering a vile oath, he lunged forward, his good hand reaching through the bars, reaching for her throat, but she stepped nimbly out of danger, a cackle of laughter spewing from her lips.

And in spite of his resolve, he found himself pleading once more. "I'm begging you, don't bring her down here, don't let her see this. Think of the child."

"Unlike my Dominique, your little street urchin is made of strong stuff," Charmion said, her words bitter. "She may scream, she may faint, but the child is well-rooted within her and will be in no danger." A cruel smile twisted her lips. "Think how pleased she will be when I tell her you are here."

Laughter bubbled from Charmion's throat, faster and faster, until he thought, hoped, prayed, she would choke on it.

"I cannot wait to see her face when she sees yours," the witch exclaimed, and with a wave of her hand, she was gone.

* * *

Kristine looked up from her sewing as Charmion entered the room. As always, a feeling of dread swept over her when she was in the witch's presence. Charmion had treated her kindly thus far, making sure she had enough to eat, that she had a comfortable bed, clothes to accommodate her rapidly expanding waistline. The witch had provided several yards of soft wool for baby sacques and gowns. She had assured Kristine of an easy delivery, claiming that there were herbs to ease the pangs of birth and bring the child speedily into the world. Kristine didn't know if the witch spoke the truth, but if so, why had the herbs not worked on Dominique?

Kristine shook the disquieting thoughts away. Charmion had been the essence of kindness, save for the fact that she was holding Kristine prisoner against her will.

"Good afternoon, Lady Kristine," Charmion said. As always, there was an edge of mockery in her tone, a glint of dislike in her eyes.

Kristine nodded. "Good afternoon."

"I have a surprise for you, my dear," Charmion said, her voice a soft purr.

"A surprise?" Kristine asked.

"Yes. Tell me, what would please you most?"

"I should like to go home."

Charmion laughed and made a dismissing gesture with one hand. "What else would please you?"

Tears burned Kristine's eyes. "I should like to see my husband."

Charmion smiled. Smiles were meant to be expressions of joy, of delight, but there was nothing of happiness in the smile the witch bestowed upon Kristine.

"And so you shall," Charmion exclaimed. She held out one hand. "Come."

"He's here?" Kristine stood abruptly, her sewing falling to the floor in her haste. "Erik is here?"

"Indeed. He is waiting for you."

She was afraid to believe, afraid to hope.

"Come along." The witch's black eyes were filled with dark merriment and expectation as she led the way out the door and down the corridor.

Kristine followed behind, her heart pounding with anticipation and dread. A part of her was filled with hope, while another, more sensible part feared that it would not be Erik she was going to see, but his body.

Fear coiled deep within her as Charmion led her down a winding staircase and into a dungeon ablaze with light.

Charmion's castle was dimly lit at best and Kristine blinked against the sudden, unexpected brightness.

Charmion paused at the foot of the stairs. "He is waiting for you. Stay as long as you wish." She smiled, a smug, immensely satisfied smile, and then she vanished.

Kristine stood there for a moment, afraid to move, afraid this was some cruel hoax and that she would not find Erik here at all, but his corpse.

She took a tentative step forward. "Erik? Erik, are you here?"

"Stay where you are, Kristine. For the love of God, stay where you are."

Weak with relief, she put a hand against the wall for support. He was here, he was alive! Thank God.

"Are you all right?" she called. "Has she hurt you?"

"I am as I was when I arrived," he replied, his voice tinged with bitterness. "Go now. Do not come down here again."

Confused, she stared down the narrow corridor. There were cells on both sides of the stone walkway. All were empty of life. All were filled with mirrors, though she could see nothing reflected in them but the light of a dozen lamps. Curious, she took a step forward.

"No!" The word, filled with panic, sounded as though it had been ripped from his throat. "Go back!"

Alarmed, she ran down the narrow corridor, her footsteps echoing off the walls. And then she saw him, standing in the far corner of a small barred cell, his back toward her, his head bowed. There was nothing else in the cell—no bed, no chair, not even a blanket, only iron bars and a cold stone floor.

"Erik?" She took a hesitant step forward, certain this was a cruel joke. "Erik, is that you?"

"Go away, Kristine. Please, if you have any feeling for me at all, go away and never come back."

She took a step closer, staring in morbid fascination at the creature standing with its back toward her. She could not see its face. The form, though human, was covered from head to foot on one side with thick black fur. Only they weren't feet, but paws.

It had to be a joke, she thought, some horrible monstrous joke. And even as she tried to convince herself that it was some cruel jest on Charmion's part, her memory spewed forth a kaleidoscope of images she had tried to forget: The sight of Erik coming home naked in the dark of a rain-swept night. The creature she had seen in the lodge the night she'd fainted, a creature who had worn a mask and whose left side had been covered with thick black fur. Nothing she had seen before, nothing Lady Trevayne had said, had prepared her for what she saw now.

It was not a trick at all. It was Erik.

"No." She felt suddenly faint and she stumbled forward, grabbing at the cell door to keep from falling. "No . . ."

At her touch, the door swung inward. With a cry, she fell forward, landing on her hands and knees inside the cell.

Erik whirled around, his gaze meeting hers, and for a moment, time ceased. He watched the blood drain from her face, watched her expression turn from fear to horror as her gaze swept over him and she saw him as he really was, saw the thick black pelt that covered the left side of his body, his wolflike ear, his feet that weren't feet at all, but paws with thick black nails. Saw it all in the bright light of a hundred flickering candles. Saw his ugliness reflected back at her a hundred times over.

Shaking her head in disbelief, she backed away from him, only to be brought up short by the cell door, which had closed behind her, trapping her inside the cell with a monster.

Laughter echoed down the corridor of the dungeon. Charmion's laughter.

Erik turned his back on Kristine, unable to abide the fear and revulsion in her eyes. He could hear the harsh rasp of her breathing, smell the sharp scent of her fear. She had scraped one of her hands on the rough stones when she fell, and the metallic odor of her blood rose in his nostrils, hot and thick and sweet. He licked his lips, horrified by the urge to lick the blood from her palm.

Silence stretched between them, a horrible silence that wore on his nerves. He sent a silent plea to Charmion, begging her to open the cell door so Kristine could escape, but the door remained closed, kept shut by another bit of witchery.

He pressed his forehead against the cold stone wall, his right hand clenched close to his side. Despair washed over him, engulfed him, and with it an all-consuming sense of shame and humiliation that Kristine had seen him as he was.

And then he heard her voice, small and frightened. "Erik?"

He closed his eyes, praying that this was a nightmare, that when he opened his eyes, he would find himself at home, in his own bed.

"Erik?"

He heard the tears in her voice and wished he could offer her some small measure of comfort, but there was nothing he could do. Nothing anyone could do.

"Erik, it is you, isn't it?" He heard the pity in her voice, the desperate need for reassurance. "Talk to me, please. Say something, anything."

"Kristine . . ." He breathed her name on a sigh, felt every muscle in his body tense as he heard her take a hesitant step toward him. "Stay there!"

"Won't you hold me? I'm so afraid."

"It's me you should be afraid of."

"You? Why?"

"Look at me!" He whirled around to face her. "Look, and tell me you're not afraid of what you see."

"I see my husband."

"You see a monster!" He thrust his left hand toward her. "Tell me this doesn't frighten you! Tell me you're not repulsed by what you see."

She shook her head, her eyes filling with tears. "I am afraid, terribly afraid, but not of you."

"Kristine, Kristine . . ." He lowered his hand and turned his back to her once more. "Don't you understand? I'm changing on the inside, too." He groaned deep in his throat. It was the dark, feral thoughts that plagued his mind more and more often of late that frightened him the most.

His breath caught in his throat when she placed her hand on his back.

"There has to be something we can do," she said quietly. "Some way to break this terrible curse. There has to be."

He shook his head, his eyes closing in pleasure as her fingertips stroked his back. He wondered how she could bear to be near him when he was in this hideous state, wondered how he had lived all these months without the tender touch of her hand.

"We've got to find a way out of here," Kristine said.

"There is no way out." Despair washed over him. He was trapped in a living nightmare, at the mercy of his worst enemy. The knowledge filled him with a strange lethargy.

"There has to be! We can't just sit here and do nothing." She placed her hands on his shoulders, the full extent of what had happened to him hitting her with renewed force as she felt smooth, warm skin beneath one hand and thick fur beneath the other. She fought down her own panic as she forced him to turn and face her.

For a moment, she could only stare at him. Without

the mask, she could see the entire right side of his face, could see what a devastatingly handsome man he had once been.

He tried to turn away from her, but she cupped his face in her hands. "No. Look at me. We have to find a way out of here. Don't you see? We have to find someone who can break Charmion's curse before . . ." She took a deep breath. "Before it's too late."

Erik stared down at his wife. She was beautiful, with her eyes flashing fire. And she was right. He couldn't waste time lamenting the inevitable. He had to get Kristine out of there before it was too late. Perhaps, if one witch could cast a spell, another could break it.

"All right, my little warrior wife," he said with a wry grin. "We'll fight our way out of here."

Or die trying.

Chapter Nineteen

Charmion sat before the fire, staring at the dancing flames. The big black cat lying in her lap purred softly, its back arching as she ran her fingertips up and down its spine.

"Vengeance is truly sweet, my pretty one," Charmion murmured. "Sweet, indeed."

Lifting one hand, she sent a trickle of power into the fire. Immediately, her daughter's image sprang to life within the flames.

"He will pay dearly for every tear you wept, my Dominique, for every drop of blood you shed."

She stared at the image until it faded from sight.

Soon she would have another child. Erik's child. She would raise it as her own, love it as her own. The babe would never know its true parents but would grow up thinking that Charmion was its mother. And Erik . . . once the transformation was complete, he would be her pet. It would give her great pleasure to watch him, to see the intelligence in his eyes, the knowledge of who and what he had been.

It would be interesting to see how long it took for

him to surrender his humanity, to forget he had once been a man and finally, fully, become a beast. In truth, she had expected him to succumb to the full effects of the curse long before now. She had underestimated him, she mused. She had known he would fight against the inner change with every fiber of his being, just as his body fought the outer transformation. She had not realized how strong his will was, how deep his instinct for survival. And yet, no matter how fiercely he resisted, in the end, he would succumb. Her victory would be complete. Her daughter would be avenged.

She smiled, pleased, knowing that the intense inner struggle must be causing him even more pain and anguish than the physical torment he experienced as his body underwent the outer transformation. And the harder he fought it, the more painful it would be.

And now the woman was here, come of her own free will. Charmion laughed softly. She had never thought of taking the child until the woman showed up at her doorstep. She had known, in that moment when she ascertained the child's sex, that she would take the babe. A baby, she thought, a baby for Christmas. It would be the best gift of all.

Sitting back in the chair, she closed her eyes. Things were turning out even better than she had foreseen.

Chapter Twenty

Charmion stood outside the cell, unable to believe her eyes. She had expected to find the girl cowering in a corner, in fear for her life. Instead, she was asleep on the floor, her head pillowed on Erik's chest.

And Erik, now more monster than man, had the gall to smile at her.

An oath hissed through Charmion's teeth. "You dare mock me?"

Erik shrugged. "Did you hope I would tear her apart?"

"Of course not!"

"Of course not," he repeated. She wouldn't want him to harm the child. "What will you do with Kristine, after the child is born?"

"When that time comes, you will no longer care."

Fear's cold, clammy hand knotted his insides. "The transformation is nearly complete, then?"

"Before the New Year, I should think."

"And when it happens, will I remember that I was once a man?"

"Oh, yes."

"Let her go, Charmion. Kristine has done nothing to you. She poses no threat. Send her away."

"I might have, had you not asked it of me."

"Please, Charmion, for the love of heaven—"

"Don't speak to me of love! Your love killed my daughter as surely as if you had plunged a knife into her heart! I have thought of her, grieved for her, these past five years. Be glad I do not destroy the mother who bore you, as well!"

With a wave of her hand, Charmion disappeared in a swirl of thick, dark smoke.

Days passed. Food appeared in the cell once each day. Raw meat for Erik; rich, nourishing meals for Kristine. Erik refused to touch the meat, though with each passing day it grew more tempting. Kristine offered to share her food with him, but he accepted only a little, not wanting to deprive her or the child of the sustenance they needed.

They clung to each other, not knowing how much time they had left, how long Charmion would allow them to be together. He watched Kristine constantly, wanting to imprint her image so deeply in his mind that, man or beast, he would never forget the smoothness of her skin, the clear green of her eyes, the beauty of her smile.

At night, while she slept, he paced the length of the narrow cell, his soul sinking deeper and deeper into despair. He could feel the curse creeping over him, feel it working its hideous magic on his body, his mind. His dreams were dark, filled with the scent of blood and death. In his dreams, he was no longer human, but fully a wolf. He dreamed of stalking his prey, of bringing it down, of burying his fangs in warm flesh and tearing it to shreds. He dreamed of Valaree, of hunting alongside her in the light of a full moon.

Valaree. Her name whispered through his mind. *I need your help again, Valaree. . . .*

Too soon, Charmion came to his cell and took Kristine away. The witch had let them spend a week together. It had not been kindness on her part, Erik knew that well enough. Never kindness. She had given him a week to bask in Kristine's love, to grow accustomed to her nearness, to the company and comfort of another human being, and then Charmion had taken her away, knowing his loneliness would be all the more awful to bear when she was gone, and he was again alone.

He howled his anger and frustration, the sound of his rage echoing off the damp stone walls, reverberating in his own ears until the wild animal sound penetrated his mind and he clamped his mouth shut, horrified that such a beastly cry had come from his lips.

Left alone, he padded restlessly back and forth, and everywhere he looked, his image stared back at him, mocking him, tormenting him. Though still manlike in stature, he was not a man. His whole body was covered with thick black fur now, his feet and his left hand were paws. His left ear was wolflike. Only his right hand and the right side of his face remained human. For now, he looked like a man in the costume of a wolf, but soon, soon . . . The horror of what he was becoming made his stomach churn, made him long for death, for the forgetfulness of oblivion.

He wrapped his right hand around one of the bars, wishing he could bend it to his will, wishing he could sink his teeth into Charmion's black heart. He cursed her for taking Kristine from him. As much as it had bothered him to have her imprisoned in the dungeon, he had treasured Kristine's company, had loved her all the more for letting him hold her when he was in such monstrous form. Sometimes, he had caught her staring at him, her beautiful green eyes filled with pity and compassion, but never with revulsion or fear. He had the feeling that her presence had been the only thing keeping him sane, feared that being alone with nothing but his own hideous reflection would soon drive him mad.

His fingers tightened around the bar of the cell, his knuckles going white with the strain. He had to get out of there!

"Please," he prayed, "if I am damned to be a wolf, then let me forget that I was once a man. Let me run wild with Valaree and her pack. Please don't leave me here, in Charmion's power, to know that she has destroyed my love, to see my babe and never be able to hold her." He groaned low in his throat. "Please, please . . ."

He wondered if Charmion would grant him the opportunity to see a priest and confess his sins before the transformation was complete. Would she think it punishment enough to condemn him to hell on earth without damning his eternal soul as well?

Without Kristine, the days passed with agonizing slowness. He paced restlessly back and forth, hour after hour, oblivious to the rough stones that scraped the pads of his feet until they bled. A harsh, bitter laugh rose in his throat. His paws, he amended as he stared at the bloody paw prints that stained the cold gray stones.

"A fine end you've come to, my lord of Hawks-bridge Castle," he muttered. "If only your father could see you now!"

He was going quietly mad, he thought, and welcomed the madness that would wipe away the memories of his past, of Kristine, of his unborn child.

He smiled as he thought of how disappointed Charmion would be if he lost his mind. She was looking forward to the time when his mind would be trapped in the body of an animal, but it would never happen if he went mad. Insanity would cheat her of her final victory.

Kristine paced her chamber, her arms wrapped protectively over her womb, her throat and eyes aching from the tears she had shed. She couldn't seem to stop crying.

She looked around the room, at the sumptuous furnishings, and thought of Erik, locked in a damp cell in the dungeon below. She had a warm bed to sleep in, a soft mattress, fluffy pillows. He had a cold stone floor. She had a wardrobe filled with dresses of the finest silks and satins and soft wools. Erik was naked. Her meals were served hot on plates trimmed with gold; she had clear, cool water or wine or tea to drink. Erik was given a bowl of water and a platter of raw meat.

She would have refused to eat, refused the comfort Charmion offered, had it not been for her child, but she could not starve herself without harming the babe, and she could not risk her child's life. Even knowing Charmion would take it from her, even knowing she would never see the baby again once it had been born, she could do nothing to cause harm to Erik's child. Charmion might kill her, might kill Erik, but their child would live, proof that they had once lived. And loved.

She sought forgetfulness in sleep, but her dreams were dark and troubled. Sometimes she dreamed that Erik was a werewolf, that he was stalking her through dark shadowed woods. Sometimes she dreamed they had escaped from Charmion's castle and returned home and that she was forced to keep Erik locked behind bars to prevent him from tearing their newborn child to shreds.

Charmion came to visit her morning and evening, making certain she was well, asking if there was anything she needed. A midwife had been summoned from the village. A nursery was being readied. Dominique's cradle was being refinished.

Kristine didn't know which was worse, the nightmares that haunted her sleep, or the waking nightmare that her life had become.

She thought longingly of Hawksbridge Castle, of Mrs. Grainger and Leyla and Lilia, of Nan and Yvette.

She missed riding Misty.

She missed falling asleep in Erik's arms. . . . Erik, Erik. Waking or sleeping, he was ever in her thoughts, her prayers.

Daily, she begged and pleaded and demanded to see him again, and finally Charmion agreed.

Kristine's heart pounded with anticipation as she followed the witch down the narrow flight of stairs to the dungeon. She had forgotten how bright it was down there with the candlelight reflected in the mirrors, candles that burned but never went out.

Charmion halted at the bottom of the stairs. "Enjoy your visit, my dear," she said, her voice filled with mockery. "I shall return for you within the hour."

Kristine nodded, the witch already forgotten as she hastened down the narrow corridor toward Erik's cell.

She knew what he looked like. His image haunted every dream, yet she stared at him in shock when she saw him, only then realizing she had been hoping that the image she saw in her dreams was only make-believe, that she would find him whole when she saw him again.

He whirled around at the sound of her footsteps. A myriad of emotions flashed across his face—joy, hope, shame, despair—as he slowly walked toward her.

"Erik."

"My Kristine." He reached through the bars, his good hand resting on her swollen abdomen. "Are you well?"

"I'm fine. Truly."

His gaze searched her face. "She's not mistreating you?"

"No." She blinked back her tears, knowing it would distress him to see her cry. Knowing that he needed her touch, needing to touch him in return, she reached through the bars and caressed his right cheek. "I miss you."

He caught her hand in his. Lifting it to his lips, he kissed her palm, then rubbed his cheek back and forth against the back of her hand. Her skin was smooth and soft, so soft. He inhaled her fragrance, remembering the evenings they had spent together in the library, the nights he had shared her bed. Desire stirred within him and he dropped her hand. Wanting her now, in his present form, seemed obscene somehow.

"You shouldn't have come here," he said.

His voice was deeper than she remembered, almost a growl. "Don't be angry with me. I had to see you. Oh!" She gasped as the baby gave a lusty kick. Reaching through the bars again, she took his hand and placed it over her womb. "Can you feel it?"

A look of wonder spread over his face as he felt his child move beneath his hand. "Does it hurt you?"

"No, it feels wonderful. I hope it's a boy, Erik. A strong, healthy boy." Fighting tears, she smiled up at him. "The next lord of Hawksbridge Castle."

"The next lady of Hawksbridge, if Charmion is to be believed."

"What do you mean?"

"She says the child is female, a girl to replace the daughter she has lost."

"A girl. You have failed, then."

"Failed?"

"You married me to beget an heir to Hawksbridge."

"I have not failed. My daughter will be my heir."

"You are not disappointed, then?"

"No."

Kristine smiled. "Perhaps we will have a boy next time."

Erik nodded. His daughter would never see Hawksbridge, and there would be no next time. He knew it, and so did Kristine, but he nodded just the same, willing to play the game if it would make her happy, even as he quietly cursed his father. But for his father, none of this would have happened. Left to his own devices, he would never have married Dominique. She would never have conceived, never died in childbirth, and he would not be here now, his body slowly being transformed into that of a beast. . . . He felt the baby move again, drew in a sharp breath as he realized that had he entered the priesthood, Kristine would have died on the gallows.

He blew out a deep sigh and realized that her life, the time they had spent together, was worth any price he had to pay.

"I won't give up hope," Kristine said. "I won't stop believing that there's a way out of here, a way to break the curse."

He smiled down at her, but his eyes were filled with sadness.

"Don't give up, Erik! Think about the baby. You want to see her, don't you? We can't let Charmion win. We can't!"

"But I've already won." Charmion materialized out of the shadows. She stared at Erik, a smug smile on her face. "Haven't I?" She glanced at Kristine. "Even if you could escape, even if you kill me, there's nothing you can do to save him." Head cocked to one side, she nodded slowly as she studied Erik. "I should say the final transformation and the child will arrive within days of each other."

Erik forced himself to endure the witch's scrutiny without turning away, though it was humiliating to stand there, without so much as a scrap of cloth to hide his nakedness. Hatred boiled up inside him, filling him, until he thought he would choke on it.

"It grows more difficult each day, does it not?" Charmion mused. "More difficult to maintain your humanity. Well," she said brightly, "soon you won't have to worry about it at all. You shall make a delightful pet. No doubt I shall have to keep you tightly muzzled at first, but you will soon learn your place, and if you don't, why, then I shall destroy you. A wolf skin would look well in front of my hearth, don't you think?"

Kristine backed away from the cell, sickened by the image conjured up by the witch's words, by the evil laughter that filled the dungeon like thick oily smoke.

A growl rose in Erik's throat, a horrible, inhuman sound filled with impotent rage.

The witch cackled with delight as he lunged forward, his left arm reaching through the bars, claws straining to reach her.

Horrified, Kristine watched Charmion taunt him, watched him throw himself against the bars in a vain attempt to reach the witch. Kristine looked away, unable to watch, found herself reaching for a heavy gilt-edged mirror. Before she was fully aware of what she was doing, she lifted the mirror and struck Charmion over the head with all the force at her command.

The witch gasped in pain, then crumpled to the ground amid a shower of broken glass.

"Erik, what have I done?" Kristine stared at him, a look of horror on her face. "Is she dead?"

Dropping to his knees, he reached through the bars to check the witch's pulse. There was none. For all their power, witches were frail creatures. He quickly searched her pockets, looking for the key to the lock, but it wasn't there.

"Kristine. Kristine!"

"She's dead, isn't she? I didn't mean to kill her."

"Kristine, listen to me. You've got to find the key or something we can use to break the lock."

She nodded. Then, with a glance at the fallen witch, she turned and hurried down the corridor.

Erik stared after her, then blew out a sigh. Charmion was dead, and all hope of breaking the curse had died with her.

He swore softly as he ran his hand over the lock. If Charmion had cast a spell over it, he would never get out.

Minutes later he heard the sound of Kristine's footsteps on the stones, and then she was there. She held up a large brass key. "I found it!"

Erik nodded. "Hurry, love." He held his breath as Kristine slid the key into the lock. An eternity seemed to pass as he waited for her to turn the key.

His breath whooshed out in a sigh of relief as the lock opened. A moment later, he was out of the cell, holding Kristine in his arms.

"Let's go," she said. "Please, Erik, let's get out of here. Now."

He nodded, as eager as she to put this place far behind them. Hand in hand, they left the dungeon.

"Find me something to wear and pack us some food," Erik said when they reached the top of the stairs. "I'll go saddle the horses."

"Hurry."

"I will." He walked through the silent house toward

the front door, the hair along the back of his neck prickling. He could feel Charmion's dark magic all around him. He paused in the hallway, his gaze drawn to a life-sized portrait of Dominique.

He stared at the painting, wondering how she had grown up in this place of evil witchcraft and still remained so pure and sweet. He knew there were witches who practiced white magic, just as there were others, like Charmion, who delighted in evil. Dominique had been born to be a witch, but she had refused to acknowledge the magic she possessed. He had never truly realized until now how difficult it must have been for her.

With a sigh, he touched a finger to her painted cheek. "Forgive me," he murmured. "I never meant you any harm."

Leave here. Hurry.

With a start, Erik glanced over his shoulder, expecting to see Dominique standing behind him, so clearly had he heard her voice. But there was no one there.

Filled with a sense of urgency, he left the house and headed for the stable. Ten minutes later both horses were saddled and he was at the back door.

"Kristine?"

"Here I am." She stepped out of the kitchen, a basket and a heavy cloak on one arm. "Here." She thrust a pile of clothing at him. "Hurry."

She felt it, too, he thought as he dressed, the need to be gone from this place as soon as possible. He wondered briefly whose clothing he was wearing and what had happened to the former owner.

When he finished dressing, he draped the heavy

cloak over Kristine's shoulders; then they hurried toward the horses. Erik lifted Kristine onto Misty's back, stuffed the contents of the basket into the saddlebags, and tossed the basket away.

Taking up Raven's reins, he swung onto the stallion's back and led the way out of the yard.

He didn't look back.

Chapter Twenty-One

They rode as fast as they dared down the narrow, winding trail. Kristine let the mare have her head, knowing Misty didn't need her hand on the reins to follow Erik's big black stallion. Tears blinded her eyes. She had killed Charmion. It didn't matter that the woman had been a witch, or that she had planned to take Erik's child, or that she had probably planned to kill Kristine, herself, once the babe was born. She hadn't wanted to kill Charmion, and yet, at the time, it had seemed there was no other choice. She couldn't have left Erik in that awful dungeon, couldn't have left him there knowing what the witch had in store for him.

A shiver raced down Kristine's spine that had nothing to do with the cold. She had never been given to violence, yet she had killed twice. No matter that the first time had been to defend her honor, the second time to defend Erik and her unborn babe. Murder was a sin, and the guilt of it weighed heavily on her conscience.

She lifted her gaze to Erik's back. The dreadful

curse had almost fully consumed him. Only the right half of his face, neck, and hand remained human. The rest of his body more closely resembled that of a man-sized wolf. And soon, too soon, the transformation would be complete and he would be lost to her forever.

What would happen to him then? What would he do? Where would he go? Would he stay with her at Hawksbridge Castle, condemned to live as a beast for the rest of his days? How would he bear it? How would she? And if he left . . . How would she go on, never knowing where he was, always wondering if he was dead or alive?

She wanted to scream out her anguish, to rail at fate, to curse Charmion for her wickedness. Sin or not, she was suddenly glad she had killed the witch.

Blinded by her tears, she almost pitched forward over Misty's neck when the mare came to an abrupt halt. Snorting softly, Misty danced sideways. It was then that Kristine saw the wolves. Four of them. Three sleek black ones and a large gray one. They stood side by side across the foot of the trail, blocking their passage. Fear slid down her spine. Were they Charmion's pets, put there to prevent their escape?

"Erik?" She gathered Misty's reins. "Erik?"

"It's all right, Kristine," he said reassuringly.

"What do you mean?" she asked, and then stared, mouth open, as one of the black wolves transformed into a beautiful young woman with luminous brown eyes. Thick, waist-length black hair fell down her back and over her bare breasts.

Feeling suddenly light-headed, Kristine clutched the reins. A gasp escaped her lips. Darkness gathered around her. "Erik . . ."

He glanced over his shoulder, then vaulted from the saddle and ran to Misty's side. He caught Kristine as she toppled from the mare's back.

Valaree came to stand beside him. "Is she all right?"

"She's fainted."

Valaree smiled. "I didn't mean to frighten her."

"It's not just you. She's been through a rather bad time in the last few weeks." He stared down at Kristine's pale face. "She killed Charmion."

"The sorceress is dead?" Valaree exclaimed. Her gaze ran over Erik, her brows drawing together in a frown. "But the curse is not broken."

"No," he replied heavily. "I fear there is no way to break it now."

"I know of a powerful mage who lives on the far side of the River Onyx. Perhaps he can help you."

With a shake of his head, Erik muttered, "I doubt it." His arms tightened around Kristine. "But I'm willing to try."

He glanced down at Kristine as she stirred in his arms. Slowly, her eyelids fluttered open. "What happened?"

"You fainted."

She stared at him a moment, and then she frowned. "The wolves . . ."

"They are friends of mine," Erik said.

"Friends? Of yours? But one of them changed into a woman. I saw her."

"They're werewolves, Kristine, but there's nothing to fear. They will not harm you."

Kristine peered over Erik's shoulder. The black-haired woman stood near Misty, her brown eyes serene.

The other wolves sat in a group, tongues lolling, ears pricked forward.

"Are you feeling all right now?" Erik asked.

"I guess so."

"Can you ride?"

She nodded.

Gently, he placed her on her feet, then put his good arm around her and drew her close to his side. "Don't be afraid, Kristine. Valaree saved my life not long ago."

Kristine looked up at him through narrowed eyes, unaccountably jealous of the affection she heard in his voice. "When? How?"

"Later." He glanced up the narrow path, a shiver of unease slithering down his spine. "Let us get away from here and find a place to spend the night."

Kristine nodded. She, too, was anxious to put as much distance between them and this place as possible. Erik lifted her onto Misty's back, then mounted his own horse. Kristine looked around for Valaree, but the girl was gone, having transformed herself into a wolf again.

With a sigh, Kristine took up Misty's reins, wondering if her life would ever be normal again.

They sought shelter in a small cave that was known to Valaree and her family. Erik tethered the horses to a nearby tree, fighting the despair that threatened to overtake him. Seeing Valaree again only served to remind him of what he would soon become. But unlike Valaree and her family, he would not have the advantage of changing into human form.

He shook the morbid thoughts from his mind and ducked inside the cave. A small fire burned near the entrance. Valaree knelt beside the fire, stirring something in a pot. A tall man rested with his back against the cave wall. One of the wolves lay beside him, its head resting on his lap, its eyes closed. A girl of perhaps two and twenty sat on his other side, brushing her hair. She sent Erik a friendly smile.

"Hello," she said, "I'm Valaree's sister, Elsbeth. This is my father, Ulric, and that," she pointed at the wolf, "is my mother, Yolanthe."

Erik nodded. "Pleased to meet you, Elsbeth." He hesitated a moment, then offered Ulric his hand.

The werewolf sniffed Erik's fingers, then took his hand. His handshake was strong and firm. "Are you certain Charmion is dead?"

Erik frowned. "As certain as I can be."

"Did you take her head and her heart?"

"No." Erik glanced at Kristine, saw the blood drain from her face.

"It is the only way to be certain she is truly dead," Ulric remarked.

"But she had no pulse," Kristine said. "No heartbeat."

Ulric smiled reassuringly. "No doubt she is dead, then. Come, let us eat."

Kristine had no appetite for food. Saying she had a headache, she went to the rear of the cave and stretched out on one of the furs spread against the back wall.

Erik sat near the fire with Valaree and her family. Valaree served up bowls of thick lamb stew. Erik recalled passing a small flock of sheep on their way to the cave, and Ulric's subsequent disappearance. No doubt Valaree's father had provided the meat for the stew.

"Your woman's time is very close," Elsbeth remarked.

"Yes," Erik said. He slid furtive glances at Valaree and her family. Save for their eyes, which were slanted and thickly lashed, they appeared quite human as they sat across from him.

Valaree had told him this was a cave they used often. They kept a supply of clothing here, along with blankets and furs and several flasks filled with water. It was, she said, just one of the many places where they had supplies.

"You have questions," Ulric said. "Ask them."

"I'm sorry, I did not mean to stare."

"It is natural for you to be curious," Ulric remarked.

Erik nodded. Curious did not begin to describe what he was feeling, thinking. Fearing.

"When you are ready to talk, we are here to listen." Ulric stood up, and the wolf stood with him. "Come," he said, gesturing to his daughters. "Let us run beneath the stars."

Elsbeth bounded to her feet, her eyes sparkling. "Will you come with us, Erik?"

"No. I should stay here, in case Kristine needs me."

"Of course," Elsbeth said.

"Valaree, are you coming?"

"No, Father. I shall stay and keep Erik company."

With a nod, Ulric left the cave, followed by his wife and daughter.

"It will not be so bad," Valaree said softly. "I have told you that you are welcome to stay with us when the transformation is complete."

Erik shook his head, unable to put his thoughts into words.

"You feel alone, as though you will be cut off from humanity, unable to speak, to communicate. But it will not be like that, if you stay with us. When we are in wolf form, we will be able to communicate with you, and you with us."

She placed her hand on his arm, her dark brown eyes intent upon his face. "If you wish, I will be your mate. Wolves mate for life, Erik. You need not be alone."

"Valaree . . ."

"You need say nothing now. I spoke only in hopes of comforting you. I know how frightened you must be, how lost you must feel. Though I was born a werewolf, there were still adjustments to be made. It is not an easy way of life, but you can find happiness, if you try. There are wild wolves who are friendly to our pack. If you stay with us, you will meet them."

Erik drew in a deep breath. "My thanks, Valaree. I will think on what you have said."

Later that night, lying beside Kristine, Erik thought about what Valaree had suggested. He did not want to spend the rest of his life as a wolf, but if it was his fate to do so, then he was fortunate indeed to have met Valaree and her family, to know there were those who would welcome him.

But it was Kristine he loved, Kristine whose life he wished to share. Turning on his side, he placed his hand over her belly, felt his child stir beneath his fingertips.

Please, please let me see my child before the transformation is complete. Please let me hold my babe in my arms just once. Please . . .

He closed his eyes as Kristine pressed herself against him, and prayed that, whatever happened to him, his wife and child would make it safely back home.

It rained the next day. Valaree had suggested staying in the cave to wait out the storm, but Erik had insisted they move on. Time was running out. They had to find the mage soon, before it was too late.

Ulric had agreed with him, a fact that chilled Erik to the core of his being. The werewolf knew, as he did, that the transformation was almost complete.

Erik glanced into the distance. The wolves loped ahead of the horses, running tirelessly, oblivious to the cold and the rain.

Kristine huddled inside her cloak, the hood pulled low over her forehead to shield her face. She had been quiet since they'd left the cave. He knew she was troubled by the presence of the werewolves, by the constant reminder of what awaited him when the curse was complete.

At noon, they paused to rest the horses. The wolves went ahead to explore the lay of the land. Erik lifted Kristine from Misty's back and they sought shelter in the lee of an overhanging rock.

"Are you going to return to Valaree if . . . when . . . ? Are you?"

"You heard what she said?"

Kristine nodded. "I didn't mean to eavesdrop."

Her gaze searched his. "Are you going to be her . . . her mate?"

"I don't know."

"I think you should." She looked up at him, tears spilling down her cheeks. "I know you won't be happy staying with me after . . . After. I don't want you to be alone."

"Kristine . . ."

"I just want you to be happy."

"Ah, Kristine . . ." Taking her in his arms, he held her close for a long time, gently rocking her back and forth, his throat thick with emotion, and knew he had never loved her more.

"How much farther is it?" Kristine asked.

"Ulric said we would reach the wizard's keep late tomorrow."

"The mage will be able to help us," Kristine said. "I know he will."

Erik nodded.

"And then we'll go home." She forced a smile. "I want our daughter to be born at Hawksbridge."

"My mother will be pleased."

"We must send for her when we get home, Erik. She's lonely at the convent."

"She is at Hawksbridge already."

"She is?"

"I went to see her. That's how I knew where you had gone. I sent Chilton to fetch her home." He let out a sigh. "It was wrong of me to send her away. Hawksbridge was her home long before it was mine."

"She understood your reasons."

"Promise you will take good care of her for me."

"You will be able to do that yourself, soon." She

smiled up at him, though her eyes were sad. "The mage will be able to help us. You must believe that. You must help me to believe," she said with quiet desperation. "Oh, Erik, I cannot bear this any longer."

"Kristine, don't. I need you to be strong for me."

"I'm sorry." She wiped her eyes with a corner of her cloak, and then she smiled up at him, her eyes luminous with unshed tears. "We should go. The sooner we find the mage, the sooner this nightmare will be over."

Chapter Twenty-Two

The River Onyx appeared as black as its name. Erik knew it was simply a trick of the light reflecting off the black stones that lined the bottom of the river; still, it was disconcerting to gaze at that murky ribbon of water and think of crossing it.

Though the water was only thigh-high, it ran swift. The horses balked at entering the dark water and only Erik's firm hand, and the stallion's trust, enabled him to lead Raven across the river. When he reached the far side, he went back for Misty. Fearing the mare might panic, Erik told Kristine to wait. In the end, he had to blindfold the mare to get her across the river.

He went back one more time to get Kristine. Lifting her in his arms to keep her from getting wet, he carried her to the other side.

Valaree and her family, in wolf form, swam across easily enough. Standing close together, they shook the water from their coats, then ran off toward the woods that edged this side of the Onyx.

"You're cold," Kristine said as Erik put her down.

"I'll be all right. We'll rest here a few minutes."

"Are you hungry?"

Erik nodded.

"Me, too." Delving into one of the saddlebags, she withdrew a loaf of brown bread and a square of yellow cheese.

Erik drew his knife and sliced the bread and cheese. It would satisfy his hunger, but what he craved was meat. Only days ago, he had insisted Valaree cook the venison she had offered him; now he found himself yearning for a hunk of meat that was raw and dripping with the juices of life. A part of his mind was disgusted by the mere idea of eating uncooked meat while another part, a part that was growing more dominant with each passing day, hungered for the taste.

"Erik?"

He glanced up to find Kristine staring at him. "What?"

She shook her head. "Nothing."

"Tell me."

She shook her head again. How could she explain it? How could she describe the feral look she had seen in his eyes? For a moment, his eyes had looked just like those of the werewolves.

They washed the bread and cheese down with wine. Kristine put the remainder of the food back in the saddlebags, and then Erik lifted her onto Misty's back. She took up the reins, watching as he climbed into the saddle. Once he had moved with effortless grace; now his movements were sometimes awkward as he tried to adjust to his changing form.

"What about Valaree and her . . . her family?" she asked.

"They'll find us. Are you ready?"

Kristine nodded. "Yes, let's hurry."

It was a dark, forbidding region they traveled through. Huge boulders dotted the landscape, looming out of the swirling mists like nightmare creatures ready to pounce. Trees rose up out of the ground, misshapen by a devil wind.

Kristine shivered, wondering if they had made a mistake in coming here. Surely nothing good could dwell in this accursed place.

She glanced at Erik. He rode beside her, careful, now that he had lost his mask, to ride on her left side so that she was spared the sight of his disfigurement as much as possible.

She had told him it was unnecessary, yet she knew it bothered him when she saw the ruined side of his face. It bothered her, too, but not in the ways he imagined. She felt only pity for him, and an increasing sense of sadness.

The setting sun had turned the sky to crimson when the wolves materialized out of the shadows. They trotted beside the horses for a few minutes, and then the big gray one barked and veered into the woods to the right.

"They must have found a place to spend the night," Erik remarked. Two of the black wolves ran after the gray, while the third kept pace with the horses.

A short time later, they reached a large cave carved out of the side of a rocky hill.

Dismounting, Erik lifted Kristine from her horse, and they went inside.

Valaree had changed into human form. She wore another long gown, this one a pale shade of blue. The other wolves sat in a half circle behind her. A small fire blazed cheerfully near the rear of the cave.

"Why don't the others change?" Kristine asked.

"It is more difficult for them than it is for me."

Kristine looked at Valaree, puzzled. "I don't understand."

"And I don't know how to explain it," Valaree replied. "Only that it is easier for some of us to change from wolf to human than it is for others. My sister prefers the wolf form."

"And your parents?"

"My mother has lost the ability to change."

"Lost it?" Erik asked. "Why?"

Valaree shrugged. "No one knows. That is why my father rarely transforms."

"Is this another of your dens?"

"Yes." Valaree glanced around. "We come here often. It is the largest. Come, sit. I will prepare something to eat. Elsbeth has killed a deer." She looked at Erik, her expression thoughtful. She started to speak, glanced at Kristine, and changed her mind. "Why don't you rest awhile, Kristine?" she suggested.

"Yes, I think I will."

"There are blankets in the back of the cave."

"I'll get them," Erik said. He stared at Valaree a moment, then walked to the back of the cavern.

There were several furs and blankets piled against the cave wall, as well as a small cask of wine. He also noted several clay jars filled with water; others held herbs and dried meat.

He picked up two thick wool blankets. "Here." He

spread one of the blankets on the floor of the cave, out of the way of the smoke.

"Thank you," Kristine replied. "I am a little tired." More than a little, she thought, but she didn't want to worry Erik. He had enough to worry about.

He brushed a kiss across her lips, then covered her with the second blanket.

"Erik?"

"What is it?"

"You won't leave me?"

"No, beloved, I won't leave you."

She smiled at him; then, with a sigh, she closed her eyes. Moments later, she was asleep.

"This journey must be difficult for her in her condition," Valaree remarked when Erik returned to the fire.

"Yes."

"Yet she never complains. She is a brave girl."

He nodded, thinking brave did not begin to describe it.

Valaree regarded him through eyes that were dark and wise, eyes that knew him better than he knew himself. She cut off three thick chunks of venison and placed them on the ground. One by one, the wolves came forward, accepted the meat, and then went outside to eat.

Valaree looked up at Erik, the knife clutched in her hand. "Do you want to have yours now, while she sleeps?"

Erik stared at Valaree, his heart suddenly beating faster. He knew what she was asking. He looked at the haunch of venison. Unable to help himself, he sniffed the air, his mouth watering as he inhaled the rich, gamy scent of the meat. For a moment, he imagined what it would be like to sink his teeth into the raw meat, to taste the warm bloody flesh and then, with a groan, he shook his head. "Cook it."

"It will be less painful for you if you stop fighting," Valaree remarked softly.

"I can't stop. I can't give in." He clenched his good hand into a tight fist. "Don't you understand? I cannot let her win."

"The witch has won already."

"No!" Erik stared at his left hand. With a low-pitched growl of pain and resignation, he turned and left the cave.

Valaree stared after him, her heart aching with sympathy and understanding.

Late that night, long after the others were asleep, Erik stood outside the cave, staring into the distance. They would reach the mage's castle on the morrow.

He refused to let himself believe the mage would be able to break the spell. Better to expect the worst. At least then he would not be disappointed. And yet a tiny spark of hope burned deep in his heart. He closed his eyes, imagining what it would be like to be a whole man again, to have the use of two good hands, to return to the company of men, to associate freely with his friends and neighbors. To make love to Kristine without fear, to feel her hands upon his flesh . . .

Kristine . . . She had made the last few months both heaven and hell. How had he ever lived without her? He prayed she would be delivered of a healthy child, that she would not grieve overlong for him, but go on with her life, find a man who would love her and be a good father to her child . . . the child he would never see. He had hoped the curse would not be complete until after the babe was born, but he feared it was not to be.

He glanced over his shoulder as a soft sound alerted him to the fact that he was no longer alone. "Valaree."

"I woke and you were gone."

He nodded.

"It will be all right," she said quietly.

"I wish I could believe you."

"You must be strong. You must have faith."

Slowly, he shook his head. "Faith? In what? The mage's ability to reverse Charmion's spell? I know it cannot be undone."

"Then why are we seeking his help?"

"Because I have to try. I'll do whatever he asks, pay whatever price is demanded, endure any pain."

"You love her very much, don't you?"

"Yes."

"I shall add my prayers to yours that he may be able to undo the witch's spell. And if he fails . . . if the spell cannot be broken, our pack will welcome you. You need not be alone."

He nodded, remembering her offer to be his mate. What would it be like, to live as a wolf, to surrender, once and for all, to the beast growing within him, to know, as he hunted prey and howled at the darkness, that he had once been a man? And if he were to relinquish the memory of his humanity, would he become, at last, fully a beast?

"Erik?"

"Leave me, Valaree."

"As you wish."

"Valaree?"

"Yes?"

"I appreciate your help, your concern."

She nodded, then turned and walked away.

He stared up at the dark sky. "Please," he whispered, "please don't let the transformation be complete until I've seen my child."

The mage's castle was located at the top of a high mountain. Witches and wizards alike seemed to have an affinity for high places, Erik mused as he climbed out of the saddle. He helped Kristine dismount and then he turned the horses loose in a fenced paddock that materialized in front of them.

"I guess he's home," Erik muttered as hay and water magically appeared.

He took Kristine's hand in his and they stared at the fortress. Three stories high and made of shimmering white stone, it seemed to glow in the faint light of the winter sun. Colorful stained-glass windows were set like rare jewels in the white stone. Alders and beeches dotted the property; wildflowers bloomed on the hillside. Several cats roamed among the bushes or basked in the sun. Brightly colored birds flew among the treetops.

"What an amazing place," Kristine whispered. "So different from Charmion's dark abode."

"Indeed."

Hand in hand, they walked up the stone steps to the castle. The door opened of its own accord.

"Ready?" Erik asked, and at Kristine's nod, they stepped inside.

"Welcome."

Erik stared at the woman before them. She was small and petite. Plain of face, she had long white hair, a beak of a nose, and golden eyes.

"I am Fidella. Caddaric has been expecting you. He bids me make you welcome. Warm baths await, as well as food and wine. If you will come this way."

The woman did not wait for their reply, did not look back to see if they followed.

After a moment, Erik and Kristine followed the woman down a wide corridor. Two doors stood open at the end of the passage.

"The one on the right is for you, my lady," Fidella said with a wave of her hand. "The one on the left is for you, my lord."

Erik felt Kristine's hand tighten on his and knew she did not wish to be separated from him.

"Your master is most generous," he said, "but we will not need two rooms."

"The rooms are connecting, my lord." The woman offered Kristine a reassuring smile. "You need have no fear, my lady. When you are ready, ring the bell, and I shall bring you refreshment."

"Thank you," Erik said. "But before we do anything else, I should like to see your master."

"He understands your impatience, my lord, and bids me tell you he will see you this evening."

"Why not now?"

"He is in the tower, in the midst of preparing a spell, and cannot be disturbed. Please, make yourself comfortable. If there is anything you need, you have only to ring the bell."

"Thank you," Erik said again.

The woman inclined her head, then took her leave.

Erik watched her walk away, then, still holding Kristine's hand in his, he stepped through the doorway on the right. The room, painted a soft shade of pink, was large and airy. And round. A canopied bed stood in the center of the floor. Three multicolored windows were set in the wall. Several thick furs covered the floor. A fire blazed cheerfully in the raised stone hearth. There was a small cherrywood table and two chairs on one side of the bed, a full-length mirror on the other side. A large round wooden bathtub stood beside the hearth; a delightful fragrance wafted from the water. There was also a small four-drawer chest covered with a fine linen cloth. A gown of soft mauve velvet was laid out on the foot of the bed.

"It's lovely," Kristine murmured.

Erik grunted softly, wondering if she meant the room or the gown. The very air reeked of magic, of power. It crawled over his skin, yet he detected no undercurrent of evil or malice.

Dropping his hand, Kristine went to test the water. It was hot, but not too hot. A froth of bubbles swirled over the top of the water, iridescent in the lamplight.

Erik crossed the room and opened the connecting door. A quick glance showed that the second room was exactly like the first, save that it was blue.

"Enjoy your bath, Kristine," he said.

"It will be all right," she said reassuringly. "You'll see."

He nodded, then went into the other room and closed the door. For a moment, he pictured her disrobing, slipping into the tub's scented water. He wished fleetingly that he could join her in the tub, that he could take the soap from her hand and—

He jerked his thoughts away from the images that

rose in his mind. Though she did not appear repulsed by his appearance, he could not bring himself to let her see him unclothed, could not endure the pity in her eyes.

He undressed and slid into the tub, noting for the first time that there was no mirror in this room, nothing to reflect his image back to him.

He washed quickly and stepped out of the tub, shaking the way a dog shakes when it emerges from water. He swore when he realized what he was doing. Reaching for a strip of toweling, he dried off, then dressed in the trousers and tunic that had been left for him. Sitting on the edge of the bed, he drew on a pair of soft leather boots that were cut to accommodate his changed feet, as well as a pair of gloves, the left one tailored to fit over his disfigured hand. There was also a mask made of fine black silk.

He picked it up and slipped it on, grateful for the mage's thoughtfulness. He had felt vulnerable, naked, without the mask.

Crossing the floor, he knocked softly on the connecting door. "Kristine?"

"Come in."

She glanced over her shoulder as he stepped into the room. Erik's gaze ran over her. The mauve gown complemented her skin and eyes. Her hair framed her face like a golden nimbus. She looked beautiful, radiant with the bloom of motherhood.

She smiled at him, and then she frowned.

"What is it?" he asked.

"Nothing."

"Tell me."

"The mask. Where did it come from?"

"The wizard provided it."

"It isn't necessary, Erik. Your face does not frighten me."

"It is not for you," he replied quietly. "It is for me."

She started to say something, but it was forgotten as a large covered tray appeared on the table.

"Oh, my," she murmured. "Fires that burn without wood. Bathtubs that disappear. And now this."

Erik glanced around the room, only now noticing that the bathtub was gone, that the fire did indeed burn without fuel of any kind. At least none that could be seen.

Kristine uncovered the tray, revealing two pewter plates heaped with food, and two goblets of sparkling red wine.

Erik stared at the meal provided—chicken and dumplings for Kristine, a slab of near-raw meat for him. The sight of it was a blatant reminder of what he was becoming.

Kristine said nothing, only looked up at him through eyes filled with sympathy and compassion and a quiet, desperate hope.

Erik turned away, his appetite gone. He knew his host had not meant to insult him, knew the venison, served very rare, was meant to be a token of hospitality. He did not stop to wonder how the mage knew his preference.

He paced the floor while Kristine ate her supper at his urging. He did not want or need her to refuse her meal because he refused his. She had the child to think of.

Kristine pushed away from the table, hiding a yawn behind her hand. She was often tired in the afternoon these days.

"You should rest," Erik said, divining her thoughts.

"I could use a nap," she agreed. Crossing the floor, she sat on the bed, patting the mattress beside her. "Will you not rest with me, my lord husband? You must be weary, as well."

It was not exhaustion but the wish to be near her that propelled him to her side. She stretched out on the bed, and he lay beside her, drawing her against him. With a sigh, Kristine pillowed her head on his shoulder. Even now, when she had seen him without his mask, without covering of any kind, he was careful to keep her on his right, careful to keep his mask in place.

She gazed up at the ceiling, noticing the painting there for the first time. Clouds seemed to drift overhead. And there, amidst the clouds, was a full moon and countless bright stars. A moon that glowed with a silver light. Stars that twinkled.

"Erik, look." She pointed upward. "'Tis the most amazing thing."

He looked up, brow furrowed. It was, indeed, amazing. And as he watched, the sight grew even more astonishing. The moon and clouds drifted across the ceiling, the moon disappeared, to be replaced by a bright golden sun. After a time, the sun went down, and dark clouds scudded across the ceiling-sky, and then a rainbow stretched above them.

"Have you ever seen anything so beautiful?" Kristine murmured.

Erik's gaze moved slowly over Kristine's face. Her deep green eyes were filled with wonder as she stared up at the ceiling. Her skin was soft and smooth, her cheeks the color of fresh peaches, her lips slightly parted.

"No," Erik replied, his gaze still on her face. "I've never seen anything so lovely in my life."

"Surely a wizard who can conjure such a wondrous thing will be able to help us."

Erik grunted softly. He didn't want to ruin her hopes, but there was a vast difference between creating an illusion and curing a spell cast by a vindictive witch.

It was an hour past sundown when the mage summoned them. Hand in hand, Erik and Kristine followed Fidella up the winding stairway that led to the mage's private quarters.

With a smile, Fidella opened the door and gestured for them to enter.

Kristine clung to Erik's hand as they stepped into the room. It was round and devoid of furnishings of any kind.

"Welcome."

Kristine glanced around, but saw no one. She looked up at Erik, who was staring at the far side of the chamber.

"What do you see?" she whispered.

"I'm not sure."

A low chuckle floated in the air. There was a shower of red sparks, and a man dressed in a flowing black robe materialized before them. He was tall and lean, with thick silver-gray hair, a short gray beard, and mild blue eyes beneath bushy black brows.

"I bid you welcome," he said. A chair covered in red velvet appeared behind him and he sat down. A wave of his hand conjured a pair of similar chairs for his guests. "Please, make yourselves comfortable."

Kristine put one hand on the back of the chair, as if to ascertain its solidity before she sat down. Erik remained standing.

"Is it cold in here?" the mage asked. Before either of his guests could answer, a fireplace appeared, complete with a cozy fire. "Wine?"

Another wave of his hand produced a small white lacquer table and a silver tray bearing three crystal goblets. "Please," the wizard said, "help yourselves."

Erik picked up the goblet nearest him and took a drink. It was honey wine, warm and sweet.

"Now," the mage said, sitting back in his chair, "what is it you wish of me?"

"Don't you know?" Erik asked.

The wizard smiled. "But of course. However, tiresome as it might be, I cannot grant your boon until you ask it of me."

"I want to know if you can break a curse cast by another."

"Perhaps." The wizard gestured at Erik's mask. "Take that off, please."

Erik hesitated; he took a step back so that Kristine could not see his face and then removed the mask, clutching it tightly in his right hand.

The wizard's eyes narrowed. Rising, he approached Erik, ran his fingertips over the left side of Erik's face and neck. "Is this the full extent of the affliction?"

"No. It covers my left side and most of my right."

The wizard grunted softly, a wave of his hand indicating Erik should disrobe.

With a sigh, Erik removed his garments, his heart pounding as he stood naked to the wizard's gaze.

"Did this come upon you all at once, or little by little?"

"Little by little," Erik replied. He stared at the back of Kristine's head, praying she would not turn around. She had seen him as he was in the dungeon, he mused, he should have been used to it, but he could not bear for her to look at him, to see what he had become.

The mage grunted again. Rising, he walked slowly around Erik, one hand reaching out to touch the thick, dark pelt that covered his back and shoulders. "I've not seen a spell quite like this one before," he remarked. "'Tis most . . . interesting. Did she say there was a way to reverse the spell?"

Erik shook his head. "She said the spell could not be broken until her daughter forgave me."

"And where is her daughter?"

"Dead these last five years."

The wizard let out a sigh, then returned to his chair and sat down. "You may dress."

Erik quickly donned his clothing and mask. Only then did he sit down in the chair beside Kristine. "Can you help me?"

"I will make you no promises. Should I be able to break this spell, what price are you willing to pay?"

"Whatever you ask," Kristine said quickly.

The mage looked at her, a speculative gleam in his mild blue eyes. "Indeed?" His gaze moved over her, resting a moment on her swollen belly. "Anything I ask?"

"Yes," she said. "Anything."

"What have you to offer?"

"I have lands and wealth," Erik said. "All are yours if you can remove this curse."

"I have lands and wealth of my own," the wizard replied.

"What is it you want, then?" Erik asked, though he feared he knew the answer.

"Your child."

Kristine gasped. "Our child?" She stared at the wizard, mouth agape. "You are jesting."

The mage shook his head. "Is it a price you are willing to pay?"

"No." Erik stood up, reaching for Kristine's hand.

"Erik, wait." Kristine looked at the wizard. "Why would you want our child?"

"I am a wizard of great repute, yet I am unable to father a child of my own. Are you willing to sacrifice your child to save your husband from the ultimate fate that awaits him?"

"It is not her decision to make," Erik said. "The child is mine. The woman is mine. I will not see them separated."

"Wait." Kristine glanced from Erik to the wizard and back again. "Erik," she said quietly. "If he can end this awful curse, we must let him do it. We can have other children. As many as you wish." Had her own mother experienced this same heart-wrenching grief when she'd chosen her lover over her daughter?

"No! How can you even consider such a thing?"

She shook her head, her eyes filling with tears. "It would break my heart to give up our child. The child of our love. But I love you with all that I am, Erik. I would do anything to help you, anything to end your pain. Anything to allow us to have a life together. After all we have been through, I cannot bear to lose you now."

"No, Kristine."

"Calm yourselves," the mage said. "I wondered only how deep your love for the woman ran, and hers for you. Sometimes love is the best magic of all." He stood up, the hem of his black robe flowing like water around his ankles. "Make my home yours. I must study on this. I must confess, I find this spell most intriguing. I myself have transformed people, but never anything like this, and never a spell that could only be broken by one who is dead." He stroked his beard, his expression thoughtful. "If I cannot help, you may need to seek out a necromancer."

"There may not be time for that," Kristine said anxiously. "Please help us."

"I shall do my best, my dear," the wizard replied kindly and then, amidst a swirl of twinkling red sparks, he vanished from their sight.

It was an awesome display, but Erik had eyes only for Kristine. "Would you truly have given him our child?"

"Yes, my lord."

"You care for my babe so little, then?"

"No, Erik, 'tis only that I care for you so very much."

"Kristine . . ." Heart aching, he drew her into his arms and held her close.

He felt the pain moving through his right shoulder, slowly, insidiously, spreading down his arm. And knew that his time was almost gone.

Chapter Twenty-Three

It was midmorning the following day when the wizard again summoned them to the tower room. The chairs, table, and fireplace of the night before were gone. The wizard sat on a high stool in the middle of the floor, hunched over a high table upon which were spread dozens of scrolls and manuscripts. A white raven with amber eyes perched on a corner of the table.

The wizard looked up as Erik and Kristine entered the room.

"Have you found anything?" Kristine asked anxiously.

The wizard stroked his beard. "I have found a few incantations that look promising but, in all honesty, I must warn you that I doubt any of them will be effective." He glanced at Erik. "Know you the name of the witch who cast this spell upon you?"

"Charmion du Lac."

"Ah."

"You know her, then?" Erik asked.

"I have seen the results of her magic in times past. Much of what I know, I learned at her hand."

"You are friends, then?"

A myriad of emotions flickered in the wizard's eyes. "Not exactly."

"What, exactly?" Erik asked.

"We once explored the ancient arts together. During that time, we became friends, but we found it difficult to maintain that relationship, so we became . . . ah . . . more than friends. I'm afraid that liaison did not work out well, either."

Kristine clutched Erik's hand, unsettled by the wizard's disclosure. "And now?"

"We are, at best, congenial enemies."

For a moment, Erik considered telling the mage that Charmion was dead, but quickly decided against it, thinking that, if the mage still had feelings for the witch, he might send them away. "Can you help me or not?"

"I shall do my best." In a fluid motion, the wizard stood. "Disrobe."

"Again?"

"Please."

Erik glanced at Kristine, then turned so that his left side was away from her. Jaw clenched, he shed his clothing. It was humiliating to stand naked before the mage, to stand exposed as if he had no more feelings than the beast he was all too rapidly becoming.

The wizard smiled at Kristine. "Stand away, my dear."

Kristine moved to the far side of the room, her hands clasped at her breast. Slowly, the wizard circled Erik. Three times to the left. Three times to the right.

With a wave of his hand, he sprinkled a handful of what looked like crushed dandelion fluff over Erik's head and shoulders. And then he began to chant softly. He had a most pleasant voice.

Kristine tried to understand the words of the incantation, but they were in a language she had never heard before.

The wizard circled Erik again, three times to the right, three times to the left, his voice rising, becoming higher and more intense. A hail of multicolored sparks flew from his fingertips; golden lights danced around the two men, enclosing them in a shimmering circle of brilliant amber fire.

Kristine folded her arms over her stomach, felt all the hair on her body rise as the wizard's power filled the room.

Erik's head fell back and a long, low groan rose from deep inside his chest.

Kristine leaned forward, her gaze fixed on the man she loved, the words *please, please, please* pounding in her head as the golden lights grew brighter, changed to swirling silver flecked with blue. The air pulsed with energy. There was a sharp crack that sounded like lightning, a sudden *whoosh* as a ribbon of rainbow fire engulfed Erik.

Her breath caught in her throat as, for the space of a half dozen heartbeats, Erik stood before her, tall and straight, his body whole, perfect, and beautiful.

The spell was broken! Relief gushed through her. And then, between one breath and the next, the rainbow fire turned black as pitch. The air filled with the acrid odor of smoke and ash.

The wizard stumbled backward, as if pushed by an invisible hand.

A cry of pain was torn from Erik's throat as his body changed back to what it had been. Fighting for breath, he dropped to his hands and knees.

For every tear my daughter wept! For every drop of blood she shed.

The words, filled with unrelenting hatred, echoed from the floor, the ceiling, the very walls of the room.

Kristine covered her ears in a vain effort to shut out that horrible, vengeful voice. She looked at Erik. He was writhing on the floor, his body convulsing beneath a hideous greenish-black aura.

"No!" She screamed the words. "Leave him alone! He's suffered enough!"

For every tear my daughter wept! For every drop of blood she shed!

The words vibrated through the air, exploded off the walls, shattered the windows.

Erik curled into a tight ball as waves of excruciating pain ripped through him.

"Lady Trevayne!" the wizard shouted. "Come to me, now!"

The urgency in his tone compelled her to his side. He put one arm around her shoulders and held her tightly against him. A wave of his hand enclosed them in a shimmering silver cloud.

"My curse cannot be broken." Charmion's voice, brimming with evil, slammed into Erik.

"Please," Kristine begged. She shook off the wizard's grip on her arm and took a step forward, intending to go to Erik, only to find that she could not move through the cloud that surrounded her. "Please. He's suffered enough."

"Not yet," the voice said. "Not yet." Hideous laughter filled the air. Power slithered through the room like a living entity. The force of it pressed against the shimmering silver cloud protecting Kristine and the wizard. She held her breath, afraid the witch's power would strike them down, but nothing happened.

An angry wail echoed off the walls, and then there was a great silence, broken only by the sound of Erik's labored breathing.

"She is gone," the wizard said.

"It can't be Charmion," Kristine said, confused. "I . . . I hit her. I killed her."

"Apparently you did not," the wizard remarked. A wave of his arm dissolved the shimmering cloud.

Kristine hurried to Erik's side, one hand reaching out for him.

"No!" He backed away from her. "Don't touch me."

"Why?"

"I can feel her power crawling over me."

"What do you mean?"

"I'm afraid for you, afraid you'll feel what I'm feeling if you touch me."

"What do you feel?"

"You don't want to know." He closed his eyes, fighting the sharp, stabbing pains that grew more intense with every breath. "She's punishing me," he said. "Punishing me for coming here, for trying to cheat her of her victory."

Kristine stared at Erik. "How can she be alive?"

He shook his head. It didn't matter how. It was enough to know Charmion still lived, that Kristine and his child were still in danger, and he was helpless to protect them.

"Erik . . ."

"Leave me."

"No."

"Please, Kristine."

"Come, child," the wizard said, "I believe he needs to be alone."

"I just want to help."

"I know," Caddaric said, his voice laced with sympathy. "I know." Draping his arm around Kristine's shoulders, he led her from the room.

Left alone, Erik collapsed on the floor, surrendering to the pain that lanced through him with his every breath, every heartbeat. They had come here seeking help. He knew now that no help would be forthcoming.

It will be less painful if you stop fighting. Valaree's words rose in the back of his mind. Was that the answer, to simply give in? If he stopped fighting the transformation, would it take place more quickly? It would be so easy to give in, to stop fighting and accept the inevitable. So easy . . .

Closing his eyes, he sank into the velvet blackness that waited for him.

"What are we to do now?" Kristine asked. They were sitting in the wizard's chambers. It was a large, square room, the walls lined with bookshelves crowded with books, scrolls, and manuscripts. Plush gray carpets covered the floor. Several flowering plants added splashes of color. The white raven regarded them from a perch in the corner.

Kristine stared into the cup of green tea the wizard had conjured for her. "It's useless to fight her, isn't it?"

"Fighting evil is never useless," Caddaric replied.

"But you can't help Erik, can you?"

The wizard blew out a deep sigh. "I'm afraid not, my child. But I might be able to help you."

"Me?"

He nodded. "I cannot reverse the curse Charmion has put upon Erik, but she has no power over me. She cannot enter my keep, nor can she harm those in my protection."

"She hurt Erik."

"Only because she had power over him already."

"It's hopeless, isn't it?"

"For Erik? I am afraid so. You are welcome to stay here, within the protection of these walls, until your child is delivered."

"I had hoped my daughter would be born at Hawksbridge."

The wizard sighed. "If you wish, I shall see you safely back to Hawksbridge. I can seal the castle against her evil. You and all who dwell there will be safe from Charmion's power so long as you do not admit her to the castle."

Kristine nodded. There was no hope for Erik. She must think now of their child. His child. "Thank you."

"I am sorry, Lady Trevayne. I wish I could do more."

"Kristine. Call me Kristine."

"And you must call me Caddaric."

She smiled faintly. "For a moment, I thought the spell had been broken. For just a moment, he looked as I had always imagined him to be, as he must have been before Charmion's evil curse."

"You have never seen him as he was?"

"No. I wish . . ." She fought back a wave of hopelessness, blinked back the tears that were ever close to the surface. "You and Charmion, you're so different, it's little wonder you did not get on well together."

Caddaric nodded. "Her magic has always been as dark as the place she calls home. Did you know we are the only two witches left in the land? I was the light to balance her darkness."

"Has she always been so . . . so evil?"

"Sadly, yes, though I thought there was hope for her when first we met. She could have done so much good, yet she preferred the dark arts. I fear they will yet be her downfall."

Kristine thought about Charmion's castle, shrouded in mist and darkness, so different from Caddaric's home. It was hard for Kristine to comprehend evil, harder still to understand why a witch as powerful as Charmion—a witch who could, with a word, surround herself with beauty—chose to live in the darkness of Cimmerian Crag.

She closed her eyes, suddenly weary.

"You should rest," Caddaric suggested.

"Yes, I think I will. Thank you for everything."

Rising, Kristine made her way to her chamber. A fire blazed in the hearth, the drapes were shut against the sun. With a sigh, she sat down in the chair beside the hearth and removed her shoes. When she stood up, she saw that the bed had been turned down, the pillows plumped.

Magic, she thought. She'd had enough of magic, both black and white.

* * *

Erik woke with a cry, the images of his nightmare all too vivid. He had been fully a beast in his dream, and yet he had been capable of human thought. He had seen himself running with Valaree, killing a deer, fighting over the fresh meat, and all the while what little humanity he still possessed had been appalled by his actions. He had run through the night, had howled his anguish at an uncaring moon. And then he had seen himself lying at Kristine's feet, his tongue licking her palm, his tail wagging as she stroked his head. . . .

Rising, he glanced around, noting that he was still in the tower room and that night had fallen. He padded toward the window, only to come to an abrupt halt when he saw himself reflected in a shard of broken glass. Nothing remained of Erik Trevayne save for the right side of his face and his right arm. The curse had swallowed up the rest of him, clothing him in coarse black fur.

Why was he fighting it?

He took a deep breath, and Kristine's scent flooded his nostrils. Kristine. She was worth the pain each breath cost him. He would endure anything to have one more day with her, one more hour.

Charmion would win the fight. He knew it, knew it was futile to resist. But he would not surrender. He might be beaten, but he would not give up.

He was reaching for his trousers when there was a rap on the door. "Lord Trevayne?"

"Enter."

Caddaric stepped into the room, and the door

closed behind him. "I am most truly sorry that I am unable to break the curse."

Erik nodded. Back turned to the wizard, he drew on his trousers and reached for his shirt.

"Kristine tells me she wishes to return to Hawksbridge. If it is agreeable, I shall take you there. As I told her, I can cast a spell that will protect your castle and all who dwell within its walls from Charmion's magic."

Erik slipped his shirt over his head and quickly secured his mask in place before turning to face Caddaric. "You can do that?"

"Yes. I regret that, since you are already under her power, I can do nothing for you."

"My life no longer concerns me. It is Kristine and the babe who must be protected now."

"Then we are in agreement?"

"Yes."

"Good. I believe we should leave on the morrow, early."

"We'll be ready."

"Kristine tells me she has never seen you as you were. Is this true?"

Erik nodded.

"I do not wish to offend you but, if you like, I can conjure a temporary spell that will enable you to be as you once were for a brief period of time."

"I am not offended." Erik looked at his left hand, felt excitement stir within him at the thought of being as he had been before the curse, of holding Kristine in his arms, of touching her and having her touch him in return.

"This evening, then?" Caddaric asked.

"Yes. How long will it last?"

"It is a difficult spell to maintain, but I believe I can assure you of an hour, say, two hours before midnight?"

Kristine looked up at Erik and shook her head. "How can he do that?"

"I don't know. Does the thought displease you?"

"Of course not. But how does it work?"

"He didn't say, only that it is a difficult spell to maintain for long."

"What time is it now?"

"Near ten."

She stared up at him, her heart pounding. To see him as he had been, to be able to touch him . . .

"Erik."

"I know."

He gazed into her eyes, hardly aware that the lights in the room had dimmed. Soft music filtered through the air. A fire sprang to life in the hearth. He heard a soft whisper, like the rustle of silk, as Kristine's dress was magically transformed into a long white sleeping gown.

He knew the moment his own transformation took place, felt it in every fiber of his being, saw it in the wonder that spread over her face, felt it in the tremor of her hand as she removed his mask and stroked his cheek. His left cheek.

"Erik," she murmured. "You're beautiful."

"Am I?"

"And I can touch you, can't I?"

He nodded, hardly daring to breathe as she lifted

his shirt over his head and flung it aside, then slid her hands over his chest, his shoulders. His reaction to her touch was immediate and evident.

"Erik, oh Erik."

He heard the wanting in her voice. Not trusting himself to speak, he swept her into his arms and carried her to bed. Lowering her to the mattress, he stretched out beside her, raining kisses on her brow, the curve of her cheek, her nose, her lips—ah, but she tasted sweet, so sweet.

And her hands. There was no hesitation in her touch, no holding back. She ran her fingertips over him, and there was no mistaking the delight she found in caressing him.

He groaned with pleasure, gasped with aching need as she removed his trousers, then shed her gown.

For a long moment, Kristine let her gaze move over him, admiring his broad shoulders and chest, his flat belly and long, muscular legs. And then she was touching him again. His skin was smooth and warm and firm. Looking at him, caressing him, made her ache deep down inside. Desire unfurled within her when she saw the visible evidence of his need, and then she was stroking him again, her hands trembling in her eagerness to touch, to explore the depth of his navel, the fine curly hair on his chest. She traced the line of hair that arrowed toward his manhood, held him in her hand.

"Kristine . . ."

She heard the urgency in his voice as he swept her into his arms and positioned her beneath him.

"I don't want to hurt you."

"You won't." She wrapped her arms around his neck and held him tight, her hands moving restlessly over his back and shoulders. Never before had she been able to caress him, to see his face as their bodies merged into one flesh. Tears burned her eyes and she blinked them away, afraid he would not understand why she wept, afraid she would not be able to explain that they were tears of joy and gratitude for this moment, of regret for the years that they might have shared, years that had been stolen away by a vindictive witch.

He claimed her lips in a long, passionate kiss as his flesh melded with hers. It had been too long since he had made love to her, too long since he had held her like this. The fire's glow cast warm golden highlights over her skin and he knew she had never been more beautiful than she was now, her eyes filled with love, her belly swollen with his child.

He wanted to savor each moment, to make it last and last, but his body betrayed him. Unable to restrain himself, he convulsed within her. Her arms tightened around him, holding him closer, closer.

When he would have rolled away, she clung to him. "Not yet."

He rested on his elbows to spare her the burden of his weight, ashamed of his lack of self-control. He had not meant to take her so quickly, had intended to caress and arouse her, but holding back had been impossible. Her touch had inflamed him and he had taken her like a boy discovering the act for the first time.

He felt her hands stroke his hair, glide over his back, slide down his thighs and over his buttocks.

Still embedded within her, he felt himself harden and knew he was ready for her again.

"Kristine?"

She moved beneath him, hips lifting in silent invitation. He made love to her slowly this time, savoring each sensation, holding back until she was clinging to him, her fevered body trembling. Together, they plunged over the abyss into ecstasy.

"Kristine!" Her name was a sob, a prayer. And then he whispered the words he had held back for so long.

"Kristine, my Kristine. You will never know how much I love you."

She sat by the window, staring into the darkness as she relived every moment of the past hour, remembering the sheer pleasure of lying in her husband's arms. Nothing could be more wonderful than being wrapped in his embrace, feeling his heated skin next to hers, being able to touch and taste him with wild abandon, to explore every inch of his body. She had never dreamed a man could be beautiful, but Erik was. Or had been.

With a sigh, she turned her gaze to the man sleeping across the way. It seemed like a dream now, the hour they had spent in each other's arms, an hour she would cherish for the rest of her life. And yet, she could almost wish it had never happened, for it only made what she had lost that much harder to bear.

She felt the baby stir in her womb and she placed her hand over her belly, grateful now more than ever for the child growing within her.

"I love you," she whispered. "I shall tell you of my love every day of my life, and of your father's love as well. I shall tell you what a handsome man he was. I shall tell you how fiercely he battled an evil witch so you will know how brave and strong he was."

"And will you also tell her how much I loved her mother?"

Kristine looked up, smiling through her tears. "I don't think I will ever find words enough for that."

"Kristine . . ."

Needing to hold him, to be held by him, she crossed the floor and climbed into bed. He stiffened as she snuggled against his side. His left side.

"Erik, don't. It doesn't matter."

"How can you bear to look at me, touch me?"

"I love you. From now on, whenever I look at you, I will see you as the man you were."

"And when the transformation is complete, what then?"

"I shall still love you."

"I want you to marry again. Hoxford, perhaps."

"No!"

"Kristine, you are a young woman. You cannot live the rest of your life alone. Promise me you will marry again, if not for yourself, then for our child."

"No, no, don't ask that of me. Please."

"I am asking. Wait a year, two if you must. But promise me you won't shut yourself up at Hawksbridge. Promise me that you will find a good man to be a father to our child. Promise me you will try. Please, Kristine, I cannot bear the thought of your being alone."

He could not bear the thought of her being with

another man, either, could not abide the idea of another holding her in his arms, caressing her, possessing her. Only the certainty that she needed a man to watch over and protect her, and the knowledge that he would not be there to see it, made it bearable.

"All right, I promise. And now you must promise me something."

"What?"

"Promise you will stay at Hawksbridge when we return."

"I cannot." How had she known he intended to leave as soon as he saw her safely back home?

"Yes, you can. At least until . . ." She choked back a sob. "Until the transformation is complete. Please, let us spend every moment we have left together."

"Very well, Kristine, I shall stay."

She flung her arms around him then, her face pressed against his shoulder as she fought her tears.

"Kristine, ah my Kristine," he murmured. "Please don't cry."

The sound of his voice, the pain and regret he could not disguise, were her undoing. She wept bitter tears, crying for his pain and her heartache, for the separation that grew closer with each passing hour, cried until she fell asleep.

He held her close, watching as the stars slowly faded from the sky, winking out like tiny candles, felt the sting of tears in his own eyes as he accepted the fact that he would never hold her like this again.

Chapter Twenty-Four

Fidella roused them at dawn with the news that Caddaric had ascertained that the signs were favorable. It was time to leave.

"Please hurry," she said. "He is most anxious to be away."

"We will, thank you," Kristine said. She smiled at the woman, then closed the door. Home. She was eager to go back to Hawksbridge, yet a little fearful of leaving the protection of the wizard's castle.

"Our breakfast has arrived," Erik remarked.

"What? Oh." Kristine shook her head as she saw the silver tray on the table. It was most disconcerting, having meals that appeared out of nowhere, fires that started with no visible means, lights that dimmed at the wave of an unseen hand.

Crossing the floor, she sat down at the table, which had also appeared by magic. She stared up at Erik, who was standing near the window, looking out. "Will you not eat, my lord husband?"

He shook his head. He had no appetite for food this morning, could think of nothing but the journey home. His mother would be waiting there. Kristine would not be alone.

He had much to do when he returned to Hawksbridge, and only a short time in which to do it. He would have to summon his solicitor. There were arrangements to be made in regard to Kristine and his mother and the child to ensure their welfare, papers to be signed while his hand could still hold a pen.

A knock at the door drew his attention. "Enter," he said.

Caddaric opened the door and stepped into the room. He wore a long black cloak over his black robe. "It is time." He glanced at Kristine. "Are you ready, my dear?"

Kristine nodded.

"Good. Come, take my hand. You, too, Erik."

"I thought we were leaving."

"We are." He smiled benignly. "Did you think we would go by horse or carriage?" He shook his head. "Mortal travel is far too slow and too tiresome for these old bones."

"I can't leave Misty," Kristine said.

"No need to worry. Your mare and the stallion are already at Hawksbridge." He extended his arms. "Come, we must away."

"Have you done this before?" Kristine asked as she placed her hand in the wizard's.

"Many times."

The wizard grasped their hands in his. "Now, you two must also join hands."

Kristine's gaze met Erik's as their fingers entwined. "I love you," she whispered.

"And I you."

"Ready?" Caddaric asked.

Kristine nodded, her hand tightening on Erik's as she felt the wizard's power flow into the room like the breath of a warm summer wind. There was a rushing sound, like the beating of mighty wings, an eerie sensation of being caught up in the middle of a storm. Breathless, she closed her eyes, her heart thundering in her breast, certain they were heading for destruction.

There was a whooshing sound, followed by a sudden calm, and when she opened her eyes again, they were in Erik's chamber.

"Oh, my," Kristine murmured. "Oh, my."

"Kristine?" Erik placed his hands on her shoulders, his eyes worried as he studied her face. "Are you all right?"

She nodded. "I guess so."

"That's my girl. Why don't you go tell my mother we've returned. And ask Mrs. Grainger to prepare a room for Caddaric."

"Aren't you coming down?"

"No."

"Erik . . ."

"Not now, Kristine. Caddaric, is there anything you need?"

"No. Will there be a problem if I wander around the estate?"

"No. Please, make my home yours."

With a nod, Caddaric took his leave.

"Erik, why won't you come downstairs with me? I know your mother is anxious to see you."

He shook his head. "I shall see her later. I have no wish to see anyone else. When you see Mrs. Grainger, tell her to send Chilton for my solicitor."

"Your solicitor?"

"Please, Kristine, just do as I ask."

It was rising between them again, that invisible wall that he hid behind when he wanted to distance himself from her.

"You remember your promise, Erik?"

"I remember."

"Please don't shut me out of your life. Please let us spend whatever time we have left together."

"It is not my intention to shut you out, Kristine, but . . ." He took a deep breath. How could he explain it to her, this need to withdraw, to pull away from those he loved most in hopes that, when the time came, it would be easier to bid them good-bye? "Please, go and do as I asked."

She stared up at him for a long moment; then, with a sigh, she rose on her tiptoes and kissed his cheek. "Is there anything you need?"

"No."

"Very well." She smiled at him, trying to pretend that everything was all right, and then she hurried out of the room before he could see her tears.

Caddaric walked through the castle. Starting from the lowest dungeon, he made his way upward, until he reached the upper rooms. It was a vast place, Hawksbridge Castle, filled with ancient memories and old ghosts. Battles had been fought here. Children had been born within these walls, some had died. An unfaithful wife had been murdered. Prisoners had died in the cold bowels of the dungeon. A servant had plunged to his death from a tower room.

The spirits of those who had perished within these

walls brushed over his skin, clinging like cobwebs. Life and death, fealty and treachery, love and hatred, joy and sorrow, courage and cowardice, all the threads of life were here, woven into a tapestry as old as time itself.

He listened to the voices, to the cries of the dead, as he walked from room to room, casting a protective spell over the castle and all those who dwelled within its walls. Only Erik was beyond his protection. Erik, who was enthralled to Charmion's evil witchery.

Charmion. She would soon discover their absence from his holdings. He could well imagine her rage, knew she would pursue them, but to no avail. Unless she found a way to breach his protective wards, she could do no harm to those who resided within the walls of Hawksbridge Castle.

He sighed, weariness overtaking him as he put the last ward in place, wondering, even as he did so, if his magic was strong enough to repel Charmion's power.

In need of nourishment, he made his way down the long, winding stairway that led from the tower to the castle's first floor.

A delicious aroma drew him toward the back of the house, into a large dining room occupied by an elderly woman clad in a severe black gown. She looked up, startled, when he entered the room.

Caddaric bowed in her direction. "Good afternoon, madam," he said. "I am Caddaric Delapre."

A faint smile curved her lips. "Your reputation precedes you, sir." She offered him her hand. "I am Edith Trevayne, Erik's mother. Please, join me. I have never met a wizard before."

Caddaric sat down in the chair to her right, his hands folded in his lap.

"Would you care for something to eat?" she asked.

"Yes, please."

She rang a tiny silver bell; a moment later, a tall, thin woman entered the room. "Yes, my lady?"

"Judith, please bring Lord Caddaric some of that excellent roast beef we had for supper last evening, and a glass of wine."

"Yes, my lady."

"Judith is a wonderful cook," Edith remarked. "She's been with the family for years. I don't know what we would do without her." She was babbling, she thought, talking of foolish, unimportant things because she lacked the courage to ask the question uppermost in her mind.

But he knew her thoughts. Gently, he took her hand in his. "My lady, I fear I can do nothing to help your son."

"Nothing?"

Caddaric shook his head. "I'm sorry. Charmion's curse is all-encompassing. There is no way for me to reverse it or break it."

"You're sure?"

Caddaric nodded. "Charmion is a most clever witch. Though it may be small consolation to you now, rest assured that I have done all in my power to seal your home against her dark magic."

He squeezed her hand as tears welled in her eyes. Rarely had he felt so helpless or wished so fervently that he could ease the pain in another's heart. Never had he felt such a need to offer comfort.

Impulsively, he rose to his feet and drew her out of her chair and into his arms. "Weep if you must," he murmured. "Often it is the only thing that helps."

She shuddered in his embrace and then, as if his

words had unleashed the floodgates of sorrow, she began to cry.

And he held her close, one hand lightly patting her back as he murmured inane words of comfort.

A discreet cough at the doorway warned him they were no longer alone.

"Forgive me, sir," the cook said, her eyes wide. "I didn't mean to . . . I . . . that is . . . oh, my." Cheeks flushed with embarrassment, she dropped the tray she was carrying on the table and hurried out of the room.

"She has gone," Caddaric said quietly.

"Whatever will she think?"

"Does it matter?"

Edith shook her head, suddenly embarrassed to find herself in a strange man's arms in the dining room in the middle of the day. But he didn't seem like a stranger; indeed, she felt as if she had been waiting for him all her life, as if everything that had gone before was simply a prelude to this moment.

"Edith."

She looked up at him and wished she were younger, prettier.

Caddaric smiled down at her. "Are you by chance a witch yourself?"

She blinked the last of her tears from her eyes. "Me? A witch?"

"I fear you have cast a spell of your own."

"You feel it, too?" she asked, her voice filled with wonder.

"I would have to be dead not to."

She stared up at him. His was an arresting face, but it was his eyes that held her gaze, mild blue eyes that looked at her with tenderness and a touch of bewilderment. "How can this be? I'm an old woman. Too old to feel like this."

Caddaric placed a finger beneath her chin. "But your heart is still young, my lady," he murmured, and then he did the unthinkable. He kissed her.

Heat spread through her, warm as sunshine, and she knew she had, indeed, been waiting for this man her whole life.

Shaken to the very depths of his soul, Caddaric loosed a deep sigh as he broke the kiss. His brief affair with Charmion had soured him on the fair sex. Grateful to have survived that liaison with a whole skin, he had immersed himself in his magic, resigned to going through life alone, never knowing the love of a good woman. But this woman, with her clear gray eyes and heartbreakingly sad smile, ah, this fragile bit of femininity tempted him sorely.

"I think, madam, that when the time is right, you and I will have much to discuss."

"Yes," she replied quietly. "When the time is right."

And though neither spoke, they both feared the time would not be right until Charmion's curse had been fulfilled.

Chapter Twenty-Five

Caddaric settled comfortably into life at Hawksbridge Castle. To Kristine, it seemed as if the wizard
had always been part of the household. He told them
amusing tales at meals, entertained them with stories
of his travels to the far corners of the world in his
never-ending quest for knowledge.

Kristine did not miss the way Lady Trevayne's eyes
lit up whenever Caddaric was in the room, or the way
the wizard always managed to find an excuse to
touch Lady Trevayne's arm, or her hand, or her
shoulder. On more than one occasion, she had come
upon the two of them in the library or the solar,
sometimes deep in conversation, sometimes just
sitting side by side in companionable silence. She
envied them the closeness they shared.

She wondered what Erik thought about the romance
blossoming between his mother and the wizard. Wondered if he had even noticed. He never left his room
now, except late at night when the household was
asleep. He refused to join them at meals or sit in the

parlor with them in the evenings. It grieved her that he no longer came to her bed at night. She missed being held in his arms, missed falling asleep with him beside her. But what disturbed her most was that he had taken to locking the door that connected her room to his.

With a sigh, she glanced at Caddaric and Lady Trevayne. They sat facing each other over a small table, a chessboard between them. Feeling as though she were intruding on their privacy, she turned her attention back to the book in her lap, but the words made no sense. She couldn't concentrate, couldn't think of anything but Erik, alone in his room upstairs, denying himself the company of those who loved him. No one had seen him outside his room since they returned to Hawksbridge. He had spent an hour with his mother the night they returned to the castle. The next day, he had spent the entire afternoon with his solicitor.

Kristine closed the book and put it aside. Why was she sitting here when she wanted to be with him? Why had she let him shut her out when whatever time remained to them could now be measured in weeks, perhaps days?

Rising, she smiled at Lady Trevayne and Caddaric. "Good night."

"Going to bed so early?" Lady Trevayne asked.

Kristine nodded.

"Are you all right, child?"

She nodded, blinking back the tears that were ever close to the surface these days.

"Good night, daughter."

"Rest well, Kristine."

"Good night," she murmured, and hurried from the room.

She climbed the stairs carefully. At the top of the landing, she drew a deep breath, one hand pressed against the small of her back. She tired so easily these days. Lady Trevayne insisted she take a nap in the afternoon and another in the evening. Mrs. Grainger made her drink endless glasses of milk.

When her breathing was normal again, she walked down the corridor to Erik's room and knocked on the door. "Erik?" She waited a moment, then knocked again, louder. "Erik, are you awake?"

Still no answer. Concerned, she lifted the latch and peered inside. The room was empty. Frowning, she went to her own room and drew on a hooded cloak. Tiptoeing past the library, she went outside. It had snowed earlier. A smooth blanket of white covered the grounds, sparkling in the moonlight. Erik's footprints were easy to follow.

Lowering her head against the wind, she followed his tracks, lengthening her stride so she could step where he had stepped.

She found him standing near the pool in the center of the rose garden.

He stood with his back toward her, and she noticed he wore neither hat nor cloak nor boots, only a thick wool shirt and loose-fitting trousers.

"Erik?"

"You should not be out here, Kristine."

"Neither should you. You must be freezing."

"Freezing?" There was a note of bitter amusement in his voice. "When I have this thick fur coat to keep me warm?"

"Erik . . ."

"Kristine, go back to the house. There is nothing for you out here."

"Don't say that. You must fight her, Erik, please. You can't just give up."

He blew out a sigh that seemed to come from the very depths of his being. "You don't know," he whispered, his voice gruff. "You cannot imagine how hard it is."

He stiffened as he felt her hand on his back. Such a small hand, filled with such gentleness, such caring. Such love. He remembered his vow never to surrender to Charmion, never to give up. At the time, he hadn't thought the pain could get any worse, hadn't realized how strong the beast within him would become. His dreams were dark, filled with images of wolves running through the snow, of blood and death. Often, he dreamed of Valaree, only to wake feeling as though he had been unfaithful to Kristine. More and more, he felt the need to be outside, to shed his clothing and run wild through the night.

"Erik?"

Slowly, he turned to face her, and she saw that he wasn't wearing his mask. It was the first time she had known him to leave his room without it.

"Kristine." His voice had grown deeper in the last few days. "Kristine."

She looked into his eyes. A world of pain, of fear, of need, was reflected in the dark depths. Smothering a sob, she gathered him into her arms and held him tight.

"Hang on to me, Kristine," he said, his voice a low growl. "Don't let me go."

"Never! I'll never let you go." She held him as tightly as she could, felt the tremors that wracked his body. She tried to imagine what he was feeling, what it must be like for him to know that he was losing a little bit more of himself with each passing day. She wished she could do something, anything, to keep the hideous change from spreading further, wished there was something she could do to ease his pain.

She felt the babe move within her womb. Their child should be born any day now. Nightly, she prayed that the baby would come before the curse reached its conclusion.

Erik drew away and placed his right hand over her belly, his fingers spread wide.

She looked up at him, felt her heart break when she saw the tears in his eyes, knew he, too, was hoping the babe would soon be born.

She shivered as the wind picked up. In the distance, she heard the long, lonely cry of a wolf.

He lifted his head, looking toward the sound. "It's Valaree."

"How can you be so sure?"

He shook his head. "I don't know."

Kristine reached for his hand and held it tight. "Let's go back to the house. I'm cold."

With a nod, he lifted her in his arms and carried her swiftly down the path toward the house.

Inside the back door, he paused. Almost as if he was sniffing the air, Kristine thought.

"My mother and Caddaric are in the parlor." Gently, he placed Kristine on her feet.

When he turned to go back outside, she caught

him by the hand yet again. "Don't run away from us, Erik. We love you."

He lifted a hand to his face, then shook his head. "No."

"You needn't hide from us. The servants have all gone to bed. There's no one to see you but us. Please. It's not good for you to be so alone."

For a moment, she thought he would refuse; then, with a sigh, he placed his hand in hers.

Lady Trevayne looked up as they entered the room, her surprise at seeing her son evident in her eyes. "Erik."

"Mother."

"I'm so very glad you're here. Come, sit beside me."

Feeling self-conscious, he padded across the floor and sat down on the damask-covered sofa. Kristine followed him, taking the seat on his other side.

He drew a deep breath and loosed it in a long, slow sigh, aware of their eyes upon him, aware that they were trying not to stare at his feet, his left hand, his face. He was a freak, he thought bitterly, a thing to be stared at, pitied. Anger boiled up inside him, and with it an urge to strike out against them, to rail against the fate that had brought him to this. And then he saw the tears in his mother's eyes, felt Kristine's gentle touch on his arm, and the anger drained out of him.

Taking a deep, calming breath, he looked at the wizard. "How long will you be staying?"

Caddaric glanced at Edith before answering. "I'm not sure. Do you wish me to leave?"

"No. If it would not be an imposition, I should very much like for you to stay until . . . until I can no longer take care of my own affairs. When that time comes, I would consider it a great favor if you would make certain that my wishes are carried out as planned."

"You needn't worry," Caddaric said. "I shall stay as long as necessary."

"My thanks."

"I only wish I could do more for you."

"Nothing can be done for me. My only worry now is for my family."

Caddaric looked over at Edith again. She met his gaze, a faint smile curving her lips, and then she nodded.

"You need have no fear. I have asked your mother to be my wife," the wizard said. "And she has accepted."

"Oh, but that's wonderful," Kristine exclaimed softly, and then she looked at Erik, wondering how he would take the news.

"I hope we can have your blessing," Caddaric said.

"You have it," Erik replied. He took his mother's hand in his and gave it a squeeze. "I hope the two of you will be happy."

"Thank you," Edith replied. "We had thought to wait until . . . to wait, but now, if you have no objection, we should like to be wed tomorrow afternoon."

"On Christmas Day," Erik murmured. He felt a rush of guilt at having denied Kristine and the household the chance to celebrate, but he'd been so caught up in his own misery, he'd given no thought to the holiday.

Edith nodded. "And I should very much like for you to give the bride away."

"I would be honored to do so." Erik lifted his

mother's hand and brushed a kiss across her knuckles. "I hope you will be happy this time."

"I shall take good care of her," Caddaric promised.

Erik nodded. "I know you will." He gave his mother a hug, then stood up and crossed the floor to shake the wizard's hand. "It will be easier for me, knowing they have someone to look after them," he said, his voice gruff, and then, without another word, he left the room.

Edith stared after him, tears running down her cheeks. Kristine blinked back tears of her own when Caddaric knelt beside Edith and took her hands in his, and then she hurried after Erik.

She found him in his room, staring out the window. "Are you upset?" she asked. "About the marriage?"

"No, I am glad of it. My mother deserves some happiness in her life."

"What do you mean?"

"She never loved my father, nor did he love her. It was a marriage arranged by their parents."

Kristine placed a hand over her belly, grateful for the child she carried, for the love she felt for its father. She understood now why Lady Trevayne's eyes had once held such sadness. She had been wed to a man she didn't love, had seen her oldest son killed in an accident. And now Erik . . . Erik.

She crossed the floor to stand behind him, slid her arms around his waist, and laid her cheek against his back. "I love you."

He swallowed hard as he placed his right hand over her arm. "And I love you. More than I've ever loved anyone else. More than my life."

Slowly, he turned and drew her into his arms. "You are a most remarkable woman, Kristine. So lovely, so brave."

"Brave? Me?" She shook her head. "I'm so afraid of losing you."

He brushed his knuckles over her cheek. "In spite of everything else that has happened, I am glad of this last year we've shared."

It had been the worst year of his life, and the best. Before Kristine, he'd had nothing to live for, had been resigned to his fate. And then he had found her, and she had turned his life upside down. The thought of losing her was tearing him apart, and yet he would not have missed the time they had spent together. Because of her, he had known love for the first time in his life. Because of her, he had an heir. Because of her, he would not be forgotten.

"It grows late," he said at last. "You should get some sleep."

"In all the time we have been together, you have never stayed the night with me, my lord husband. Do you not think it is time?"

"Past time, perhaps," he replied, amazed anew that she did not find him repulsive, that she did not turn away from the sight of his face, from the horror that was spreading over his body.

He watched her disrobe, his gaze moving lovingly over her slender form, lingering on the swell of her belly. She was beautiful, so beautiful.

She slid into bed, waiting for him to join her. Crossing the floor, he extinguished the light beside his bed, then slipped out of his shirt and trousers.

She was watching him, waiting for him, her eyes shining with love and acceptance.

He had never thought to hold her close again. With a sigh, he slid into bed beside her and drew her into his arms. She cradled him to her breast as if he were a child, her hand stroking his hair.

There were no bad dreams that night.

Chapter Twenty-Six

Erik sought out Caddaric in the morning. He found the wizard in the tower rooms he had taken for his own.

"We have more comfortable chambers than this," Erik remarked, glancing around.

Caddaric shrugged. "Surely you must know I can make this as comfortable as I wish."

Erik nodded. At the moment, the room was furnished with only a large desk made of dark red wood and a matching chair. The white raven perched on the windowsill.

"Have you come to speak of my marriage to your mother?"

"No."

"It does not displease you, then?"

"I think you will be good for her," Erik replied. He regarded the wizard a moment. "And that she will be good for you."

"She told me of her marriage to your father, that it was not a happy one. That he was, on occasion, unkind to her."

"Unkind? He beat her when he was angry. And when he was young, he was often angry."

"And yet you vowed to give him an heir."

"It was his dying wish," Erik said flatly. "I could not deny him."

"So, what would you have of me this day?"

"When I am fully a beast, will Charmion still have power over me?"

Caddaric frowned. "I'm not sure I understand your question."

"You said your magic would not work on me because I was under her power. Will I still be under her power when her spell is accomplished?"

"I cannot say for certain, but I would think that her power would be even stronger once the transformation is complete."

"Is there nothing you can do to render me invulnerable to her dark magic?"

"Invulnerable?" The wizard stroked his beard, his expression thoughtful. "Why? Do you think she will decide to turn you into a toad?"

"I don't know. I only know that Kristine and my child will not be safe so long as Charmion lives."

"Ah." Understanding sparkled in the wizard's eyes. "Do you truly think you can destroy her?"

"I don't know, but I intend to try."

"It will not be easy. She rarely leaves Cimmerian Crag."

"I will go to her."

"And do what?"

"Become her pet, as she intended. I will crawl on my belly, and lick her feet, and do whatever else she asks of me."

The wizard nodded slowly. "It is a plan so simple,

so wise, it may very well work. And yet it is not without risk. Should you fail, her vengeance will most likely be swift and cruel."

Erik lifted his left hand. "More cruel than this?"

"I shall see if I can conjure a spell that will offer you some measure of protection, but it is doubtful. And even should I find one, there would be no way to prove its effectiveness until you are face-to-face with Charmion, and then it will be too late."

"It is a risk I am willing to take."

To the wizard's credit, he did not try to dissuade him. "I shall protect Kristine and your mother with my life. Do not fear for their safety."

"You will not tell either of them we had this conversation." It was not a question.

"No."

With a nod, Erik left the tower room.

Caddaric stared after the lord of Hawksbridge Castle, thinking he had never known a man of such courage.

With a sigh, he went to his desk and sat down. "So, my Fidella," he said. "We must find a spell that will withstand Charmion's power. But first we must bring a bit of Christmas cheer to this sad household."

Cawing softly, the white raven flew across the room to perch on the wizard's shoulder.

Kristine couldn't believe her eyes when she went downstairs late that morning. Christmas had come to Hawksbridge. An enormous tree trimmed with glittering baubles, silver garlands, and tiny candles stood in one corner of the great hall. Smaller trees were scattered around the room. Vases filled with flowers that didn't bloom in the winter added splashes of color to the room. Garlands of holly draped the walls. A fire crackled in the hearth.

After a quick look around, Kristine ran up to Erik's room. "Erik, you must come downstairs, now!"

The door opened a crack. "Is something wrong?"

Reaching through the doorway, she tugged on his arm. "Come! You have to see this!"

Unable to resist the excitement in her voice or his own curiosity, Erik allowed her to lead him downstairs.

For a moment, he wondered if he was dreaming. But one look at the broad grin on Caddaric's face and Erik knew the wizard had been hard at work.

His mother, sitting at Caddaric's side, smiled at him. "Merry Christmas, Erik."

He nodded. "And to you, as well."

"It's wonderful!" Kristine exclaimed. "Caddaric, did you do this?"

"Of course he did," Erik muttered. "We have our own Father Christmas."

"Guilty as charged," the wizard said. "So, what shall it be first? Breakfast? Or . . ." He waved his hand and several gaily wrapped packages materialized under the tree. "Presents?"

Kristine and Edith looked at each other. "Presents!" they exclaimed.

The gifts were opened quickly—a delicate silk scarf and a pair of gloves for Edith, a pair of warm slippers for Kristine, a robe for Erik, a new cloak for Caddaric.

When Caddaric and Edith went to see about breakfast, Erik reached into his pocket and withdrew a silver box. Handing it to Kristine, he said, "This one is from me."

"What is it?"

"Open it and see."

Trembling with excitement, Kristine lifted the lid. Inside, nestled on a bit of blue velvet, was a silver filigree heart on a slender silver chain. "Oh, Erik," she breathed. "It's exquisite." She quickly put it on. "How does it look?"

"Not as beautiful as you."

She gazed up at him, her eyes sparkling brighter than the candles on the tree, her cheeks flushed with excitement. Taking his hand in hers, she pressed it to her breast. "Thank you, Erik. I'll wear it always."

Erik felt his throat tighten later that day as he watched his mother become Caddaric's wife. Kristine stood at his side, her hand in his, while silent tears slipped down her cheeks.

Seated behind them in the small chapel, he heard Mrs. Grainger sobbing quietly. Her husband and sons sat around her. Leyla and Lilia sat across the aisle from the Graingers, tears welling in their eyes. The white raven perched on the back of the front pew, amber eyes unblinking as the wizard repeated his wedding vows.

Erik felt Kristine's hand squeeze his, knew she was remembering the day she had become his bride. Did she ever regret it, he wondered as he squeezed her hand in return. He slid a glance at her, thinking, as always, how beautiful she was, how precious she had become to him. The sea-green gown she wore made her eyes glow like emeralds. Her hair gleamed like fine gold in the light of the candles. It was long enough now that he could see how wondrous and thick it had once been. He would have liked to see her hair before it had been cut, to have held her in his arms clad in nothing but the mantle of her hair, to have felt the silky fall of golden tresses slide over his skin when they made love.

He shook the thought aside. It was useless to wish for that which could never be. He closed his eyes as the priest offered a prayer, and added one of his own, giving thanks for the woman beside him, for the love she had given him, for the child she carried beneath her heart. No matter what the future held for him, he knew that, man or beast, he would always carry the memory of Kristine's love.

The priest said the final amen and Erik watched as his mother embraced her new husband. Never had he seen his mother look so happy, so serene. She smiled as she turned toward him.

"Be happy, my mother," he murmured, and enfolded her in his arms.

"Thank you, Erik."

He held her close for a long moment, regretting again that he had sent her from him, that he had denied himself the comfort she might have offered him. One more regret, when he already had so many.

He released her so that Kristine could offer her own good wishes, and then they left the chapel to partake of the supper Mrs. Grainger had prepared.

Erik sat at the head of the table, his mask again in place in deference to the priest and the household staff. He declined anything to eat, merely sipped a glass of wine.

He knew, without knowing how he knew, that the curse would be fulfilled before morning, and so he sat there, his gaze on Kristine's face, imprinting her image firmly in his mind, memorizing the sound of her voice, her laughter, knowing he would have only his memories to sustain him in the long, lonely days ahead.

Kristine woke slowly, smiling as she felt the baby move. Soon, she thought, soon her child would be born. Knowing how Erik loved to feel their baby move, she reached for his hand, only to realize that she was alone in bed.

Where had he gone off to so early, she wondered and then, with a sigh, she closed her eyes, remembering the night past. He had held her tenderly, his dark eyes filled with love. He had caressed her, his hand gentle, not to arouse her, but simply, he had said, for the pleasure of touching her. They had looked at each other and smiled as the baby gave a vigorous kick. Though the curse was much in their thoughts, they had not spoken of it. Instead, they had spun dreams for the future, dreams they had both known would not come true. Later she had fallen asleep in his arms.

Suddenly overcome by the need to see him, she slid out of bed. She was reaching for her robe when she saw the note on her dressing table.

Her name, written in Erik's bold hand, was written across the top. Her heart seemed to skip a beat as she picked up the letter.

My dearest Kristine,

*My time grows short and so, while I am still able,
I take pen in hand to tell you how much I love you,
how I have cherished these days as your husband,
how sorry I am for the grief and pain I have caused
you. Be assured that your future is secure. I have
made full provisions for you and the child.
Hawksbridge is yours for as long as you wish.
Should you marry and wish to leave, then it will go
to our child.*

*Do not grieve for me, beloved. It is my wish that
you be happy always, that you will remember your
promise and find another husband to protect you
and be a father to our child. Know that my every
thought will be only for you for as long as human
reason remains. Know that . . .*

The words ended in a scrawl and a splash of ink.

She frowned, wondering why the letter ended so abruptly and then, with a cold, clear certainty, she knew. Slowly, feeling as though she were caught in the icy grip of a nightmare, she turned around.

He was lying on the floor at the far side of the bed, his great black head resting on his paws.

The letter fell from her fingers as she wrapped her arms around her belly. A sob rose in her throat as she stared down at him. His eyes, still gray, still *his* eyes, looked up at her.

"Erik, oh Erik."

He whined low in his throat.

She shook her head, not wanting to believe, praying that she was having a bad dream, that she would awake to find him sleeping beside her.

Dropping to her knees, she wrapped her arms around his neck. "Oh, Erik," she whispered.

He whined again. The sound tore at her heart and she buried her face in his fur. Tears stung her eyes and burned her throat, coming faster and faster, until she thought she might cry into eternity.

He whined again, and then she felt the rough velvet of his tongue on her face, licking her tears.

Slowly, she sat up. "It is you, isn't it?" She shook her head as she stared into the dark gray eyes she knew so well. He was there, inside the wolf's body. "All this time, I knew it was going to happen, and still I hoped it would not."

How did it feel, she wondered, to be able to think like a man, to know you were a man, and be trapped inside the body of a wolf? She could not imagine the horror of it.

She didn't know how long she sat there, her mind numb, tears running down her cheeks as she stroked the thick fur. She couldn't seem to stop crying. It seemed so impossible that this huge black wolf could be the man she loved.

A knock at the door propelled her to her feet. Dashing the tears from her eyes, she called, "Who is it?"

"Nan. Mrs. Grainger sent me to tell you that breakfast will be ready shortly. She asked me to see if you would be coming down to join Lady Trevayne, I mean Lady Caddaric, and the wizard."

"No. Please send something up. And Nan, would you ask Mrs. Grainger to send up a good portion of the roast beef we had for dinner last night?"

"Roast beef, ma'am? For breakfast?"

"Just do it, Nan, please."

"Yes, my lady."

Feeling numb inside, Kristine took off her sleeping gown and put on a day dress of dark gray silk. She was ever conscious of the wolf—of Erik—lying on the floor, his eyes watching her every move.

How long would he stay here, she wondered. How long before he forgot who he was? Would he seek out Valaree and her family? It pained her to know that he would probably be happier with the werewolf clan than here, with her.

She placed a hand over her belly as she felt the baby's lusty kick. *Poor little babe*, she thought. *Never to know your father. How shall I ever explain it to you?*

"Lady Kristine?"

She opened the door to Caddaric. His gaze searched her face. "It's happened, hasn't it?"

She nodded and stepped back so he could enter the room.

Caddaric drew a sharp breath as Erik stood up. "Have you tried talking to him?" the wizard asked. "Does he understand you?"

"I don't know."

"Erik, bark once if you understand me."

The wolf barked once, his gray eyes filled with frustration and anger.

"I cannot bear it," Kristine said softly. "Is there nothing you can do?"

"I'm afraid not."

There was another knock at the door. Kristine blinked back her tears as she crossed the floor to admit Nan. The maid's eyes grew wide when she saw the wolf standing beside the bed.

"It's all right, Nan," Kristine said, taking the tray from the girl's hands. "Thank you."

Nan pointed at the wolf with a hand that trembled. "Where did that come from?"

"He is my pet," Caddaric said smoothly. "You needn't be afraid. He won't harm you."

"Your pet? I've never in all my life seen a wolf that big! Why, he's as big as a pony. How did he get here?"

Caddaric raised one brow. "I conjured him, of course. I am, after all, a wizard."

Nan glanced at Kristine, at the wolf, at Caddaric, then hurried out of the room.

"Do you intend to tell the staff about this?" Caddaric asked.

Kristine shook her head. "No. I shall tell them that Erik was called away on business."

"Yes, perhaps that would be best," the wizard agreed. He let out a heavy sigh. "I do not look forward to telling Edith."

Kristine nodded, glad she would not have to tell Erik's mother that the transformation was complete.

She set the tray on the table and removed the lid. The sight of the roast beef somehow made it all real. She put the plate on the floor and stepped back.

The wolf looked at it, then looked up at her. With a shake of his head, he ran out of the room.

Moments later, there was a scream from the kitchen followed by the crash of crockery.

Caddaric and Kristine hurried downstairs to find Erik scratching at the back door. Mrs. Grainger stood with her back to the wall, her face as white as her apron.

"It's all right, Mrs. Grainger," Kristine said. She opened the door and the wolf ran outside. "He's harmless."

"Harmless! I've never in all my life seen a wolf as

big as that one. However did the beast get into the house?"

"He belongs to Caddaric. Didn't Nan tell you?"

Mrs. Grainger shook her head. "Will it be staying here, in the house?"

"Yes."

Mrs. Grainger sank down onto one of the kitchen chairs. A moment later, Yvette came bursting into the room. "There's a huge black wolf in the yard!"

"It's all right, Yvette," Kristine said. "He's quite tame."

Caddaric grinned. "I think I had best go and inform the rest of the staff."

Kristine nodded. "Thank you."

"Talk to the staff about what?"

All heads turned as Edith appeared in the kitchen doorway.

"Whatever is going on?" Edith glanced at Mrs. Grainger's pale face, at Kristine's red-rimmed eyes, at the grave expression on her husband's face. "Oh," she exclaimed softly.

"Come, my dear," Caddaric said, and wrapping one arm around Edith's shoulder, he led her out of the room.

Kristine patted Mrs. Grainger's hand. "I doubt if anyone will be having breakfast this morning," she said. "You might send some tea up to Erik's mother."

"Yes, my lady." Mrs. Grainger stood up.

Heavy-hearted, Kristine left the kitchen and returned to her room. Finding a sheet of paper, she sat down and began to write.

It was the most difficult letter she had ever written.

* * *

He ran effortlessly, tirelessly. Two days had passed since the transformation. The reality of it was his worst nightmare come true. He ran for miles. He killed a rabbit, devouring the poor creature in three quick bites. The meat and blood were sweet on his tongue. He drank from the stream that ran behind the castle, basked in the sun. And all the while his mind screamed that it could not be true. Each morning he woke in Kristine's room, hoping it had all been a dream. And each morning he faced the truth in her eyes.

He had thought himself prepared for the final transformation. For days before it happened, he had known it would soon be upon him and still he had not been prepared for the reality of it, the sheer unadulterated horror of it. The pain of it. He recalled the look of shock, of pity, in Kristine's eyes when she had first seen him. He had yearned to tell her he loved her, that he was sorry he had involved her in this nightmare, but of course he could not.

A low whine rose in his throat as he recalled the sight of her tears, the feel of her hands gently stroking his fur. Charmion had said he would always remember that he had been a man; now he prayed he would forget, prayed that the beast would take over his mind as well. As much as he feared losing the memory of his humanity, he knew it would be a blessing. It was too painful to be near Kristine, to see the pity in her eyes, to know he would never again hold her in his arms, that he would never be a father to their child.

He had promised to stay until the transformation was complete, and he had fulfilled that promise. He rose each morning with the intention of leaving

Hawksbridge, and each day Kristine begged him to stay until the babe was born. And because he had nothing else to give her but his presence, because he could not bear the sadness in her eyes, he stayed. As soon as the child was born, he would leave. He would go to Charmion, and he would destroy her, or be destroyed himself.

Throwing back his head, he began to howl, the feral cry filled with all the grief in his heart, all the anguish in his soul.

Chapter Twenty-Seven

Caddaric and Edith stared at Kristine in stunned silence.

Edith shook her head. "You did what?"

"I thought you should know. I sent a letter to Charmion, offering to give her my child if she would break the spell."

Kristine took a deep breath. She had torn up the first letter she had written. And the second. Three days had passed since the awful transformation, three long days, and lonely nights. This morning, she had written a new letter. Even now, Brandt was carrying her missive to Charmion.

"You cannot mean it," Edith said, her face pale with shock.

"I do."

Caddaric stroked his beard thoughtfully. "You do not intend to invite her into the house?"

"I don't know. I hadn't thought about that. I only know I cannot go on like this. I cannot bear to see Erik as he is. I cannot bear to see the pain in his eyes.

It's worse than anything I ever imagined. He's so unhappy."

"And what of Erik?" Edith asked quietly. "Do you think he would approve of this?"

Kristine shook her head. "I'm sure he would not."

"Have you asked him?"

"No. I know what his answer would be."

They were able to communicate with him, so long as they asked him questions that could be answered yes or no. But she would not ask for his permission. This was something she had to do, even if he hated her for the rest of his life.

She pressed a hand to her back, massaging the dull ache that had been plaguing her since early morning.

"And if the witch agrees, what then? Do you think she can be trusted?"

"I don't know," Kristine replied. "I only know I have to try."

"Caddaric?" Edith looked at her husband.

He shook his head. "I have never known her to have any honor." He began to pace the room. "She wants the child. She will know that, should she revoke the spell, Erik will not rest in his efforts to get the child back." He stopped in front of Kristine. "You cannot bargain with her. We can only hope that, should she come here, the wards I have placed around the castle will be strong enough to repel her."

"I cannot believe you made this decision without consulting us," Edith said.

"I'm sorry."

"How long ago did you send the letter?"

"I sent Brandt early this morning."

Caddaric grunted softly. "I think we must lock Erik up."

"What? How can you even suggest such a thing?"

"It's for his own good," Caddaric explained. "He spends most of his time outside. Brandt will have arrived at Cimmerian Crag by now. Charmion could arrive here at any moment. I do not think it would be wise for wolf and witch to confront each other."

Kristine shook her head. "I cannot. I cannot lock him up."

"I will take care of it. Call him."

Kristine left the room and went out the back door. Was there no end to this nightmare? Cupping her hands around her mouth, she called Erik's name.

Several minutes passed, and then she saw him running toward her. She forced a smile as he rubbed against her legs.

"Come," she said, "Caddaric wishes to see you."

The wolf looked up at her, a question in his dark gray eyes. It was disconcerting, seeing Erik's eyes in the face of the wolf.

"I don't know what he wants." Fighting back tears, she laid her hand on his head. "I love you."

Whining softly, he licked her hand.

Caddaric was waiting for them in the library. He closed the door once Erik and Kristine were inside.

Erik stared up at Kristine.

"It's all right," she said.

"Erik, look at me," Caddaric said, his voice soft, hypnotic.

The wolf looked at the sorcerer, his eyes filled with suspicion.

"Erik, you must trust me," Caddaric said. "Listen to my voice."

The wolf shook his head, his hackles rising.

"Erik, it will be all right." Kristine knelt beside him and wrapped her arms around his neck. "Please, you must do as he says."

The wolf looked at her, a look of such love, such trust, she thought her heart would break.

She heard the wizard's voice, speaking in a language she did not understand, felt his power coalesce, felt it brush against her skin. There was a gentle whooshing sound, and Erik was gone.

She looked up at Caddaric, her eyes wide with panic. "What have you done?"

"Nothing, my lady. I have only sent him to the dungeon. It is the only place I could think of where he cannot escape. We dare not keep him in one of the rooms. One of the maids might accidentally open the door, or he might leap through a window."

"The dungeon," Kristine said, her voice tinged with despair.

"He will be comfortable there. There are furs for him to rest on. Fresh meat. Water. Clean straw on the floor."

"But to lock him up . . ."

"Kristine, it is for his own good. I had promised not to tell you this, but now I fear I must. It was Erik's intent to go to Charmion, to become her pet, to let her think he was fully her creature, and then try to destroy her. He had asked me if I could find a spell to protect him from her." Caddaric shrugged. "I found one that might have worked, but there is no way to be sure."

"What kind of wizard are you, anyway?" Kristine cried.

Caddaric drew himself up to his full height. "I do the best I can, Lady Trevayne, but the truth is, Charmion is the most powerful witch I have ever known."

Erik paced the cell, his anger growing, spreading, until he thought he would vomit it up. So she had decided he was nothing but an animal after all, to be locked away in a cage.

He howled his fury until the cold stone walls echoed with his rage, all the while remembering another dungeon, one filled with mirrors.

He had to get out of here, had to find Charmion, had to destroy her before the child was born.

He heard the sound of the dungeon door opening, footsteps on the cold stones. Her footsteps.

"Erik?" Kristine knelt at the door, her beautiful green eyes glistening with tears. "I'm sorry, so very sorry."

She reached through the bars.

And he growled at her. Growled his anger, his frustration, his helplessness.

She jerked her hand back, her eyes wide and afraid. "Erik?"

Dropping to his belly, he crawled toward her, whining softly.

"Oh, Erik," she breathed. "Caddaric told me you were going to try to destroy Charmion. That's why we locked you up." It was not fully a lie, she thought, nor fully the truth. "We couldn't let you go. Please forgive me, but I cannot bear to lose you."

He stared up at her, the need to speak clawing at his throat. So much to tell her. *I love you. I love you. . . .*

"Caddaric said he thought he had found a spell to protect you from her evil, but he said there was no way to be sure it would work. You understand, don't you? I couldn't let you go. I just couldn't."

She reached through the bars again, and he licked her hand. *Kristine, Kristine, know that I will always love you. . . .*

"Kristine? Are you down here?"

"Yes, Caddaric."

He was at her side in minutes, his face flushed. "I think I may have found the solution." He glanced at Erik, then tapped her on the shoulder. "Come upstairs, we need to talk."

Kristine glanced at Erik. "All right," she said, but when she started to rise, the wolf took her hand in his mouth and tugged softly. "I don't think he wants us to go."

Caddaric looked at the wolf, disconcerted, as always, to see human eyes in the wolf's face. "I think we should discuss this upstairs."

Erik growled low in his throat.

"All right," Kristine said. "We'll stay."

"Kristine . . ."

"This involves Erik, too. He has a right to know."

"Very well. Brandt returned moments ago with a message from . . ." Caddaric glanced at the wolf. Erik still held Kristine's hand in his mouth. "Charmion has agreed to your terms."

Erik tugged on Kristine's hand, a growl that sounded very much like a question rising in his throat.

"I sent Charmion a note," Kristine explained. "I

told her I would . . . I would give her our baby if she would revoke the curse."

Erik shook his head, a sharp growl of protest rumbling deep in his throat.

"Erik, it's the only way," Kristine said. "Do you think this is easy for me? Do you think I want that witch to have my child? Our child?" She sniffed back her tears. "You can hate me if you wish, I don't care! I don't care. I have to do this. Please understand."

He released her hand, his tongue stroking lightly over the marks his teeth had left in her tender flesh. *Forgive me, beloved, forgive me.*

And then, with a growl, he shook his head again, needing to make her understand, desperate for her to know that there was no way to break the spell, that anything Charmion promised would be a lie. Only Dominique had the power to revoke the hideous curse.

He tried desperately to form the words, howled with frustration when he could not.

Caddaric helped Kristine to her feet and drew her away from the bars. "Come," he said. "I think our presence is upsetting him."

"I'll come to see you later," Kristine said. Blinded by her tears, she let the wizard lead her away.

"What solution have you found?" Kristine asked.

"I do not trust Charmion," Caddaric replied. He sat on a low sofa beside Edith, holding her hand. "We cannot allow you to go to her with the child. In her own realm, her power is far too strong. She could take the babe and destroy Erik, and there would be nothing you could do to stop her. Nor can we allow her to come here, to Hawksbridge."

Edith looked up at her husband. "Caddaric, what are you trying to say?"

"We need to find neutral ground, someplace where her dark magic will have no power."

"Where might that be?" Edith asked.

"You are certain you wish to do this, Kristine? Certain you want to exchange your child for Erik's life?"

"Yes."

"Very well. Her evil magic is of little effect within the sanctuary of holy ground. We will meet at the chapel near Hawksbridge Cross. The priest there will be entrusted to hold the child and instructed to give the babe to Charmion only when Erik has been returned to his human form."

"But if her magic is of no effect in the chapel, how will she revoke the spell?"

"Revoking an evil spell is not considered evil magic. There is a room in the cellar of the church. We will put Erik there. Once Erik is human again, the priest will give the babe to Charmion. When she is gone, we will free Erik."

"How will we keep Erik from going after her?"

"That, my dear, will be up to you. However, if I know Charmion, she will not return to Cimmerian Crag."

"Why not? It's her home."

"Only one of many. I think she will take the child to her holding in the south. It is a far more cheerful place, if any place where that witch dwells can be considered cheerful. Dominique was born there." Caddaric drummed his fingers on the ebony table beside the sofa. "The other alternative is to put a spell on Erik that will make it impossible for him to find Cimmerian Crag, should she return." The wizard grunted softly. "That may be the wisest thing to do, in any case."

Kristine nodded. Would the wizard's plan work, she wondered, and then thrust all doubt from her mind. It had to work.

It was their only hope.

Chapter Twenty-Eight

It started at midmorning, a dull ache low in her back, gradually escalating, until she knew it wasn't just another pain, but the onset of labor.

She rang for Leyla and Lilia, who smiled and patted her hands, then went to gather fresh linens.

Edith and Caddaric came to sit with her, but it was Erik she wanted. Erik she needed. Wolf or man, he was her husband and she needed him beside her.

"I want Erik." She clasped Edith's hands in hers. "Please, I want Erik."

Edith sent the two silent women from the room. "Bring him," she told her husband. "If it will ease her mind to have him here, then bring him."

Caddaric shook his head. "How can you suggest I bring him here? We know not how he will react to her cries, or to the scent of blood."

But as the hours passed and Kristine's labor grew more intense, when she writhed helplessly on the bed, crying Erik's name, screaming Erik's name, the wizard relented. A wave of his hand brought the wolf to Kristine's bedside.

Erik rested his head on the edge of the mattress, eyes closed as Kristine's hand moved restlessly over his head, clutched the fur at his neck as another contraction ripped through her. It grieved him to see her in pain, to hear her soft cries. He damned Charmion for the hideous curse she had placed on him, railed at the fate that had transformed him into a beast, making it impossible for him to hold his wife's hand, to speak words of assurance and comfort to her, to promise her that all would be well.

Mute, he stared at her, at the perspiration that dampened her brow, at the lines of stress and pain around her eyes and mouth, and wished he could endure the pain in her place.

Fear engulfed him as he recalled the last time he had watched a woman labor to bring forth his child. Kristine's whimpering tore at his heart, reminding him of Dominique's last, heart-wrenching cries.

Lifting his head, he howled his frustration, felt Kristine's hand stroke his head.

"It will be all right," she said. "I will not leave you as she did."

Whining low in his throat, he licked her hand, howled again as she cried out in pain.

After another half a dozen contractions that he was sure would rip Kristine in two, the child was born.

The scent of the blood, the afterbirth, filled his nostrils and he backed away from the bed, watching as Edith bathed the child, then wrapped it in a soft blanket and laid the babe in its mother's arms.

He growled, drawing the wizard's attention.

"'Tis a healthy girl," the mage said.

A girl. As Charmion had predicted. Erik padded

toward the bed and placed one paw on the edge of the mattress.

Kristine blinked back her tears as she lifted the child so Erik could see his daughter. "I shall call her Erika, after her father."

Erika. She was tiny and perfect, with dark blue eyes and thick black hair. Rising on his haunches, his forelegs resting on the mattress, he breathed in the child's scent, then gently licked one tiny dimpled hand.

"She is beautiful, isn't she?" Kristine murmured.

"You should rest now, daughter," Edith said.

Kristine nodded. "Erik . . ."

"I'll look after him," Caddaric said.

"Let him stay."

"Kristine, he'll be safer back in the dungeon."

"No. He doesn't like being locked up."

"It's for the best."

"No."

Caddaric took a deep breath, prepared to argue as long as necessary, when there was a knock at the door.

"Yes?" Edith called. "What is it?"

"A message," Nan replied. "From Lady Charmion."

A low growl rumbled in Erik's throat at the mention of the witch's name.

"What is the message?" Caddaric asked.

"She wishes to see the child."

"Where is she?"

"She is without the gates, awaiting your reply."

Caddaric blew out a sigh of relief. If she was outside the castle, then the wards he had put in place were holding. "Did she say anything else?"

"No, my lord."

"She wasted no time in getting here," Caddaric muttered.

"What will we do now?" Edith asked.

Caddaric shook his head. "Kristine, are you sure you want to do this?"

Tears spilled down Kristine's cheeks as she brushed a kiss across her daughter's brow. Of course she didn't want to do this, she thought, but what other choice did she have? She looked at Erik. Hackles raised, teeth bared, he paced the length of the room, back and forth, back and forth.

"Kristine?"

"Yes," she said. "I'm sure. Tell her . . . tell her we will meet her tomorrow night, in the chapel."

The wolf shook his head, a growl rising from deep within his throat. Padding toward the door, he barked, then scratched the wood, obviously wanting to be let out.

"Perhaps you had better send him back to the dungeon," Kristine said.

Caddaric nodded. "I think that would be for the best," he said. A wave of his hand, and the wolf vanished from sight. "And I think tomorrow morning might be better for our purposes. Evil is not so strong in the light of a new day."

"Very well," Kristine said. "Nan, tell Lady Charmion we will meet her in the chapel at ten tomorrow morning."

"Yes, my lady."

"After you have delivered the message to Lady Charmion," Edith said, "please send Leyla and Lilia up with clean bedding and a cup of hot tea laced with chamomile."

"Yes, my lady," Nan replied.

"The chapel at Hawksbridge Cross," Edith remarked after the maid left the room. "It was one of Dominique's favorite places. She often went there to meditate." Edith glanced out the window. "I can feel the witch's presence," she said, shivering. "It hangs over the castle like thick black smoke."

Caddaric nodded. "Aye. It is her evil magic you feel. She is testing the wards, searching for a weakness. Pray she finds none."

Erik paced the floor of the dungeon. Occasionally, he threw his weight against the iron door. The civilized part of his mind told him it was futile, a waste of time and energy. But another part—the savage part that yearned to run wild and free through the woods, the part that compelled wolves to gnaw off a foot rather than remain in a trap—that part compelled him to try.

A low whine rose in his throat as he hurled his body against the door. He wanted to be with Kristine. He wanted to be able to hold his daughter. He wanted to sink his teeth into Charmion's throat.

The man he had been warred with the beast he had become.

He howled and howled again, the feral cry filled with rage and frustration, his anger and his helplessness rising, growing stronger.

The mournful cry rang off the walls and echoed through the stone passageway.

Kristine . . .

Chapter Twenty-Nine

Kristine held her daughter all through the night, memorizing the softness of her skin, the silkiness of her hair, wondering if her eyes would stay blue, or turn green, like her own.

"You will never know how much I love you," Kristine murmured. "Never know how wonderful your father is. Charmion will tell you lies, but I hope you won't believe them. I hope you will know that I would never have sent you away if I'd had any other choice, but I must do it, my darling child. It is the only way to save your father from Charmion's curse." Tears burned Kristine's eyes. "And I love him so much. Too much to leave him as he is. I hope that someday, when you are older, you will understand and forgive me."

As I must forgive my own mother.

Slowly, the hours of night turned to day.

Leyla and Lilia brought her a tray, but she had no appetite.

Edith came in to see if there was aught she could do.

Kristine refused help with Erika. She bathed her daughter, dressed her in a clean gown. Conscious of the minutes quickly ticking away, she kissed each tiny finger and toe, caressed her daughter's cheeks, stroked the fine silk of her hair.

Too soon, the clock chimed the quarter hour and it was time to go meet the witch.

Kristine wrapped her daughter in a blanket and then, with Caddaric and Edith following her, she made her way to the dungeon.

Erik howled when he saw her. The feral cry tore at her heart. As clearly as if he had spoken, she heard his words in her mind: *No, Kristine. You must not do this.* But it was the only way to save him.

Caddaric unlocked the cell and they all stepped inside, closing the door so Erik could not get out. Caddaric slipped a collar over Erik's head and attached a thick rope, and then they formed a circle around Erik. Caddaric glanced at each of them, then lifted his arms and began to chant.

Darkness surrounded Kristine. She clutched Erika close to her breast, her senses reeling.

When she came to herself again, she was standing in front of the altar in the chapel. Edith and Caddaric stood beside her.

Kristine glanced around, then looked at Caddaric. "Where is Erik?"

"In the cellar."

A moment later, the priest entered the chapel.

Kristine hugged her daughter and then, blinking back her tears, she handed the child to the priest. No sooner had she done so than she felt a dark sense of foreboding.

Between one thought and the next, Charmion stood before them. Her dark gaze swept over the child in the priest's arms. "Give her to me."

"Not until Erik stands here before me as a man," Kristine said.

"The child first."

"No," Kristine said. "Caddaric, take us home. We waste our time here."

Charmion glared at Kristine, her gaze malevolent. "Where is the beast?"

"Erik is in the cellar."

"Summon him."

Caddaric waved his hand and Erik stood before them, teeth bared, hackles raised. He crouched, a growl rising in his throat. Caddaric quickly grabbed the rope affixed to the wolf's collar to keep him from lunging at the witch.

"Change him," Kristine demanded.

"I cannot," Charmion said. Evil laughter filled the air as she plucked the child from the arms of the priest and quickly murmured a spell that bound them together. "Try to harm me," she said to Caddaric, "and you harm the child."

Kristine looked at Caddaric. "What is she saying? You said her magic would be of no effect in a sacred place!"

"I am sorry, Kristine. This is something I did not foresee."

"What are you saying?"

"Her evil is of no effect, but the spell she has cast is not evil. It is a spell of protection and she has used it to bind the child to her. Any harm that befalls her now befalls the child as well."

"No." Kristine shook her head. "No!"

The wolf strained against the leash. It took all Caddaric's strength to hold him in check.

"A wolf you are," Charmion said, cackling. "A wolf you will ever remain."

"No!" Kristine's anguished cry filled the chapel. "No!"

Charmion nodded, her eyes dark with evil delight. And then, slowly, her eyes widened and she took a step backward. "No," she gasped. "No, it cannot be." The color drained from her face, and she shook her head back and forth in violent denial. "No. No. No!"

As one, Kristine, Caddaric, and Edith turned to see what was causing the witch such anguish.

Charmion's cries turned into a dull moaning as she clutched the child to her breast.

Kristine stared at the vision floating in the air above her, unable to believe her eyes. A beautiful young woman clad in a long white gown hovered near the altar. The light from a dozen candles shimmered from two candelabras, but the candlelight paled in comparison to the ethereal glow that shone all around the woman. Rich, dark hair framed a pale oval face. Her eyes were bluer than the sea, filled now with silent condemnation as she gazed at the witch.

The wolf whined low in its throat.

"Dominique." The name was a tortured whisper on Charmion's lips.

Kristine drew a deep breath. Erik's first wife.

The wolf tugged against the rope in Caddaric's hand and the wizard let him go.

"Erik." The woman hovering near the altar held out her hand and the wolf went to her, rubbing its head against her thigh. She ran her hand over his head, her eyes filled with unbearable sorrow, and then she fixed her gaze on her mother's face. "What have you done?"

"No." Charmion shook her head. "It cannot be. It cannot be."

Dominique smiled at the wolf, her expression one of such tender love and devotion, it brought tears to Kristine's eyes.

"Erik. My husband. I know you never loved me as I loved you. I thought you incapable of such a tender emotion." She glanced at Erik's daughter. "Yet even though you never loved me, I see that you love this child, as you would have loved our own." A single tear slid down her cheek. "I forgive you for not loving me, my husband. I forgive you with my whole heart and soul. I loved you in life. I love you now. I will love you . . . forever."

Dominique's gaze settled on her mother's face again. "But you . . ." She shook her head, her eyes filled with reproach. "Unless you return the child to her father, I will never forgive you for what you have done. Not in this life. Not in the next."

Her image faded, her voice grew distant, and she was gone.

Kristine stared at Erik, her eyes wide, her breath trapped in her throat as the wolf transformed, his body stretching, changing, until he stood naked before them, tall and strong and perfect. And human.

Erik's gaze moved over all of them. And then, without a word, he went to stand before Charmion.

She stared up at him a moment, her face as pale as death, and then she placed the child in his arms.

A wave of her hand, and the witch was gone.

"Erika." He murmured his daughter's name aloud for the first time. "Erika."

Chapter Thirty

Kristine hurried forward, her eyes damp with tears as she placed her hand on Erik's arm. At last, they were all together, as they were meant to be.

"She's beautiful," he said, "just like her mother."

Edith gestured at her son, then nudged her husband. "Do something."

"What? Oh, of course." With a wave of his hand, Caddaric clothed Erik in a shirt of white lawn, buff-colored breeches, and a pair of kidskin boots.

Erik glanced over his shoulder, a wry grin curving his lips. "Thank you."

Caddaric nodded, his eyes twinkling.

Erik handed his daughter to her grandmother, then drew Kristine into his arms. "And you," he murmured, his voice thick with unshed tears. "How can I ever thank you for your trust, your unfailing devotion?"

"Oh, Erik." She clung to him, her hands running over his back and shoulders, moving over his face.

He was beautiful, so beautiful. And whole again, at last.

"Tell me," Caddaric said, "do you remember what it was like to be a wolf?"

Erik nodded. "But I would rather forget."

Edith poked her husband in the ribs. "No more questions!" she exclaimed. "Can you not see they wish to be alone?"

"What? Oh, of course," Caddaric said. Ushering his wife and the stunned priest out of the room, he quietly closed the door behind them.

"Kristine." Ah, the joy of speaking her name.

"Erik." Tears welled in her eyes. "Oh, Erik, I was so afraid I had lost you forever."

"I missed you," he said. "More than you will ever know."

"No more than I missed you."

Blinking back his tears, he hugged her to him. "Thank you, Dominique," he murmured.

A warm breeze that felt oddly like a kiss brushed his cheek and was gone.

"It's over," Kristine said. "At last."

"Ah, Kristine, do you know how much I love you?"

"As much as I love you?"

"More," he said.

"No," she said, smiling at him through her tears. "I love you more."

Laughter welled up from deep inside him as he twirled her around the room.

"Come, my sweet Kristine," he said, setting her on her feet. "We can argue about it at home."

Home! She sighed as she cupped his face in her

hands. "Ah, my lord Erik, don't you know that you are my home?"

"And you, my love, are my life," he said fervently, and he kissed her there, in the middle of the chapel, with the golden rays of the sun shining down on them through the window like a benediction.